aus der Reihe:

Innovationen mit Mikrowellen und Licht

Forschungsberichte aus dem Ferdinand-Braun-Institut,
Leibniz-Institut für Höchstfrequenztechnik

Band 50

Bassem Arar

GaAs-based components for photonic integrated circuits

Herausgeber: Prof. Dr. Günther Tränkle, Prof. Dr.-Ing. Wolfgang Heinrich

Ferdinand-Braun-Institut
Leibniz-Institut
für Höchstfrequenztechnik (FBH)
Gustav-Kirchhoff-Straße 4
12489 Berlin

Tel.   +49.30.6392-2600
Fax   +49.30.6392-2602

E-Mail fbh@fbh-berlin.de
Web   www.fbh-berlin.de

Innovations with Microwaves and Light

Research Reports from the Ferdinand-Braun-Institut, Leibniz-Institut für Höchstfrequenztechnik

Preface of the Editors

Research-based ideas, developments, and concepts are the basis of scientific progress and competitiveness, expanding human knowledge and being expressed technologically as inventions. The resulting innovative products and services eventually find their way into public life.

Accordingly, the *"Research Reports from the Ferdinand-Braun-Institut, Leibniz-Institut für Höchstfrequenztechnik"* series compile the institute's latest research and developments. We would like to make our results broadly accessible and to stimulate further discussions, not least to enable as many of our developments as possible to enhance everyday life.

To bring quantum optical sensors out of quantum optics labs, compactness, robustness, and reliability of the existing hardware have to be improved significantly. Whereas state-of-the-art hybrid micro-integration provides laser modules that are sufficiently compact, essential building blocks (e.g. phase modulators, fiber couplers) of a quantum sensor's optical setup are still not available with the required form factor. Miniaturization of passive components is therefore a prerequisite for field and space deployment. In this work, building blocks for photonic integrated circuits targeting applications at 780 nm and 1064 nm were developed. Modelling, manufacturing, and testing of GaAs-based phase modulators and waveguide couplers are presented. Further, a novel experimental method for investigating the electro-optic properties of phase modulators is demonstrated.

We wish you an informative and inspiring reading

Prof. Dr. Günther Tränkle
Director

Prof. Dr.-Ing. Wolfgang Heinrich
Deputy Director

The Ferdinand-Braun-Institut

The Ferdinand-Braun-Institut researches electronic and optical components, modules and systems based on compound semiconductors. These devices are key enablers that address the needs of today's society in fields like communications, energy, health and mobility. Specifically, FBH develops light sources from the visible to the ultra-violet spectral range: high-power diode lasers with excellent beam quality, UV light sources and hybrid laser systems. Applications range from medical technology, high-precision metrology and sensors to optical communications in space. In the field of microwaves, FBH develops high-efficiency multi-functional power amplifiers and millimeter wave frontends targeting energy-efficient mobile communications as well as car safety systems. In addition, compact atmospheric microwave plasma sources that operate with economic low-voltage drivers are fabricated for use in a variety of applications, such as the treatment of skin diseases.

The FBH is a competence center for III-V compound semiconductors and has a strong international reputation. FBH competence covers the full range of capabilities, from design to fabrication to device characterization.

In close cooperation with industry, its research results lead to cutting-edge products. The institute also successfully turns innovative product ideas into spin-off companies. Thus, working in strategic partnerships with industry, FBH assures Germany's technological excellence in microwave and optoelectronic research.

GaAs-based components for photonic integrated circuits

vorgelegt von
Master of Science
Bassem Arar
geb. in Daraa

von der Fakultät IV − Elektrotechnik und Informatik
der Technischen Universität Berlin
zur Erlangung des akademischen Grades

Doktor der Ingenieurwissenschaften
− Dr.-Ing. −

genehmigte Dissertation

Promotionsausschuss:

Vorsitzender: Prof. Dr. Bernd Tillack
Gutachter: Prof. Dr. Günther Tränkle
Gutachter: Prof. Dr.-Ing. Klaus Petermann
Gutachter: Prof. Dr.-Ing. Rainer Michalzik (Universität Ulm)

Tag der wissenschaftlichen Aussprache: 25. Januar 2019

Berlin, 2019

Bibliografische Information der Deutschen Nationalbibliothek
Die Deutsche Nationalbibliothek verzeichnet diese Publikation in der
Deutschen Nationalbibliografie; detaillierte bibliographische Daten
sind im Internet über http://dnb.d-nb.de abrufbar.
1. Aufl. - Göttingen: Cuvillier, 2019
Zugl.: (TU) Berlin, Univ., Diss., 2019

© CUVILLIER VERLAG, Göttingen 2019
Nonnenstieg 8, 37075 Göttingen
Telefon: 0551-54724-0
Telefax: 0551-54724-21
www.cuvillier.de

ISBN 978-3-7369-9976-3
eISBN 978-3-7369-8976-4

Abstract

Semiconductor lasers based on GaAs/AlGaAs double heterostructures have recently received increasing interest for atomic spectroscopy applications. For example GaAs/AlGaAs double heterostructure laser radiation at the wavelengths of 780 nm and 1064 nm is used for rubidium spectroscopy, and for molecular iodine spectroscopy (at 532 nm using frequency-doubling techniques), respectively. Optical systems used for these applications should feature compact, mechanically stable, and highly efficient components in order to be suitable for operation in harsh environments (e.g. quantum optic precision experiments in drop towers or in space). State-of-the-art optical systems use micro-integrated laser modules with a small footprint. However, passive components that are necessary for the manipulation of the laser light such as phase and amplitude modulators, fiber couplers, and beam splitters are only commercially available on macro-scales. These components are then integrated into the laser systems platforms where additional opto-mechanical components are indispensable. Because of their excessive request for space, commercially available laser systems and electro-optic setups are not suitable for deployment in the field or in space. The miniaturization of passive components for reduction of mass and form factor of electro-optical systems as well as for improving the overall robustness and reliability of the latter is a prerequisite for field- and space deployment of quantum sensors.

This work presents GaAs/AlGaAs double heterostructure electro-optic phase modulators for the first time at the wavelength of 780 nm and at the wavelength of 1064 nm. The specifications of the phase modulators meet the micro-integration requirements into hybrid laser modules and spectroscopy modules with respect to optical aperture and electrical interface. Details related to design and fabrication of the phase modulators are included. The characterization of the electric and electro-optic properties of the phase modulators is then presented. The GaAs/AlGaAs double heterostructure of the phase modulators is further used to develop, design, and realize waveguide couplers. Multi-mode interference (MMI) couplers for applications at the wavelength of 780 nm are presented for the first time. MMI couplers can replace fiber-based couplers in complex optical systems and are core building blocks for photonic integrated circuits (PICs). The compatibility of the double heterostructure phase modulators and MMI couplers for implementation of PICs is then demonstrated through a monolithically-integrated Mach-Zehnder-intensity modulator at 780 nm for the first time.

Further, a method based on heterodyne interferometry is developed for the in-depth investigation of phase modulators including phase and amplitude modulation response, including modulation efficiency, residual amplitude modulation, and signal distortion in GaAs-based phase modulators. During hybrid integration of a phase modulator chip into an electro-optical hybrid system, this method can be applied to optimize the coupling efficiency in real time while at the same time reducing the residual amplitude modulation. The method further provides the means to separate linear and the non-linear effects in the phase modulation signal. It is shown how this provides the means to determine separately linear and quadratic electro-optics in GaAs/AlGaAs double heterostructures. For the first time, the quadratic electro-optic coefficient is determined without having to calculate the contribution of free carriers effects to phase modulation.

This thesis work is organized as follows:

First, the fundamentals of guided wave optics are presented (chapter 2). Electro-magnetic wave propagation in planar waveguides is described, conditions for guided optical modes are provided, and concepts for waveguide couplers are discussed. Then the electro-optic properties of GaAs are presented and phase modulation in GaAs/AlGaAs double heterostructures due to electro-optic effects is introduced (chapter 3).

Next, the design of GaAs/AlGaAs double heterostructure phase modulators (chapter 4) and waveguide couplers (chapter 5) is presented. For the design of the phase modulators we study the state-of-the-art GaAs-based electro-optic phase modulators at the wavelength of 1.31 nm and transfer these concepts to the wavelengths of 780 nm and 1064 nm. Efficient GaAs/AlGaAs double heterostructures with phase modulation efficiencies larger than 15 deg /(V · mm) are designed. The design of low loss and polarization maintaining waveguide couplers and phase modulators then allows for the development of a Mach-Zehnder intensity modulator (chapter 6) at the wavelengths of 780 nm.

In the experimental part of this work, after fabrication (chapter 7), the electro-optic performance of these devices is characterized experimentally. The performance of phase modulators, waveguide couplers, and MZI modulators is determined (chapter 8). The modulation efficiency of 16 deg /(V · mm) is demonstrated for phase modulators at 780 nm and at 1064 nm. The propagation losses amount to 1.2 dB/cm at 780 nm and to 4.3 dB/cm at 1064 nm (which corresponds to an improvement beyond state-of-the-art for GaAs-based phase modulators at 1064 nm). For the Mach-Zehnder-intensity modulator, the extinction ratio of more than 10 dB and excess loss of less than 3 dB are demonstrated. Further, the novel heterodyne analysis method for in-depth characterization of the electro-optic performance of phase modulators is developed and implemented (chapter 9). As an application of the heterodyne analysis method, the linear and the quadratic electro-optic coefficients of GaAs/AlGaAs double heterostructures are determined. For the linear electro-optic coefficient we find results that are in agreement with literature. However, the results for the quadratic electro-optic coefficients differ from values given in the literature. The discrepancy is discussed and suggestions to solve it are provided.

Kurzfassung

Halbleiterlaser auf Basis von GaAs/AlGaAs Doppelheterostrukturen erhalten in letzter Zeit zunehmend Interesse für Anwendungen in quantenoptischen Experimenten, z.B. in der Atomspektroskopie. Zum Beispiel wird mit GaAs/AlGaAs Diodenlasern erzeugte, kohärente Strahlung bei den Wellenlängen von 780 nm und 1064 nm für die Rubidium- und Iodspektroskopie eingesetzt. Elektro-optische Systeme für diese Anwendungen müssen aus kompakten, mechanisch stabilen, und hocheffiziente Komponenten aufgebaut sein, um den Einsatz in rauen Umgebungen (z.B. in Falltürmen oder im Weltraum) zu erlauben. In aktuellen optischen Lasersystemplatformen werden mikrointegrierte Lasermodule mit geringem Platzbedarf eingesetzt. Jedoch sind passive Komponenten, die für die Manipulation des Laserlichts notwendig sind, wie z.B. Phasen- und Amplitudenmodulatoren, Faserkoppler und Strahlteiler, kommerziell nur auf Makroskalen verfügbar. Diese Komponenten werden dann in die Lasersystemplattformen integriert, was zusätzliche opto-mechanische Komponenten erforderlich macht. Aufgrund ihres erheblichen Platzbedarfs sind State-of-the-Art Lasersysteme für den Einsatz im Feld oder im Weltraum nicht geeignet. Die Miniaturisierung von passiven Bauelementen zur Reduzierung von Masse und Formfaktor von elektrooptischen Systemen sowie zur Verbesserung der Robustheit und Zuverlässigkeit der Systeme ist eine Voraussetzung für den Einsatz von Quantensensoren im Feld oder im Weltraum.

Im Rahmen dieser Arbeit werden GaAs/AlGaAs Doppelheterostruktur elektrooptische Phasenmodulatoren zum ersten Mal für die Wellenlänge von 780 nm und für die Wellenlänge von 1064 nm realisiert. Die Entwicklung, Herstellung, und anschließend die Charakterisierung der elektrischen und elektrooptischen Eigenschaften der Phasenmodulatoren wird in Details präsentiert. Die GaAs/AlGaAs Doppelheterostruktur der Phasenmodulatoren wird außerdem verwendet, um Wellenleiterkoppler zu entwickeln und zu realisieren. Multi-Mode-Interferenz (MMI) Koppler und Richtkoppler für Anwendungen bei der Wellenlänge von 780 nm werden zum ersten Mal vorgestellt. MMI Koppler können Faser-basierte Koppler in komplexen, Optischesystemen ersetzen und sind Kernbausteine für photonische integrierte Schaltungen. Die Kompatibilität der Doppelheterostruktur Phasenmodulatoren und MMI-Koppler für die Realisierung photonischer integrierten Schaltungen wird außerdem durch die Realisierung eines Mach-Zehnder-Intensitätsmodulators bei der Wellenlängen von 780 nm zum ersten Mal demonstriert.

Darüber hinaus wird ein auf heterodyner Interferometrie basierendes Messverfahren zur Untersuchung der Modulationseffizienz, der Restamplitudenmodulation, und der nichtlineare Signalverzerrung in Phasenmodulatoren entwickelt. Während der hybriden Integration eines Phasenmodulatorchips in ein elektrooptisches Hybridsystem kann dieses Verfahren angewendet werden, um in Echtzeit die Kopplungseffizienz zu optimieren und gleichzeitig die Restamplitudenmodulation zu reduzieren. Außerdem können mit diesem Verfahren linearer und nicht-linearer Response im Phasenmodulationssignal getrennt werden. Es wird gezeigt, wie dies die Möglichkeit bereitstellt, lineare und quadratische elektro-optische Koeffizienten in GaAs/AlGaAs Doppelheterostrukturen unabhängig voneinander zu bestimmen: zum ersten Mal kann der quadratische elektrooptische Koeffizient bestimmt werden, ohne dass der Beitrag der freier Ladungsträger zur Phasenmodulation ab initio berechnet werden muss.

Diese Arbeit ist wie folgt strukturiert:

Zunächst wird die Physik der geführten Wellenoptik vorgestellt (Kapitel 2). Die elektromagnetische Wellenausbreitung in planaren Wellenleitern wird beschrieben, Bedingungen für geführte optische Moden werden bereitgestellt, und Konzepte für Wellenleiterkopplern werden diskutiert. Schließlich werden die elektrooptischen Eigenschaften von GaAs vorgestellt und die elektrooptischen Effekte in GaAs/AlGaAs Doppelheterostrukturen beschrieben (Kapitel3).

Im Anschluss werden Phasenmodulatoren (Kapitel 4) und Wellenleiterkoppler (Kapitel 5) basierend auf GaAs/AlGaAs Doppelheterostruktur entworfen. Für das Design der Phasenmodulatoren wird der Stand der Technik bei GaAs-basierten elektrooptische Phasenmodulatoren analysiert und ausgehend davon die Übertragung der für 1.31 µm bestehenden Konzepte auf die Wellenlängen 780 nm und 1064 nm vorgenommen. Das Design von Phasenmodulatoren basierend auf einer GaAs/AlGaAs Doppelheterostruktur wird erarbeitet. Die Simulationen versprechen eine Modulationseffizienz von mehr als $15\,deg\,/(V \cdot mm)$. Schließlich wird das Design der Doppelheterostruktur genutzt, um das Design von Wellenleiterkoppler zu erstellen, so dass diese Komponenten zusammen mit dem Phasenmodulator für das Design eines Mach-Zehnder Intensitätsmodulator (MZI) genutzt werden können. Das Design des MZIs folgt in Kapitel 6.

Im experimentellen Teil werden die Strukturen nach der Herstellung (Kapitel 7) charakterisiert. Die Phasenmodulatoren, die Wellenleiterkoppler, und die MZI Mdulatoren werden experimentell untersucht (Kapitel 8). Die für 780 nm und 1064 nm realisierten Phasenmodulatoren zeigen eine Phasenmodulationseffizient von $16\,deg\,/(V \cdot mm)$. Die Ausbreitungsverluste betragen $1.2\,dB/cm$ bei 780 nm und $4.3\,dB/cm$ bei 1064 nm und stellen daher eine Verbesserung gegenüber dem Stand der Technik ($12\,dB/cm$ für GaAs/AlGaAs Phasenmodulatoren bei 1.06 µm.) dar. Mit dem Mach-Zehnder-Intensitätsmodulator werden ein Extinktionsverhältnis von mehr als 10 dB und zusätzliche Verluste (*excess loss*) von weniger als 3 dB demonstriert. Ferner werden die Phasenmodulatoren mit dem Heterodynanalyseverfahren untersucht (Kapitel 9). Mithilfe des neuartigen Messverfahrens werden lineare und nichtlineare Effekte in dem Phasenmodulationssignal getrennt. Daraus können der lineare elektro-optischen (LEO) und der quadratische elektro-optische (QEO) Koeffizienten der GaAs/AlGaAs Doppelheterostrukturen bestimmt werden. Für den LEO Koeffizienten finden wir Ergebnisse, die in guter Übereinstimmung mit der Literatur stehen. Die Ergebnisse für den QEO Koeffizienten unterscheiden sich jedoch von den in der Literatur beschriebenen Werten. Die Diskrepanz wird diskutiert und Vorschläge zu ihrer Lösung werden skizziert.

وقل اعمَلُوا فَسَيَرَى اللَّه عَمَلَكُم ورسُولُه وَالمُؤمِنُون

To my Parents, then to Rima

إِلَى أَبِي وأُمِّي، ثُمَّ إِلَى رِيمَا

Acknowledgments

First and foremost I want to express my sincere gratitude to Professor Günther Tränkle who gave me the opportunity to accomplish this thesis at the Ferdinand-Braun-Institut, Leibniz Institut für Höchstfrequenztechnik (FBH) which has been of a great value for me, both, academically and personally. I also thank him for his generous professional supervising and constant support.

It has been a great honor for me to work with Dr. Andreas Wicht, an exceptional scientist whose commitment to research have inspired me every day. I greatly appreciate his personal qualities and his openness and I thank him for his constant support, his patience, and his contribution to this work. I also thank his invaluable help proofreading my thesis.

I am grateful to Dr. Hans Wenzel for sharing his robust experience in the theory of semiconductor lasers and his valuable contribution to this work.

I thank Dr. Reiner Güther for the valuable discussions and for his contribution to understanding the electro-optic properties of GaAs.

I would like to thank Dr. Harendra H. J. Fernando from Leibniz Institute for Astrophysics Potsdam, for introducing me to the simulation software RSoft CAD.

I deeply thank Dr. Olaf Brox for the wafer layout design and processing, Dr. Andre Maaßdorf for growing the structures, Dr. Peter Ressel for the AR-coating, Arnim Ginolas and Sabrina Kreutzmann for mounting of the passive waveguide chips.

My warm gratitude goes to all members of the group 'Lasermetrologie' for the motivating, inspiring, and warm working atmosphere. I thank my colleagues Christian Kürbis and Christoph Pyrlik for the valuable discussions at different stages in this work. I also thank Heike Christopher, Max Schiemangk, Dr. Ahmad Bawamia, and Robert Smol for their support and continuous willingness to help whenever required.

Thank you Rashed AlToma, my friend, for your support and encouragement.

I gratefully acknowledge the funding sources that made my Ph.D. work possible. I would like to thank the DLR for the funding under the grant number 50WM1141.

My deepest thanks to my family who have always encouraged me and believed in me. Words can not express how grateful I am to my father Mohammad Arar and my mother Fatima Kewan. My two brothers and best friends, Moammer and Thabet whose unconditional support have always accompanied me. My sisters Samah, Hiba, Wafa, and Rawda. And finally, thank you my dear wife Doaa, with love.

Contents

Motivation

Preamble

The way air traffic has revolutionized our life is indispensable. We check into the boarding machines to travel thousands of miles taking time-saving and safety for granted. In their cockpits, pilots relay on navigation systems, e.g. the global positioning system (GPS), to determine their position and navigate safely into the crowded air corridors. However, the GPS navigation does not provide an error-free transmission of information. The main source of error in GPS navigation systems is the inaccurate time keeping by the clock of the receiver[1]. The key solution for a new generation of navigation systems are quantum sensors. Atom interferometry-based quantum sensors can be used for precise measurement of acceleration and rotation providing the basic platform for ultra-precise navigation systems [1]. They can also be employed for navigation in harsh environments such as in deep-space or under water where the GPS may be extremely disturbed or even unavailable [2]. Further, atom interferometry-based quantum sensors are used for fundamental physics experiments under microgravity (in drop towers or in space) [2], [3]. In order for quantum sensors to be ready to leave the laboratory, appropriate space-qualified and portable laser systems should be available. This explains the increasing interest over the last decade in building compact and robust micro-integrated laser systems for quantum sensors [3].

As an example for applications of quantum sensors, figure 1 shows the laser platform for the QUANTUS-2 laser system[2] for testing the equivalence principle by using ultra-cold rubidium and potassium atoms [4]. In principle, the setup is divided into two parts. The first part uses laser light at the wavelength of 780 nm for the manipulation of rubidium and the other part uses a laser light at 767 nm for the manipulation of potassium. Both parts fill a platform with a total diameter of 65 cm which is integrated in a "capsule". The corresponding quantum sensor experiment is carried out inside the "drop tower" (*Fallturm*) in Bremen[3]. During the experiment, the capsule is dropped inside the evacuated chamber (micro-gravity during free fall on the order of 1×10^{-6} g) of the drop tower. This requires the laser platform to be robust enough to withstand the mechanical stress it is subjected to during the catapult launch and deceleration when caught in polystyrene pellets. For this purpose, the laser system of the QUANTUS-2 experiment uses miniaturized Master-Oscillator-Power-Amplifier (MOPA) laser modules (figure 1). Micro-integrated laser modules are compact devices

---

[1]GPS accuracy and error sources: see for example http://www.mio.com/technology-gps-accuracy.htm
[2]High resolution interferometry with ultra-cold mixtures in microgravity https://www.iqo.uni-hannover.de/iqo_quantus2.html?&L=1
[3]https://www.zarm.uni-bremen.de/de/fallturm.html

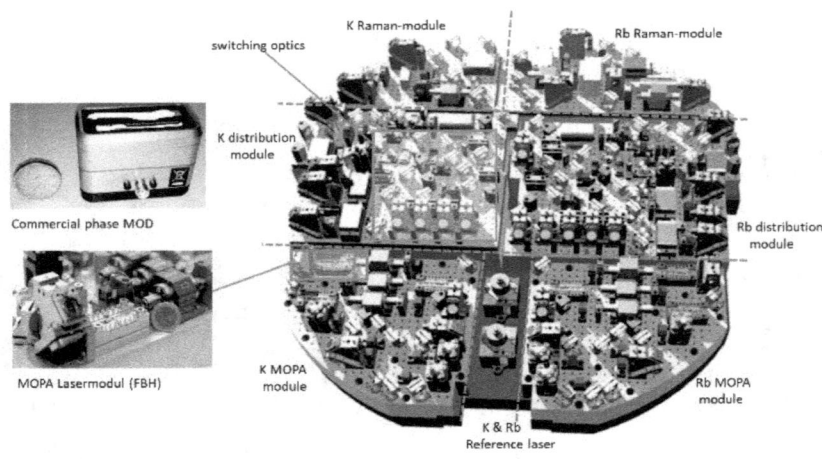

Figure 1: CAD model of the catapult-capable laser system of the QUANTUS-2 experiment for testing the equivalence principle by means of atom interferometry with ultra-cold rubidium (Rb) and potassium (K) atoms.

with a very small footprint. Typically, a micro-integrated laser module consists of a semiconductor laser chip, micro optics, and the corresponding electronic interface. All these elements are micro-integrated on a suitable platform, e.g. aluminum nitride (AlN) ceramic. Hybrid integration techniques (adhesive bonding, soldering) are used to integrate these components on the smallest footprint possible as well as with the highest degree of mechanical stability that can be achieved. The latter calls for omitting any adjustment possibilities after bonding, i.e. any movable parts are omitted. Mechanical stability is achieved through micro-integration simply for geometrical reasons: as the dimension d of an object shrinks down, its mounting surface scales like d^2 while its mass scales like d^3. Further, misalignment through bending scales like d or d^2.

Even with the successful micro-integration of laser modules, the total size of the laser system platform is actually defined by the passive components for signal processing such as beam splitters, fiber couplers, phase and amplitude modulators. In the actual quantum sensor experiments, these devices are only commercially available. The resulting complexity and volume requirement for their integration into laser system platforms are very huge. For example, for the micro-integration of a laser module, typically a footprint of $60 \times 50\,\mathrm{mm}^2$ is required (e.g. the MOPA module in the QUANTUS-2 laser system). The footprint of a (macroscopic) commercial phase modulator for applications at the wavelength of $780\,\mathrm{nm}$ is typically about $25 \times 50\,\mathrm{mm}^2$ (see photo on the upper left side of figure 1), where also additional space is required for the deflecting mirrors and lenses for beam collimation. Besides, the macroscopic modulators require high-power drivers (a few *Watt* RF-power) which increases the space requirement of about $350 \times 250 \times 100\,\mathrm{mm}^3$. Further, phase modulators are usually combined with couplers, splitters, and other optical and mechanical components for manipulation of the laser light to generate the necessary signals for the experiments. These "distribution modules" are extremely complex and volume-consuming which is not appropriate for applications in space. Hence, the miniaturization of couplers, phase and amplitude modulators, e.g. by realizing them on the basis of semiconductors (GaAs-based) should reduce the place and power requirements, as well as the complexity of the total optical system which is a prerequisite for field-capable and space-qualified quantum sensors.

For the realization of the GaAs-based components one may benefit from the rich experience that has been made in the field of optical telecommunications (InP-based photonic integrated circuits (PICs) for applications in the range of 1.3 - 1.6 µm wavelength) in which a high level of complexity has been achieved [5]. This requires to adjust the semiconductor technology for the modulators and coupler devices from the telecommunication field into new wavelength ranges, for example, for quantum sensors applications at the wavelengths of 780 nm (for rubidium spectroscopy) and at 1064 nm (hyperfine transitions in molecular iodine at 532 nm [4]).

In this work, GaAs-based phase modulators and couplers should be developed. The aperture of the components should be compatible with the state of the art GaAs-based edge-emitting lasers. This should make it feasible to realize micro-integrated laser and spectroscopy modules that combine passive photonic components (e.g. phase modulators) with active components (e.g. edge emitting lasers). The successful demonstration of these two basic photonic components (GaAs-based phase modulators and couplers) should in the future allow to integrate them on the chip (monolithic integration) which should further decrease the complexity of the system and drastically improve its robustness and reliability.

Micro-integrated laser systems, state of the art

When the passive optical components from this thesis are demonstrated, the next milestone for the future work is to employ these components into the state of the art micro-integrated laser modules.

Micro-integrated laser modules for applications in field and in space have already been demonstrated [3]. For example, an extended cavity diode laser (ECDL) module for potassium spectroscopy is shown in figure 2. The diode laser chip, micro optics, electronic interface, and a micro-thermoelectric cooler (μ-TEC) that carries a volume holographic Bragg grating (VHBG) are all micro-integrated on an AlN ceramic micro-optical bench. The footprint of the device corresponds to $25 \times 80 \, mm^2$ [3].

The deployment of micro-integrated laser modules in fundamental physics experiments in space has been successful. For example, the MOPA platform have been employed in the first optical atomic frequency reference in space, on a sounding rocket [6] (the FOKUS experiment [5]). Shortly thereafter extended cavity diode lasers have been demonstrated in space on-board a sounding rocket and demonstrated reliable frequency stabilization to the potassium D2 line as well as to each other through a

---

[4] Optical frequency standard based on molecular iodine for sounding rockets https://www.physics.hu-berlin.de/en/qom/research/jokarus

[5] REXUS 9 and 10, see for example: http://www.dlr.de/desktopdefault.aspx/tabid-6840/86_read-29274/

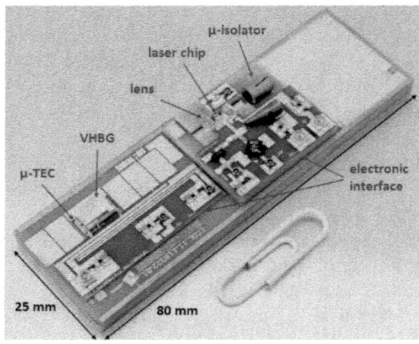

Figure 2: Extended cavity laser module for Potassium spectroscopy. VHBG: volume holographic Bragg grating, μ-TEC: micro-thermoelectric cooler. (taken from [3]).

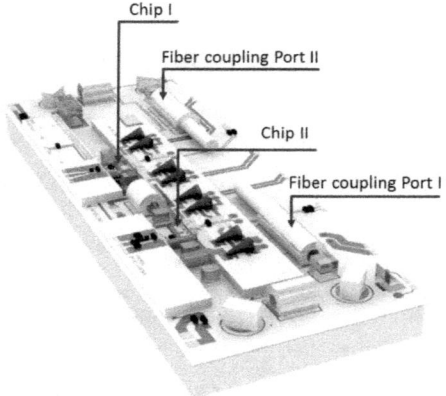

Figure 3: Laser modules based on the Milas technology. The platform allows the integration of two arbitrary SC chips, all together with micro-optics, electronic interfaces, and integrated fiber couplers.

frequency- offset stabilization [7] , and KALEXUS experiment [6]). Both the FOKUS and KALEXUS experiment were sponsored by the German Space Agency (DLR).

However, the platform of the laser module in figure 2 allows for micro-integration of a single chip. To bring the micro-integration technology to the next level, the new platform for micro-integrated optical systems in figure 3 has been developed by FBH within the Milas[7] project. The new platform allows for micro-integration of arbitrary combinations of two semiconductor chips. These combinations may include active components (e.g. diode laser or amplifier chips), as well as passive components (like GaAs chip-based phase modulators). Further, the platform has two fiber coupling ports for input into and output from the laser module using polarization maintaining single mode optical fibers. The Milas technology offers a suitable platform for the micro-integration of the GaAs-based phase modulators that are developed within this work.

---

[6]TEXUS 53, see for example: http://www.dlr.de/dlr/desktopdefault.aspx/tabid-10081/151_read-16493/#/gallery/21758

[7] Mikrointegrierte Diodenlasersysteme (Milas): supported by the German Space Agency DLR with funds provided by the Federal Ministry of Economics and Technology (BMWi) under grant number 50WM1141.

Chapter 1

Introduction

1.1 Developments in III-V semiconductor phase modulators

Milestones in the development of III-V semiconductor-based phase modulators are summarized in chronological order in table 1.1. The last three results are essential results of this work.

Table 1.1: The chronological development of GaAs-based and InP-based electro-optic phase modulators. The last 3 papers are based on this this thesis work.

author	year	waveguide	substrate	junction	λ [µm]	Mod. Eff.** [$1/(V \cdot mm)$]	losses dB/cm
[8]	1964	GaP	InP	p-n	0.550	75°	-
[9]	1983	InGaAsP/InP	InP	p-n	1.32	-	>10
[10]	1986	GaAs/AlGaAs	GaAs	P-n-N	1.06	56°	-
[11]	1987	GaAs/AlGaAs	GaAs	P-i-N	1.09/1.15	38°/36°	>13
[12]	1987	InGaAs/InP	InP	P-i-N*	1.52	12°	9.8
[13]	1988	GaAs/AlGaAs	GaAs	P-p-n-N	1.06	96°	>12
[14]	1988	GaAs/AlGaAs	GaAs	P-p-i-n-N	1.55	2.9°	1.2
[15]	1989	GaAs/AlGaAs	GaAs	P-I-i-I-N	1.09	28°	20
[16]	1992	InP/GaInAsP	InP	P-I-n-N	1.55	11°	1.0
[17]	1997	GaAs/AlGaAs	GaAs	P-p-i-n-N	1.31	35°	0.6
[18]	2003	InGaAs/InP	InP	P-p-n-N	1.55	34°	<4.5
[19]	2013	GaAs/AlGaAs	GaAs	P-p-i-n-N	0.780	11°	<1.4
[20]	2014	GaAs/AlGaAs	GaAs	P-p-n-N	0.780	23°	<1.4
[21]	2017	GaAs/AlGaAs	GaAs	P-p-n-N	1.064	16°	<2.7

* Multi-Quantum-Wells (MQWs) inside the guiding region.
** Phase modulation efficiency (phase shift in $\deg/(V \cdot mm)$)

The first III-V semiconductor electro-optic phase modulators were demonstrated a few decades ago [8]. In 1964, D. F. Nilson and F. K. Reinhart observed for the first time phase modulation of the light signal guided in a reversed biased gallium phosphide p-n junction on InP substrate and related the modulation to the linear electro-optic (LEO) effect. Twenty years later in 1983, H. J. Bach et al. demonstrated phase

6

modulation at the wavelength of 1.32 µm in double heterostructures using InGaAsP p-n heterojunctions for the first time [9]. The authors were also the first to describe the quadratic electro-optic (QEO) effect in p-n diodes. Later in 1986, the first electro-optic GaAs/AlGaAs double heterostructure phase modulator waveguide for integrated optics was demonstrated [10] (operation at the wavelength of 1.06 µm). Since then, GaAs-based phase modulators have received increasing interest for optical intercon- nects and fiber coupling [22]. The year after, in 1987, J. Faist and F. K. Reinhart reported the orientation dependence of the phase modulation in the GaAs/AlGaAs double heterostructures for laser radiation at the wavelength of 1.09 µm [11]. They measured phase modulation for both, the TE and TM modes for light propagating in the [110] and [1$\bar{1}$0] crystallographic directions in a P-i-N (with an intrinsic (i) core and P (p-doped) and N (n-doped) cladding layers) phase modulator. No difference was found between the measurements for the TM modes in both directions. However, for the TE mode, the LEO effect was found to add in the [1$\bar{1}$0] direction and subtract in the [110] direction. Later in 1988, J. G. Mendoza-Alvarez et al. quantified the contri- bution of carrier density-related effects to the modification of the refractive index in highly-doped GaAs/AlGaAs double heterostructures. They presented phase modula- tors at the wavelength of 1.06 µm with a high modulation efficiency (phase shift per volt per unit length) [13] due to contribution from the LEO effect, the QEO effect, and the carrier density-related effect.

As shown by table 1.1 the performance of different phase modulators is characterized by two parameters: the phase modulation efficiency and the propagation losses. For some of these devices, the high modulation efficiency is accompanied with extremely large propagation losses which are caused by electro-optic and free carriers absorp- tion (see for example [13] and [11] in table 1.1). An efficient phase modulator was demonstrated in 1997 by Y. T. Byun et al. [17]. The authors used a so-called W-shape P-P-p-i-n-N-N double heterostructure ridge-waveguide phase modulator and demon- strated a phase modulation efficiency of 34 °/(V · mm) and very low propagation losses (0.6 dB · cm^{-1}). This means that for example for a 2 mm long phase modulator (a typi- cal length of a GaAs-based chip), a phase shift of 180° can be achieved by only applying 1.32 V. The corresponding propagation losses of about 0.24 dB are negligible compared to the coupling losses (typically 2.2 dB for 60% coupling efficiency) which makes this structure very suitable for micro-integration applications. We carefully studied this particular double heterostructure and applied the elements of the W-shaped concept to develop the phase modulators in this work.

1.2 Thesis objectives: GaAs-based passive photonic compo- nents

GaAs-based phase modulators require a careful design of the GaAs/AlGaAs double heterostructure in order to efficiently use the electro-optic effects and the free carriers effects in GaAs. For compatibility reasons, GaAs-based couplers in this work are realized based on the GaAs/AlGaAs double heterostructures of the phase modulators. With the successful demonstration of phase modulators and waveguide couplers, as an application of monolithic integration of passive photonic components for future works, an integrated intensity modulator can be realized in the simplest layout of a Mach-Zehnder Intensity (MZI) modulator.

As a medium term target, the passive components that are developed in this work are intended to meet the micro-integration requirements on the hybrid laser modules. These requirements and the specifications of individual components are discussed in details in the following parts of this section.

1.2.1 Objective: GaAs-based phase modulators

The first objective of this work is to realize GaAs/AlGaAs double heterostructure phase modulators.

Principles of phase modulation in GaAs-based waveguides should be investigated. The GaAs/AlGaAs double heterostructures from the literature should be studied to acquire the knowledge to design phase modulators at two different wavelengths (780 nm and 1064 nm). An efficient design requires to model the electro-optic response of the modulator double heterostructure. The design criteria are the phase modulation efficiency (the amount of phase shift per volt per mm), the propagation losses (free carrier-absorption losses, modal losses, and losses arising from the lateral waveguide structure), the polarization maintenance, and the spectral dispersion of the phase modulator.

The waveguide should be achieved based on a ridge waveguide concept. The design should be optimized so that coupling a coherent light signal (laser beam) into and out of the modulator can be achieved using the state of the art micro-optics and micro-integration approaches.

The next step is to realize the phase modulators in the GaAs technology. The realized devices should be characterized. For the characterization, a coherent light signal from a diode laser should be coupled into the modulator and the transmitted power, the polarization, the phase modulation, the residual amplitude modulation, and the modulation bandwidth should be measured. We emphasize here that some of the characteristic parameters of GaAs-based phase modulators such as phase and amplitude non-linear distortion has not previously been investigated in the literature. This is why efforts have to be made within this work to develop new methods for in-depth characterization of GaAs-based phase modulators. These methods should be experimentally implemented.

The required performance of the phase modulator at 780 nm and the phase modulator at 1064 nm is specified as the following:

- single mode waveguides: the ridge parameters (ridge width and etching depth) should be selected for the waveguide to support only the fundamental guided optical mode. This is a requirement for a well-defined phase modulation [19], [23].

- the far field of the modulator's output signal must satisfy the requirements for hybrid integration with active and passive optical elements. Typical divergence angles (95%) are for example 15° in the lateral and 25° in the vertical direction. At these values, the beam can be collimated using commercial lenses to provide a beam diameter that is as close as possible to the optimal value of 0.6 mm [24].

- The 3-dB modulation bandwidth (3 dB/45° phase delay) should be at least 8 MHz (for example for the generation of the sidebands for Rb spectroscopy at 780 nm).

The design of the electrical connection to the modulator should allow for modulation frequencies of at least 8 MHz.

- the half-wave voltage (with direct driving) shall be smaller than 5 V to dispense the demand for diving electronics (a driving voltage of 5 V can be achieved even at bandwidths up to 10 MHz).

- polarization maintaining waveguide: the polarization extinction ratio (PER) is defined as the ratio of optical powers of perpendicular polarizations. The PER should exceed 60 dB provided that the injected beam features a PER of 60 dB or better.

- very low propagation losses: typical values from the literature for low propagation losses in GaAs/AlGaAs double heterostructure phase modulator waveguides are between $0.6\,\mathrm{dB\,cm^{-1}}$ at $1.31\,\mathrm{\mu m}$ [17] and $1.2\,\mathrm{dB\,cm^{-1}}$ at $1.2\,\mathrm{\mu m}$ [14]. The objective is to reduce the propagation losses of the phase modulators in this work beyond the state of the art.

1.2.2 Objective: GaAs-based couplers

The second objective is to realize waveguide couplers. Ridge waveguide couplers should be realized based on the layer structure of the phase modulators. This facilitates the monolithic integration of phase modulators together with couplers for the realization of complex devices such as intensity modulators. A waveguide coupler generally consists of three sections: The input waveguide/waveguides (usually referred to as the *access waveguides*), the coupling section in which the mechanism for transmission of the field into the output channels is determined, and the output waveguide/waveguides. An M to N (or M×N) coupler describes a device with M input waveguides and N output waveguides. In their simplest layout, 2 to 1 (2×1) couplers can be used to combine the optical field from two different input devices into one output path, or as a 1×2 coupler also to split the optical field into two different paths (splitters). Another common coupler concept is the 2×2 3dB coupler with two input waveguides and two output waveguide. The optical field from either of the input waveguides is divided equally (nominally) between the two output waveguides. For the optimum design of ridge waveguide couplers, different coupling concepts from the literature (e.g. evanescent coupling or self-imaging in multi-mode waveguides) should be compared. Wave propagation in 1×2 couplers and 2×2 3dB couplers should be modeled. The design criteria are the excess losses and the accuracy of the splitting ratio of the input field into the output waveguides (imbalance).

Following to the design, the waveguide couplers should be realized and characterized. A coherent light signal from a diode laser should be coupled into the couplers and the transmitted power (the excess loss as a measure), the polarization, and the imbalance between output ports should be measured.

The specifications for the couplers are given as the following:

- operation at the wavelength of 780 nm.

- single mode access waveguides for which the far field of the output signal must satisfy the requirements for hybrid integration with active and passive optical elements (divergence angles (95%) are 15° in the lateral and 25° in the vertical direction in similar lines to the waveguide of the phase modulators).

- excess loss: for the couplers in this work, the excess losses should be small enough so that when they are used to realize an integrated MZI modulator, the total loss of the modulator is comparable to the state-of-the-art. The excess loss of state-of-the-art GaAs/AlGaAs double heterostructure MZI modulator corresponds to about 8 dB [25]. The MZI is realized using 2 couplers and 2 phase modulators at the actives arms. The length of the phase modulators is typically 2 mm to 4 mm. Assuming that the propagation losses in one phase modulator waveguide are less than 0.5 dB (this follows from the assumption that the propagation losses in the phase modulator waveguide are about $1.2\,\mathrm{dB\,cm^{-1}}$ [14]). If we further assume that the coupling losses are 1 dB or better, the excess loss of the each of the two waveguide couplers should not exceed 3.0 dB.

- imbalance: the imbalance of the input couplers for an MZI modulator translates directly into cross-talk and extinction ratio. For example, the power imbalance of 0.2 dB limits the extinction ratio to 33 dB [26]. Therefore, the imbalance (the splitting ratio) for 1×2 splitter (typically the input coupler of the MZI modulator) should not exceed 0.2 dB in order not to limit the performance of the Mach-Zehnder intensity modulator. A typical value for the imbalance of 2×2 3dB couplers is 0.2 dB to 0.6 dB [26].

1.2.3 Application: GaAs-based amplitude (intensity) modulator

As a proof of concept, the monolithic integration of two phase modulators and two waveguide couplers is demonstrated in the application of a MZI modulator. The optical field fed into the first (input) coupler is divided between the two phase modulators (arms of the MZI modulator) and then the two arms are recombined using the second (output) coupler. The connection between the couplers and the phase modulators (active arms of the MZI modulator) is typically realized using bent waveguides such as S-bends [26]. S-bends are required to guarantee a sufficient lateral spacing between the two active arms so that the modulating electric field can be applied separately on each arm. The design criteria for the MZI modulator are the extinction ratio and the excess losses. In the S-bends, losses may arise due to radiation losses at the bend structure or reflections due to the optical mode mismatch between the straight and the bend waveguides. The S-bends should be modeled and a suitable structure with minimal losses should be found. A suitable concept should be chosen for the input and output couplers of the MZI modulator.

Next, the MZIs should be fabricated and characterized. A coherent light signal from a diode laser should be coupled into the MZI modulator input coupler and the transmitted power (the excess loss as a measure) and the extinction ratio when a modulating electric field is applied should be measured.

We specify the MZI modulator as the following:

- operation at the wavelength 780 nm.

- single mode access waveguides. The far field of the output signal must satisfy the requirements for hybrid integration with active and passive optical elements (as in the phase modulators and couplers).

- the excess loss must be comparable to or less than 8 dB (excess loss of state-of-the-art GaAs/AlGaAs double heterostructure MZI modulators [25]).

- extinction ratio: extinction ratios of GaAs/AlGaAs MZI modulators in the literature range from 3.0 dB in [25] to 24 dB in [27]. Future applications of the MZI modulators, for example in high-speed IQ modulators, require to reach extinction ratios beyond 20 dB to achieve a sufficient signal-to-noise ratio at high data rates, see [28]. As a proof of concept, the MZI modulators in this work should provide an extinction ratio well beyond 3 dB. The improvement of the extinction beyond 20 dB should be feasible.

1.3 Structure of the thesis

Based on the discussed objectives for this work, the rest of the thesis is structured as follows:

- in chapter 2 we briefly present the fundamentals of guided wave optics. The physics of wave propagation in planar waveguides and the cut-off conditions for guided modes in single mode and multi-mode ridge waveguides are introduced. Concepts of waveguide couplers are discussed. These are then used later in chapter 4 and in chapter 5 for the design procedure of the waveguides for the phase modulators and coupler devices.

- the electro-optic properties of GaAs are discussed in chapter 3. These properties are used to optimize the design of the GaAs/AlGaAs double heterostructure of the phase modulators in chapter 4. The design requires to model the distribution of both electrical and optical fields inside the double heterostructure in order to calculate the contribution of different effects to phase modulation.

- in chapter 4 details to the design of the waveguides for electro-optic phase modulators at 780 nm and 1064 nm including the calculation of the electro-optic coefficients of the double heterostructures, developing the multi-layer structure for the vertical design, and the lateral design of single mode ridge waveguides are presented.

- the developed multi-layer structure for the phase modulator at 780 nm in chapter 4 is considered for the design of waveguide couplers. Details related to the design of two different couplers concepts (directional couplers and MMI couplers) are presented in chapter 5.

- as an example of the monolithic-integration of GaAs-based phase modulators and GaAs-based couplers, the applications of a Mach-Zehnder intensity modulator in chapter 6.

- chapter 7 is dedicated to the fabrication details of the designed GaAs-based passive components.

- in chapter 8 the standard characterization of the GaAs-based phase modulators is presented. The electrical properties, the phase modulation efficiency, and the propagation losses of phase modulators at 780 nm and at 1064 nm are experimentally investigated using established methods. Then, the performance of GaAs-based waveguide couplers is characterized. Finally, as an application the main performance factors of Mach-Zehnder intensity modulators are characterized.

- a novel method for the in-depth characterization of GaAs-based phase modulators is presented in chapter 9. The mathematical model of the method and its experimental implementation are described. The experimental results of a phase modulator at 780 nm and a phase modulator at 1064 nm are presented and followed by a discussion of the results.

- finally, the conclusion and outlook are given in chapter 10.

Chapter 2

Fundamentals of guided-wave optics

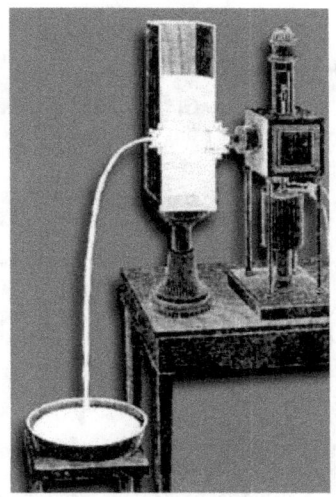

J. Tyndall (1820-1893) was the first to demonstrate
guiding of a light beam within a falling water stream
(http://i-fiberoptics.com/pdf/12_0120-if_514.pdf)

An optical waveguide is a medium in which the optical signal remains confined due
to total internal reflection. To meet the requirements for total internal reflection, the
light guiding material (core) is imbedded in the (cladding) material with a refractive
index that is smaller than the refractive index of the core. Examples are optical fibers
for long distance propagation and planar (dielectric) waveguides. Planar waveguides
are of particular importance for integrated optics. The possibility to integrate planar
active devices such as diode lasers and ridge waveguide amplifiers (RWAs) with passive
components (phase modulators, couplers,...) make planar waveguides very attractive
for the realization of compact devices and complex PICs.

13

In this chapter, the basic principles of wave propagation in planar waveguides are introduced. These principles provide a guidance to rely on for the design procedure which follows later in chapter 4 and in chapter 5. The derivation of guided modes of a simple planar waveguide from the wave equation and the corresponding boundary conditions are briefly presented. Then, the requirements for single mode and multi-mode waveguides are discussed. Further, the properties of multi-mode waveguide couplers are concluded.

2.1 Electro-magnetic wave propagation in planar waveguides

Maxwell's equations describe the propagation of electro-magnetic waves in vacuum as well as in any kind of matter. In the following, wave propagation in homogeneous non-magnetic plane (lossless, infinitely extended) is considered. The light source (e.g. laser beam) is assumed to have a harmonic time dependence with angular frequency ω.

2.1.1 Planar electro-magnetic waves

In a homogeneous, linear, and lossless dielectric medium, the wave equation for the electric wave vector $\tilde{\mathbf{E}}(x, y, z, t)$ as derived from the Maxwell's equations follows the following form [29, p. 22–24]:

$$\nabla^2 \tilde{\mathbf{E}}(\mathbf{r}, t) = \mu \mu_0 \epsilon \epsilon_0 \frac{\partial^2 \tilde{\mathbf{E}}(\mathbf{r}, t)}{\partial t^2} \tag{2.1}$$

where $\mathbf{r} = (x, y, z)$ the position vector, μ and μ_0 are the relative permeability and the vacuum permeability, respectively, ϵ the relative dielectric constant, ϵ_0 the vacuum permittivity, and the operator $\nabla^2 = \partial^2/\partial x^2 + \partial^2/\partial y^2 + \partial^2/\partial z^2$.

By considering a non-magnetic material with $\mu = 1$, the wave equation is then given by:

$$\nabla^2 \tilde{\mathbf{E}}(\mathbf{r}, t) = \frac{\bar{n}^2}{c^2} \frac{\partial^2 \tilde{\mathbf{E}}(\mathbf{r}, t)}{\partial t^2} \tag{2.2}$$

with $c = 1/\sqrt{\mu_0 \epsilon_0}$ is the vacuum speed of light and $\bar{n} = \sqrt{\epsilon}$ is the refractive index.

A simple solution of the wave equation is a plane wave with a harmonic time dependence of $\tilde{\mathbf{E}}$ according to $\exp{(i\omega t)}$ that is given by:

$$\tilde{\mathbf{E}}(\mathbf{r}, t) = \mathbf{E}(\mathbf{r}) \exp{(i\omega t)} + \mathbf{E}^*(\mathbf{r}) \exp{(-i\omega t)} \tag{2.3}$$

with $\mathbf{E}(\mathbf{r}) = (E_x, E_y, E_z)$, $\mathbf{r} = (x, y, z)$ is a complex function that depends only on the position. $\mathbf{E}(\mathbf{r})$ is called the phasor. The wave equation of the plane wave in equation 2.3 can then be described by the Helmholtz equation [30, p. 36]:

$$\nabla^2 \mathbf{E}(\mathbf{r}) + \frac{\bar{n}^2 \omega^2}{c^2} \mathbf{E}(\mathbf{r}) = 0 \tag{2.4}$$

Let us now consider a monochromatic, plane wave with a constant amplitude vector $\mathbf{E}_0$ propagating in the direction of the wave vector $\mathbf{k} = (k_x, k_y k_z)$. The corresponding phasor of this wave is written as:

$$\mathbf{E}(\mathbf{r}) = \mathbf{E}_0 \exp{(-i\mathbf{k}\mathbf{r})} \tag{2.5}$$

By inserting equation 2.5 in 2.4, the so-called *separation condition* [30, p. 37] is achieved:

$$k_x^2 + k_y^2 + k_z^2 = \bar{n}^2 k^2 \tag{2.6}$$

with $k = \omega/c$ is called the vacuum wave number.

2.1.2 Reflection of planar waves

Let us consider two homogeneous, lossless media with a planar boundary at $x = 0$. A plane wave E_i, with a linearly polarized monochromatic electric field $\mathbf{E} = (E_x = 0,\ E_y \neq 0,\ E_z = 0)$ is propagating in the first medium with the refractive index $\bar{n}_1$ and is obliquely incident with the propagation vector $\mathbf{k}_i$ at the planar boundary as shown by figure 2.1.

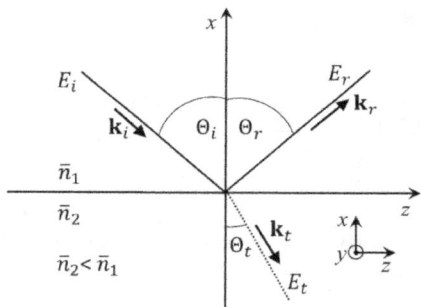

Figure 2.1: Reflection of a linear monochromatic plane wave obliquely incident on a planar boundary between two homogeneous, lossless media.

$$E_i = E_{0i} \exp\left(-i\mathbf{k}_i\mathbf{r}\right) \tag{2.7}$$

The refractive index of the second medium $\bar{n}_2$ is assumed to satisfy $\bar{n}_2 < \bar{n}_1$. Thus, the incoming wave is reflected at the interface between the two media. The reflected wave is then given by:

$$E_r = E_{0r} \exp\left(-i\mathbf{k}_r\mathbf{r}\right) \tag{2.8}$$

The wave vectors of the incident and reflected waves can be extracted from figure 2.1:

$$\begin{aligned}
\mathbf{k}_i &= (-k_{x,i},\ 0,\ k_{z,i}) = (-\bar{n}_1 k \cos\Theta_i,\ 0,\ \bar{n}_1 k \sin\Theta_i) \\
\mathbf{k}_r &= (k_{x,r},\ 0,\ k_{z,r}) = (\bar{n}_1 k \cos\Theta_r,\ 0,\ \bar{n}_1 k \sin\Theta_r)
\end{aligned} \tag{2.9}$$

In the second medium with the refractive index $\bar{n}_2 < \bar{n}_1$, the refractive wave propagates with the wave vector $\mathbf{k}_t$ at an angle Θ_t that is different from the incidence angle Θ_i:

$$E_t = E_{0t} \exp\left(-i\mathbf{k}_t\mathbf{r}\right) \tag{2.10}$$

with $\mathbf{k}_t$ given by:

$$\mathbf{k}_t = (-k_{x,t},\ 0,\ k_{z,t}) = (-\bar{n}_2 k \cos\Theta_t,\ 0,\ \bar{n}_2 k \sin\Theta_t) \tag{2.11}$$

Note that the wave vectors $\mathbf{k}_i$, $\mathbf{k}_r$, $\mathbf{k}_t$ in equations 2.9 and 2.11 necessarily satisfy the corresponding separation conditions (equation 2.6).
By taking into consideration the continuity of the tangential component of the electric field at the planar boundary, equations 2.7 to 2.11 yield at $x = 0$:

$$E_{0i} \exp\left(-i\bar{n}_1 kz \sin \Theta_i\right) + E_{0r} \exp\left(-i\bar{n}_1 kz \sin \Theta_r\right) = E_{0t} \exp\left(-i\bar{n}_2 kz \sin \Theta_t\right) \quad (2.12)$$

Equation 2.12 is valid for all values of z. This requires the phase components of the quantities in equation 2.12 to be equal:

$$n_1 \sin \Theta_r = n_1 \sin \Theta_i = n_2 \sin \Theta_t \quad (2.13)$$

The left-hand equality gives the reflection law ($\Theta_i = \Theta_r$) whereas the right-hand equality corresponds to the refraction law, namely ($n_1 \sin \Theta_r = n_2 \sin \Theta_t$). By inserting these two conditions in equations 2.9 and in 2.11, we find:

$$k_{z,i} = k_{z,r} = k_{z,t} = k\bar{n}_1 \sin \Theta_i \quad (2.14)$$

Further, from the reflection law and the refraction law, the relation between the amplitudes from equation 2.12 is donated by:

$$E_{0i} + E_{0r} = E_{0t} \quad (2.15)$$

It can be further shown (see [29, p. 35]) that the continuity of the tangential component of the magnetic field at the boundary between the two media delivers the following equation:

$$E_{0i}\bar{n}_1 \cos \Theta_i - E_{0r} n_1 \cos \Theta_r = E_{0t} n_2 \cos \Theta_t \quad (2.16)$$

With the conditions provided in equations 2.13 to 2.16, a common solution delivers the relations between the magnitudes of the indecent and reflected waves:

$$E_{0r} = \frac{\bar{n}_1 \cos \Theta_i - \bar{n}_2 \cos \Theta_t}{\bar{n}_1 \cos \Theta_i + \bar{n}_2 \cos \Theta_t} E_{i0} \quad (2.17)$$

with Θ_t related to Θ_i by:

$$\cos \Theta_t = \mp\sqrt{1 - \frac{\bar{n}_1^2}{\bar{n}_2^2} \sin^2 \Theta_i} \quad (2.18)$$

Since $\bar{n}_2 < \bar{n}_1$, i.e. $\Theta_i > \Theta_C$ with $\sin \Theta_C = \bar{n}_2/\bar{n}_1$ and Θ_C denoting the critical angle for internal reflection, then the total reflection condition is achieved. At this condition, the refraction angle in equation 2.18 becomes pure imaginary:

$$\cos \Theta_t = -i\sqrt{\frac{\bar{n}_1^2}{\bar{n}_2^2} \sin^2 \Theta_i - 1} \quad (2.19)$$

The corresponding wave vector is therefore rewritten as $\mathbf{k}_t = (-ik_{x,t}, 0, k_{z,t})$. This means physically that the wave continues to propagate in the second medium along the z-direction with an exponentially decaying component in the x-direction according to $\exp\left(x/x_p\right)$ where $x_p = 1/k_{x,t}$ is called the penetration depth since the electric field decreases to $1/e$ of its value at the interface between the two media. By inserting equation 2.19 into 2.17 we find:

$$E_{0r} = \frac{\bar{n}_1 \cos \Theta_i + i\sqrt{\bar{n}_1^2 \sin^2 \Theta_i - \bar{n}_2^2}}{\bar{n}_1 \cos \Theta_i - i\sqrt{\bar{n}_1^2 \sin^2 \Theta_i - \bar{n}_2^2}} E_{i0} \qquad (2.20)$$

It is clear from equation 2.20 that the intensities of the incident and reflected waves are equal $|E_{0r}|^2 = |E_{0i}|^2$. This means that the entire incident power is reflected. Further, their amplitudes are equal $|E_{0r}| = |E_{0i}|$ and their phases differ which corresponds to a standing wave in the positive x-direction. It is typical to write equation 2.20 in the form:

$$E_{0r} = E_{0i} \exp\left(2i\Phi_r\right) \qquad (2.21)$$

where the phase shift Φ_r is given by:

$$\tan \Phi_r = \frac{+\sqrt{\bar{n}_1^2 \sin^2 \Theta_i - \bar{n}_2^2}}{\bar{n}_1 \cos \Theta_i} \qquad (2.22)$$

The evaluation of equations 2.7, 2.8 and 2.10 under the condition of total reflection corresponds to a wave that propagates in the z-direction (see equation 2.14) with a period that is given by $\lambda_z = \lambda/(\bar{n}_1 \sin \Theta_i)$ where $\lambda = 2\pi c/\omega$. In the positive x-direction a stand wave (equations 2.21 and 2.22) with the period $\lambda_x = \lambda/(\bar{n}_1 \cos \Theta_i)$ is formed whereas it decays exponentially in the negative x-direction (equation 2.19).

The previous analysis can be applied to understand wave propagation in planar waveguides. If the reflected wave from figure 2.1 faces a second planar boundary to another lossless homogeneous medium that has $\bar{n}_3 < \bar{n}_1$, the wave shall be reflected again and thus continue to propagate in a zig-zag pattern along the first medium (with the refractive index $\bar{n}_1$). This is the case of wave guiding which is interesting for real applications. In this case, solutions of the wave equation necessary satisfy both boundary conditions and are referred to as *guided modes*.

The analysis of the wave guiding in planar waveguides leads to guided modes that are classified into Transverse Electric (TE) and Transverse Magnetic (TM) waves. For the TE waves only the y-component of the electric field is non-zero ($E = (0, E_y, 0)$). For the TM modes, only the y-component of the magnetic field is non-zero, or ($H = (0, H_y, 0)$). In the following, we explicitly consider the solution of the TE plane wave. The solution for the TM waves follows along similar lines.

2.1.3   Planar waveguides

The simplest form of a planar waveguide is a 3-layer slab waveguide. The guiding core is sandwiched between a cladding and a substrate. Such a planar waveguide is shown in the GaAs/AlGaAs material system in figure 2.2. The GaAs layer forms the waveguide core and has a refractive index $\bar{n}_f$ that is larger than the refractive indices of the cover layers: the substrate at $x = 0$ with the refractive index $\bar{n}_s$ and the cladding at $x = d$ with the refractive index $\bar{n}_c$. All the three layers are assumed to extend infinitely in the y-direction and in the z-direction and form a so-called *slab*

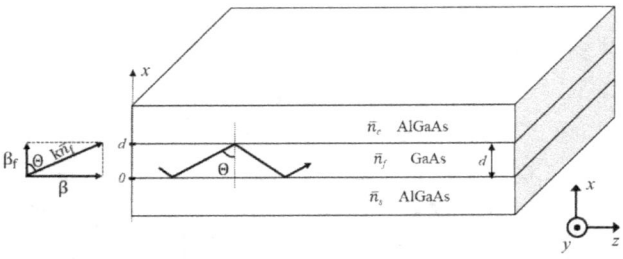

Figure 2.2: Cross-section of a GaAs/AlGaAs planar waveguide and the phase constant $k\bar{n}_f$ of a guided mode propagating in the core layer in the z-direction. The orientation of the wave vector is indicated by the arrow direction.

waveguide. We further consider a TE plane wave that propagates along the z-direction with the phasor $E_y(x,z) = E_0(x) \exp(-i\beta z)$, with $\beta = k\bar{n}_f \sin\Theta = k_z$ and $k_y = 0$ (no dependency on the y-coordinate). Optical wave propagation in the cover layers is for practical reasons not much of interest and it is expected to be absorbed or radiated out of the waveguide. Therefore, we restrict our analysis to cases where the field propagates along the core region (guided modes).
The Helmholtz equation 2.4 for the considered TE plane wave can be written as:

$$\left(\frac{\partial^2}{\partial x^2} + \frac{\partial^2}{\partial z^2}\right) E_y(x,z) + \bar{n}^2 k^2 E_y(x,z) = 0 \tag{2.23}$$

Let us consider the wave propagation as depicted in figure 2.2. For a guided wave in the film region, the propagation angle to the x-axis Θ satisfies the requirement for total internal reflection, i.e. $\Theta > \Theta_C$. Thus, the wave continues to propagate along the z-direction. Due to total internal reflections at the interfaces between the GaAs core and the AlGaAs cover layers, a standing wave is created along the x-direction. In this case the field distribution inside the core varies sinusoidally along the x-axis with $\beta_f = k\bar{n}_f \cos\Theta$. In the cladding (or substrate) layers on the other hand, the signal is reflected at the cladding-core (or substrate-core) interface and it decays exponentially with $\alpha_c = 1/x_{p,c}$ and $\alpha_s = 1/x_{p,s}$, where $x_{p,c}$ and $x_{p,s}$ are the penetration depths of the fields in the cladding and in the substrate, respectively. This condition is valid for all values of z, which means the confined power flow of the optical signal (in x-direction) follows the propagation direction z and corresponds to a guided mode.

The optical field described here corresponds to a plane wave which is a solution of the Helmholtz equation. Therefore, the resulting separation conditions according to equation 2.6 can be written for both, the cover and core layers as the following:

for the cover layers (cladding and substrate)

$$\begin{aligned} k_{x,c}^2 + k_{z,c}^2 &= \bar{n}_c^2 k^2 \\ k_{x,s}^2 + k_{z,s}^2 &= \bar{n}_s^2 k^2 \end{aligned} \tag{2.24}$$

and for the core region

$$k_{x,f}^2 + k_{z,f}^2 = \bar{n}_f^2 k^2 \tag{2.25}$$

with $k_{z,c} = k_{z,s} = \beta_m = \beta$ (propagation along the z-direction), $k_{x,f} = \beta_f$ (propagation inside the film region), and $k_{x,c}^2 = -\alpha_c^2$, $k_{x,s}^2 = -\alpha_s^2$ (exponentially decaying field in the x-direction into the cladding and into the substrate layers, respectively), equations 2.24, 2.25 can be rewritten as:

for the cover layers

$$\begin{aligned}
\bar{n}_c^2 k^2 - \beta^2 &= -\alpha_c^2 \\
\bar{n}_s^2 k^2 - \beta^2 &= -\alpha_s^2
\end{aligned} \tag{2.26}$$

and for the core region

$$\bar{n}_f^2 k^2 - \beta^2 = \beta_f^2 \tag{2.27}$$

The solution of the Helmholtz equation 2.23 that satisfies the separation conditions in equations 2.26 and 2.27 is then a guided TE wave that decays exponentially in the cladding and the substrate. Such a solution can be written as:

$$E_y(x, z) = \begin{cases} E_c \exp\left(-\alpha_c\left(x - d\right)\right) \exp\left(-i\beta z\right) & x > d \\ E_f \cos\left(\beta_f x - \Phi_S\right) \exp\left(-i\beta z\right) & 0 \le x \le d \\ E_s \exp\left(\alpha_s x\right) \exp\left(-i\beta z\right) & x < 0 \end{cases} \tag{2.28}$$

with E_f is being the real field amplitude in the core, E_c and $E_s = E_c$ are being the real field amplitudes in the cladding and in the substrate, respectively. Φ_S is the half-phase shift at the interface between the core layer and the substrate (see equation 2.22).

The terms in the first and third lines in equation 2.28 correspond to the decaying optical field in the cover materials, whereas the term in the second line corresponds to the standing wave in the core material. In order to fully describe the guided TE modes, the boundary conditions at the interfaces between the core and the cover have to be solved. We enforce the continuity of the tangential components of E_y and $\partial E_y / \partial x$ at the interfaces (at $x = 0$ and $x = d$). The following equations is then achieved:

$$\tan\left(\beta_f d - \Phi_S\right) = \tan\left(\Phi_C\right) \tag{2.29}$$

with $\tan\left(\Phi_C\right) = \alpha_c / \beta_f$ is the half-phase shift at the boundary between the core and the cladding at $x = d$. Both of Φ_C and Φ_S are calculated according to equation 2.22 for TE modes.

By considering the periodicity of the tangent function, the so-called characteristic equation of the guided modes [30] can be found:

$$\beta_f \cdot d - \Phi_C - \Phi_S = m\pi \tag{2.30}$$

The characteristic equation reveals the discrete nature of guided modes. Please refer to [29, p. 56-60] for more details to the derivation of equation 2.30.

The electric field distribution of some guided TE modes is shown in figure 2.3. Note that with $\beta_f = \bar{n}_f k \cos\Theta$, according to the characteristic equation 2.30 the number of guided modes is determined by three parameters which are the waveguide width d, the refractive index step between the guide and the cover material, and by the frequency $\omega = kc$. Each of the guided modes inside the core can be attributed to

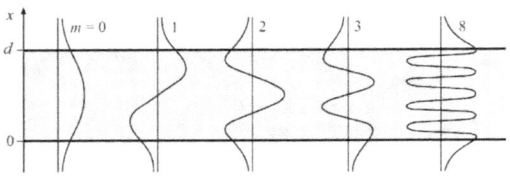

Figure 2.3: Schematic electric field distribution of some guided TE modes. m is the order of the guided mode. Original image [30, p. 44].

a propagation constant $\beta_m = k\bar{n}_f \sin \Theta_m$ with the incidence angle $\Theta_m > \Theta_C$. The mode with the lowest index m is usually referred to as the *fundamental mode*. As a rule of thumb $\Theta_m > \Theta_{m+1} > \Theta_C$ which means that the oscillation period in the x-direction (see section 2.1.2) $\lambda_{x,m} = \lambda/(\bar{n}_f \cos \Theta_m)$ for the mode m is larger than the oscillation period of the mode $m + 1$. We define the effective refractive index $\bar{n}_{eff}$ as a characteristic parameter of the guided mode $\bar{n}_{eff,m} = \beta_m/k$ for all values of m (all the guided modes). Please not the $\bar{n}_{eff}$ for any guided mode necessarily satisfies:

$$\bar{n}_{s,c} < \bar{n}_{eff} < \bar{n}_f \tag{2.31}$$

Further, since the guided optical modes have a finite penetration depth into the cladding and into the substrate, we define the effective waveguide width d_{eff} as:

$$d_{eff} = d + x_{p,c} + x_{p,s} \tag{2.32}$$

For a waveguide with a sufficiently large refractive index step $(\bar{n}_f - \bar{n}_{s,c})$, the effective width d_{eff} can replace d in the characteristic equation 2.30.

2.1.4 Ridge waveguides

The planar waveguide depicted in figure 2.2 is assumed to be infinitely extended along the y-direction. The electrical field is confined along the x-direction. However, for the design of photonic integrated circuits (PICs) the guided optical signal has to be well-defined in two transverse directions (in the xy-plane) which corresponds to a two-dimensional (2D) waveguide geometry. Some 2D waveguides geometries are the strip waveguide, embedded strip, and the ridge waveguide (see figure 2.4). Lateral wave guiding (lateral mode confinement) in these structures is achieved due to the effective refractive index step between the central region (the strip, embedded strip, or the ridge) and the region on the sides which is usually referred to as the slab region. The ridge waveguide structure is easy to fabricate and thanks to the advances in the III-V material technology it is easy to control the lateral and vertical index profile for optimum design [31]. This is why ridge waveguides are the most interesting structures for the design of PICs. On the other hand, the modeling and analysis of ridge waveguides becomes complicated due to the vector nature of the electromagnetic field and the simultaneous presence of various boundary conditions that arise at the various interfaces. In the literature, ridge waveguides were investigated either using approximate analytical approaches, e.g. the effective index methods [32] or using numerical

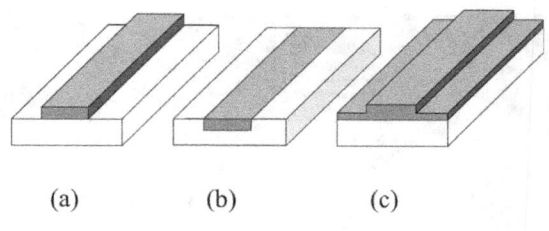

(a) (b) (c)

Figure 2.4: Some types of 2D waveguide geometries: (a) strip, (b) embedded strip, (c) ridge waveguide.

methods such as the finite difference (FD) and finite element (FE) methods [31]. The later methods are computationally intensive but they have been widely used due to their accuracy in comparison to the effective index methods.

Many efforts have been made in the literature to describe the design rules of single mode ridge waveguides [33], [34]. The term single mode means here that only a single lateral guided TE and (or) TM mode is supported. This is a very important requirement for the design of single optical components such as chip-based phase modulators or for the design of PICs in order to control the propagation of the optical field through the PIC and for further coupling of the light into single mode fibers. Multi-mode ridge waveguides that support a finite number of guided TE or TM modes are also used for certain applications, e.g. for the realization of multi-mode interference (MMI) couplers [26].

2.1.5 Bent waveguides

Bent waveguides are indispensable for the design of PICs. They are used to adjust the lateral position or the direction of ridge waveguides to achieve complex devices at a small foot-print (optical systems on the chip [35]). A widely used bent structure is the S-bend (see figure 2.5). For example in ridge-waveguide based MZI modulators, S-bends are used at the output of the couplers to increase the spatial distance between the active arms of the MZI modulator.

The S-bend, despite its simply appearing structure, raises a more challenging modeling problem than the straight ridge waveguide [36]. The propagation vector $\mathbf{k}$ of the S-bend has a non-vanishing lateral component ($k_y \neq 0$). Thus, the analysis of S-bends should account for the transition losses between a straight and a bent waveguide and the phase constants of the field upon propagation in the bend.

2.2 Planar waveguide couplers

Couplers are used in PICs to combine, i.e. spatially overlap optical fields or divide (splitters) the field from one waveguide into two or more paths. Based on ridge waveguides, waveguide couplers can easily be realized.

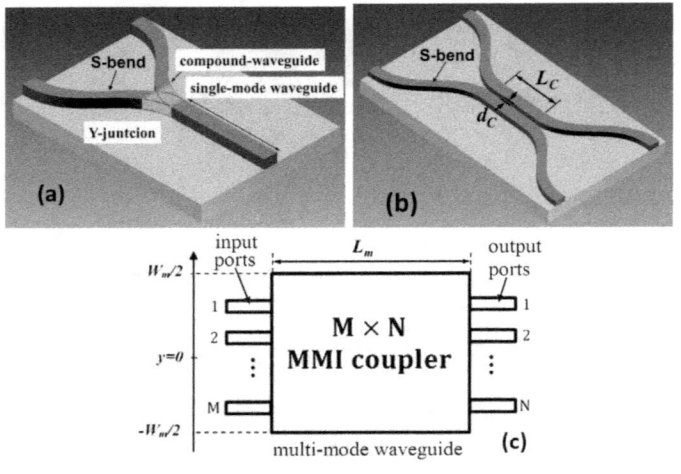

Figure 2.5: Ridge waveguide couplers. (a) 1×2 Y-coupler with S-bends, (b) 2×2 directional coupler with S-bends, and (c) the schematic of the lateral layout of a general M×N MMI coupler.

2.2.1   Concepts for ridge waveguide couplers

The Y-coupler

For the realization of ridge waveguide couplers, different coupling concepts can be applied. The simplest concept is the Y-junction (or Y-coupler) which is shown in figure 2.5 (a). This device can for example be used as a power splitter or combiner. In the splitter regime, the input waveguide supports a single guided mode. The optical power is entirely stored in this *eigenmode*. At the Y-junction , the waveguide expands and begins to support a second guided mode. At the end of the Y-junction a compound waveguide structure is created (see figure 2.5(a)). The optical power is adiabatically tapered into the fundamental mode of this compound waveguide and is then divided into the output waveguides with nominally equal power and equal phases [37]. Bent waveguides are then used to introduce a sufficient lateral separation of the output waveguides.

If the device is used as a power combiner, the optical power is adiabatically tapered from the fundamental mode of the compound waveguide into the eigenmode of the single mode waveguide. The Functionality of the power combiner is directly affected by the differences between the phases of the incoming optical fields at the Y-junction (assuming equal amplitudes). Phase-matched optical fields maximize the power stored in the eigenmode of the single mode waveguide at the end of the junction whereas fields with a π phase difference cancel each other [38, p. 524].

The performance of the the the Y-junction depends on the quality of the compound waveguide which is defined by means of the lithography process. Due to fabrication artifacts, reflection and radiation losses may arise which make this kind of couplers less desirable for PICs.

The directional coupler

This concept is shown in (figure 2.5(b)). The directional coupler uses two identical parallel waveguides. Bent waveguides are used to bring the cross-sections of the two

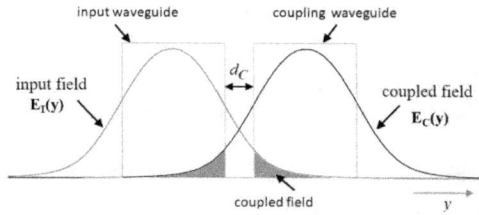

Figure 2.6: Principle of the overlap of the input optical field from the input waveguide with the coupling mode of the coupling waveguide of a directional coupler.

waveguides at a distance d_C that is small enough such that the evanescent optical field from one waveguide can couple into the guided mode of the neighboring waveguide [37, p. 264]. This type of couplers is called a directional coupler since only modes which are traveling in the same direction and with about the same velocity can couple [39, p. 342]. The waveguides spacing d_C (see figure 2.5(b)) is maintained for a certain longitudinal length L_C that is called the coupling length. The bent waveguides at the output side increase the waveguides spacing to terminate the coupling effect.

Directional couplers have a characteristic parameter that is referred to as the transfer distance L_0 [37, p. 267] which is defined as the shortest coupling length at which the injected input power is fully coupled from the input waveguide to the coupling waveguide. Different functionalities of the couplers can be realized at fractional lengths of L_0. For example, at a coupling length $L_C = L_0$ a cross-coupler is achieved, whereas at $L_C = L_0/2$ the function of a 3dB coupler is realized. In fact, $1/L_0$ is proportional to the overlap of the input field E_I and coupled field E_C under the ridge region of the coupling waveguide. Both fields with their corresponding lateral expansion under the ridge (in y-direction) are shown in figure 2.6. The overlap of both fields is calculated using the coupling coefficient Γ_C [37, p. 265] which is given by:

$$\Gamma_C = \frac{1}{2}\left(\bar{n}_{eff}^2 - \bar{n}_c^2\right) \cdot \frac{2\pi\bar{n}_{eff}}{\lambda} \int_{W_r} E_I(y)E_C(y)dy \tag{2.33}$$

where $\bar{n}_{eff}$ is the effective index of the guided TE fundamental mode (equal for both input and couple fields) and $\bar{n}_c$ is the effective refractive index of the slab region at the sides of the ridge (see section 2.2.2 for the determination of the effective refractive index of a slab region). The integral in equation 2.33 is carried out along the width of the coupling waveguide W_r. The corresponding transfer distance is given by:

$$L_0 = \pi/(2\Gamma_C) \tag{2.34}$$

The larger Γ_C is, the shorter the transfer distance L_0, which then enables to realize short couplers. The experiment shows that the performance of directional couplers is very sensitive to the fabrication variations.

The multi-mode interference coupler

A widely used coupler device is the multi-mode interference (MMI) coupler [26] which is shown in figure 2.5 (c). The so-called self-imaging (see the next section) in multi-mode waveguides is used to realize MMI couplers with multiple input/output channels. MMI couplers are known to be more tolerant to fabrication tolerances/variations in comparison to couplers such as directional couplers or Y-junctions [26]. The MMI couplers are the most interesting devices to realize MZI modulators [40]. The self-imaging principle of MMI couplers is discussed in the following section.

2.2.2   Self-imaging in multi-mode interference couplers

In an MMI coupler, the input signal from one or more single mode input (access) waveguides (waveguides 1 to M in figure 2.5 (c)) is launched into the multi-mode waveguide of a width W_m and a length L_m that supports a number of m guided lateral modes $(m \geq N)$. At the length L_m, a number N of images of the input fields is generated by means of the self-imaging mechanism.

To simplify the description of self-imaging in multi-mode ridge waveguides, the 2D geometry (in the xy-plane) of the multi-mode waveguide is reduced to one dimension (1D). Such a 1D structure can be achieved by applying the effective refractive index method [32]. In this method the cross-section of a ridge waveguide is divided into three regions (see figure 2.7), each region is attributed to a characteristic parameter that is the effective refractive index of the fundamental guided mode of an infinite planar waveguide. The planar waveguide is assumed to have the same vertical structure of the considered region. The lateral discontinuities of the original 2D structure (which cor-

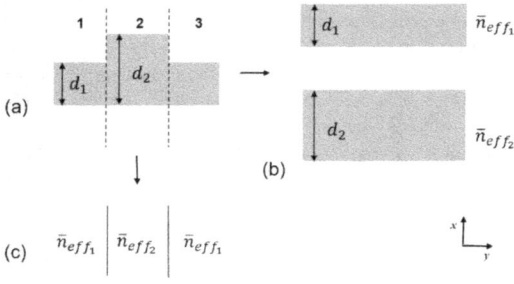

Figure 2.7: Effective refractive index method. (a) ridge cross section, (b) two slab waveguides, (c) corresponding effective refractive indices of the slab waveguides.

respond to the ridge boundaries) define the 1D region with different effective refractive indicies as can be seen by figure 2.7(a) and (b). This new structure can be regarded as a planar waveguide along the y-direction that has a core with the refractive index

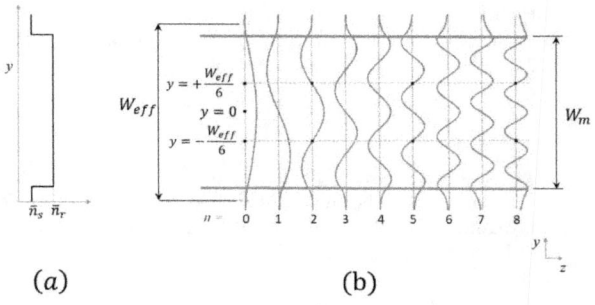

Figure 2.8: Two dimensional (2D) representation of a multi-mode ridge waveguide. (a) the (effective) refractive index profile ($\bar{n}_r = \bar{n}_{eff_2}$, $\bar{n}_s = \bar{n}_{eff_1}$), (b) top view of the ridge boundaries with examples of modal field distributions E_n of the guided modes 0, 1, $\cdots$ 8. (Reproduced photo, original taken from [26]).

$\bar{n}_{eff_2}$ and cover layers with the refractive index $\bar{n}_{eff_1}$. Thus, the analysis of the guided optical modes follows in similar lines to the guided waves in a planar waveguide that was presented in section 2.1.

The multi-mode ridge waveguide of a width W_m is represented by the effective refractive indices of the ridge $\bar{n}_r = \bar{n}_{eff_2}$ and the slab regions $\bar{n}_s = \bar{n}_{eff_1}$ as shown by figure 2.8(a) and supports m guided lateral modes. Each of these modes should satisfy the separation condition for the guiding region:

$$k_{y,n}^2 + \beta_n^2 = \bar{n}_r^2 k^2 \tag{2.35}$$

with β_n the propagation constant of the guided lateral mode with the index n and $n = 0 \cdots m - 1$. The corresponding characteristic equation is given by:

$$k_{y,n} = \frac{(n+1)\pi}{W_{eff}} \tag{2.36}$$

Equation 2.36 results from the characteristic equation 2.30 by using the following:

- $\Phi_C = \Phi_S$ for a symmetric waveguide.

- the effective refractive index step is large enough to assume that the optical guided mode is well confined under the ridge. Hence, W_m is well approximated by W_{eff}.

By considering that the optical field is TE polarized, equation 2.22 applies to calculate the phase shift Φ_C at the interfaces. The second condition above implies that the incidence angle at the interfaces between the ridge region and the side regions satisfies $\Theta \to 0$ and thus $2\Phi_C \to \pi$. This implies that the amplitude of the electric field at the interfaces is too small so that the evanescent field from the ridge region into the side regions $E_t = E_i - E_r \to 0$ which corresponds to $E_t = E_i - E_r \to 0$ (see figure 2.1).

At a sufficiently large multi-mode waveguide width W_m so that $W_m \gg \lambda$ with $\lambda = 2\pi/k$ a binomial expansion with $k_{y,n}^2 \ll \bar{n}_r^2 k^2$ can be applied. In this case, by inserting 2.35 in 2.36, the propagation constants of the guides modes are given by:

$$\beta_n \cong \bar{n}_r k - \frac{\pi(n+1)^2 \lambda}{4\bar{n}_r W_{eff}^2} \tag{2.37}$$

Now let us consider an optical field that is imposed at $z = 0$ in figure 2.8(b). Suppose $E_n(y), n = 0, 1, 2, \cdots m - 1$ are the modal field distributions of the guided modes in the multi-mode waveguide. The imposed optical field at lateral position (y, z=0) can then be decomposed into the $E_n(y)$ space [26]:

$$E(y, 0) = \sum_{n=0}^{m-1} a_n E_n(y) \tag{2.38}$$

The estimation of the coefficients a_n follows using the overlap integrals:

$$a_n = \frac{\int E(y, 0) E_n(y) dy}{\int E_n^2(y) dy} \tag{2.39}$$

based on the field orthogonality relations [26].

Equation 2.38 is valid if the imposed field E is totally contained within the multi-mode waveguide effective width W_{eff} which can be approximated by W_m for waveguides with a sufficiently large effective refractive index step ($\Delta \bar{n} = \bar{n}_r - \bar{n}_s$). In other words, the field E should have a spatial spectrum that is narrow enough such as that only the guided modes are excited which is a condition that is satisfied for all practical applications [26], since the power of the radiation modes leaks out pf the guide rapidly [51].

Each of the guided (lateral) modes propagate in the z-direction according to β_n. At a position $z > 0$, the optical field becomes a superposition of the propagating guided modes. Thus, by assuming an implicit harmonic dependence according to $\exp(i\omega t)$, the field at position $z > 0$ is written as:

$$E(y, z) = \sum_{n=0}^{m-1} a_n E_n(y) \exp(-i\beta_n z) \tag{2.40}$$

Now, by taking the propagation constant of the fundamental mode β_0 as a common factor and then dropping it (without loss of generality), equation 2.40 can be written as:

$$E(y, z) = \sum_{n=0}^{m-1} a_n E_n(y) e^{i(\beta_0 - \beta_n)z} \tag{2.41}$$

We define the beat length L_π of the fundamental and first order guided modes:

$$L_\pi = \frac{\pi}{\beta_0 - \beta_1} \tag{2.42}$$

where $\bar{\beta}_0$, β_1 are the propagation constants of the fundamental mode and first order guided mode, respectively. By inserting equations 2.37 and 2.42 in 2.41, we find:

$$E(y, z) = \sum_{n=0}^{m-1} a_n E_n(y) e^{i\frac{n(n+2)z}{3L_\pi}} \tag{2.43}$$

Equation 2.43 means that at a certain distance $z = L$ the filed $E(y, z = L)$ becomes a reproduction (self-image) of $E(y, 0)$ if:

$$e^{i\frac{n(n+2)L}{3L_\pi}} = 1 \ \ or \ (-1)^n \tag{2.44}$$

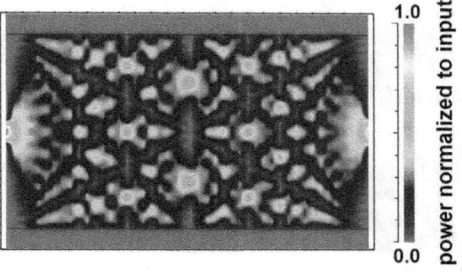

Figure 2.9: Self-imaging in multi-mode waveguides. Interference pattern of the injected optical field into a multi-mode waveguide (Simulation using a 2D beam propagation method). Input field launched at the center of the multi-mode waveguide.

This property of multi-mode waveguides is called *self-imaging*. If for example the first condition in 2.44 was fulfilled, i.e. $(\exp(i\frac{n(n+2)L}{3L_\pi}) = 1)$, this means that all guides modes overlap at the position $z = L$ with phase differences of multiples of 2π. The resulting field is then called a direct image of the input field. The second condition in 2.44 correspond to phase differences alternatively changing between odd or even multiples of π. As a result, the self-image is a mirrored-image -with respect to the center of the multi-mode waveguide- of the input field $E(y, 0)$ (or a direct image of $E(-y, 0)$). The conditions in equation 2.44 are satisfied at lengths $L_l = l \cdot 3L_\pi$, $l = 0, 1, 2, \ldots$ (a direct image at l *even*, mirrored image at l *odd*). It can also be shown (see [26]) that N images of the input field $E(y, 0)$ occur at $L_l = l \cdot 3L_\pi/N$ with $l = 1, 3, 5, \ldots$. For the special case of $N = 2$, two images with the equal amplitudes $1/\sqrt{2}$ (3dB power divider) are created at $L_l = l \cdot 3L_\pi/2$, $l = 1, 3, 5, \ldots$.

2.2.3 Interference mechanisms of self-imaging

Generally, if the y-position of the input field is set arbitrarily, the first N-images of the input occur at lengths of $L_N = 3L_\pi/N$. This interference mechanism is called a *general* interference mechanism [26]. However, by carefully selecting the y-position of the input field E, it may be possible to excite only a certain number of the guided modes (selective excitation). This mechanism is referred to as a *restricted* interference mechanism. It enables to reduce the periodicity of the phase factors in equation 2.43 which makes it feasible to create single or multiple images at fractional lengths of the beat length [26]. The most commonly applied restricted interference mechanisms in the literature are the *symmetric* interference mechanism and the *paired* interference mechanism:

- **The symmetric interference mechanism:** this is the simplest restricted interference mechanism. It is usually applied to realize $1 \times N$ MMI couplers. Here the field is launched at the center of the multi-mode waveguide which then excites only the even symmetric modes [26]. This means that the coefficients $a_n = 0$ for $n = 1, 3, 5, \ldots$ in equation 2.43. By noting that $mod_4 \left(n \cdot (n + 2) = 0 \right)$ for n even, the length L_N for the first N-fold images is given by:

$$L_N = \frac{3L_\pi}{4N} \tag{2.45}$$

which is 4-times shorter than the multi-mode waveguide length achieved by using the general interference mechanism.

- **The paired interference mechanism:** this mechanism is usually applied to realize 2×2 MMI couplers. It is achieved when the input optical field is launched at a position $y = \mp W_m/6$. It can be shown that at this y-position the modes with the indices $n = 2, 5, 8, \ldots$ don't contribute to the self-imaging (see figure 2.8). In this mechanism, each excited even mode leads to its odd partner. Mode pairs are for example $\{0, 1\}$, $\{3, 4\}$. At the propagation length $L_{3dB} = L_\pi/2$, the phase differences between the paired modes are $\pi/2$ which leads to the 3dB coupler. Cross couplers are realized at L_π where the phase differences between the paired modes are equal to π. Generally, the length of the multi-mode waveguide that produces N-fold images using the paired interference is given by:

$$L_N = \frac{L_\pi}{N} \tag{2.46}$$

The symmetric and paired interference mechanism will be applied in order to realize 1×2 MMI splitters and the 2×2 MMI couplers as will be later shown in chapter 5.

2.2.4 Characteristics of waveguide couplers

Generally, the performance of different types of waveguide couplers is characterized by two parameters: the access loss, and the imbalance. The excess loss describes the amount of optical power that does not emerge from the output ports of the coupler due to propagation losses and radiation losses (coupling losses are not included). In a coupler with a number N of output ports, if the optical power P_{in} at $z = 0$ is injected into the coupler, and the power that is transmitted to each output port is $P_1, P_2, \cdots P_N$ the excess loss (in dB) is given by [40]:

$$excess\, loss\,[\text{dB}] = 10 \times \log \frac{P_{in}}{P_1 + P_2 + \cdots + P_N} \tag{2.47}$$

The imbalance is the splitting ratio of the output power into the output ports. It can be measured directly at the output ports of a coupler device. By assuming equal coupling losses at all the output ports, the imbalance (in dB) is given by:

$$imbalance\,[\text{dB}] = 10 \times \log \frac{P_{out_{max}}}{P_{out_{min}}} \tag{2.48}$$

where $P_{out_{max}} = max\,(P_1, P_2, \cdots P_N)$, and $P_{out_{min}} = min\,(P_1, P_2, \cdots P_N)$.

Chapter 3

Theory of GaAs-based electro-optic phase modulators

Applying an external electric field across certain materials (electro-optic (EO) materials) can distort the orientation, position, or the shapes of the molecules building these materials [37, p. 697]. As a result, their optical properties are modified. For example, the refractive index of an electro-optic material can be perturbed with an electric field. The resulting effect is called the electro-optic effect. This effect is used in electro-optic phase modulators [23]. Electro-optic phase modulators can be for example realized using single electro-optic crystals such lithium niobate (LiNbO$_3$) or using compound semiconductor material systems such as GaAs-based double heterostructures [23].

Chip-based electro-optic phase modulators based on GaAs/AlGaAs double heterostructures are of particular interest due to the unique integration properties of GaAs with electronic devices. Besides, they reduce space and power requirements in comparison to LiNbO$_3$ phase modulators which is very important for the realization of micro-integrated optical devices and PICs.

In the GaAs/AlGaAs double heterostructure phase modulators, a waveguide in a multi-layer epitaxial structure (double heterostructure) is realized and the optical field is confined inside the guiding region of this waveguide. For the different layers a suitable doping profile is selected such that an external electric field is applied on the guiding region to modify the refractive index in this region. Further, in the GaAs-material the spatial distribution of the free carrier density inside the GaAs-based double heterostructure can be modified by applying an electric field. The presence of the free carriers in the GaAs (or AlGaAs) material also modifies the refractive through the Kramers-Krönig relations [23]. This effect is called the free carrier effect (also the carrier density-related effects).

In this chapter, we give a brief introduction to the electro-optic properties in GaAs which include both the electro-optic effects and the free carriers effects. Further, we discuss the properties of GaAs/AlGaAs double heterostructures and their deployment for the realization of electro-optic phase modulators.

3.1 Electro-optic effects in GaAs

3.1.1 Linear and quadratic electro-optic effects

In electro-optic materials, the change of refractive index $\bar{n}$ with the electric field E is small enough such as that it can be expanded into the Taylor series [37, p. 698]:

$$\bar{n}\,(E) = \bar{n} + (d\bar{n}/dE)\,|_{E=0}E + \frac{1}{2}\left(d^2\bar{n}/dE^2\right)|_{E=0}E^2 + \cdots, \tag{3.1}$$

where the linear electro-optic (LEO) and the quadratic electro-optic (QEO) effects arise in the second and third terms in equation 3.1, respectively. Higher order terms in equation 3.1 can be safely ignored. For the derivation of the electro-optic coefficients it is useful to derive from equation 3.1 an expression:

$$\Delta\eta = \Delta\left(\frac{1}{\bar{n}^2}\right) = -\frac{2}{\bar{n}^3}\,(d\bar{n}/dE)\,|_{E=0}E - \frac{1}{\bar{n}^3}\left(d^2\bar{n}/dE^2\right)|_{E=0}E^2 \tag{3.2}$$

where $(\eta = \epsilon_0/\epsilon = 1/\bar{n}^2)$ is the electrical impermeability of the electro-optic material. The LEO coefficient or Pockels (Friedrich Pockels (1865-1913)) coefficient is given by $\bar{r} = -\frac{2}{\bar{n}^3}\,(d\bar{n}/dE)\,|_{E=0}$ and the QEO coefficient or Kerr (John Kerr (1824-1907)) coefficient $\bar{R} = -\frac{1}{\bar{n}^3}\left(d^2\bar{n}/dE^2\right)|_{E=0}$ [37, p. 696–700]. Equation 3.2 can then be written as:

$$\Delta\eta = \bar{r}E + \bar{R}E^2 \tag{3.3}$$

3.1.2 The index ellipsoid

The index ellipsoid is a geometric construction that can be used to describe the optical properties of anisotropic materials [37, p. 712]. For example, the description of the electro-optical properties of GaAs using the index ellipsoid is given by [37, p. 712–719]:

$$\sum_{ij}\eta_{ij}x_ix_j = 1, \quad i,\,j = 1,\,2,\,3 \tag{3.4}$$

Using the ellipsoid, the refractive indices of two normal modes $\bar{n}_a$ and $\bar{n}_b$ of an optical wave propagating in a given direction $\mathbf{k}$ can be derived (see figure 3.1). η_{ij} are elements of the impermeability tensor $\boldsymbol{\eta} = \epsilon_0/\boldsymbol{\epsilon}$, and $\boldsymbol{\epsilon}$ is the permittivity tensor.
If an electric field $\boldsymbol{E} = (E_1, E_2, E_3)$ is applied, the elements of the tensor $\boldsymbol{\eta}$ become functions of the electric field, i.e., $\eta_{ij} = \eta_{ij}\,(E_1, E_2, E_3)$. Thus, each of these elements can be expanded in a Taylor's series about $\boldsymbol{E} = \mathbf{0}$:

$$\eta_{ij}\,(\boldsymbol{E}) = \eta_{ij}\,(\mathbf{0}) + \sum_k \bar{r}_{ij,k}E_k + \sum_{kl}\bar{R}_{ij,kl}E_kE_l, \quad i,j,k,l = 1,\,2,\,3 \tag{3.5}$$

with $\bar{r}_{ij,k} = \frac{\partial\eta_{ij}}{\partial E_k}|_{\boldsymbol{E}=0}$, $\bar{R}_{ij,kl} = \frac{\partial^2\eta_{ij}}{\partial E_k\partial E_l}|_{\boldsymbol{E}=0}$ are the components of the LEO and QEO tensors $[\bar{\mathbf{r}}]$ and $[\bar{\mathbf{R}}]$, respectively, which can be regarded as generalization of the electro-optic coefficients in equation 3.3.

To describe the electro-optic coefficients of GaAs using the index ellipsoid, let's consider the unit cell of the GaAs crystal which is shown on the right side of figure 3.1. The principal axes of the GaAs crystal correspond to the ellipsoid's principal axes

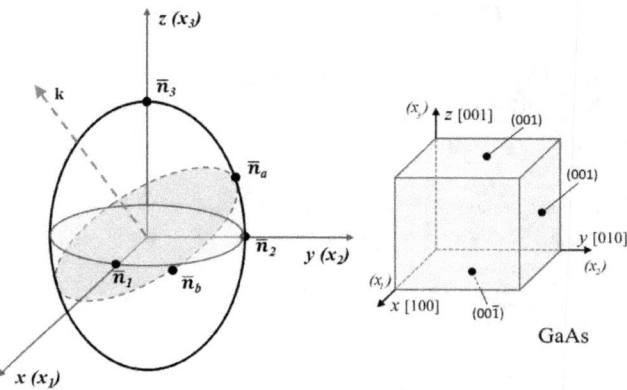

Figure 3.1: (left) Index ellipsoid. The principal axes match the coordinates (x, y, z). $\bar{n}_1$, $\bar{n}_2$, $\bar{n}_3$ are the principal refractive indices. $\bar{n}_a$ and $\bar{n}_b$ are the refractive indices of two normal modes of the wave traveling in direction $\mathbf{k}$. See [37, p. 713]. (right) GaAs crystal with $[iii]$ being the crystallographic directions and (iii) the principal planes and $i \in \{0, 1, \bar{1}\}$.

$(x = x_1, y = x_2, z = x_3)$. The principal refractive indices are $\bar{n}_1$, $\bar{n}_2$, and $\bar{n}_3$. Being a cubic crystal of the group $\bar{4}3m$, the GaAs crystal possesses only a single Pockels component $\bar{r}_{41}$ (or $\bar{r}_{32,1}$) [41] and three Kerr components, namely, $\bar{R}_{11}$, $\bar{R}_{12}$, and $\bar{R}_{44}$ [42]. They can be written as the complex third-rank tensor $[\bar{r}]$ and the fourth-rank tensor $[\bar{R}]$ as follows:

$$[\bar{\mathbf{r}}] = \begin{bmatrix} 0 & 0 & 0 \\ 0 & 0 & 0 \\ 0 & 0 & 0 \\ \bar{r}_{41} & 0 & 0 \\ 0 & \bar{r}_{41} & 0 \\ 0 & 0 & \bar{r}_{41} \end{bmatrix}, \; [\bar{\mathbf{R}}] = \begin{bmatrix} R_{11} & R_{12} & R_{12} & 0 & 0 & 0 \\ R_{12} & R_{11} & R_{12} & 0 & 0 & 0 \\ R_{12} & R_{12} & R_{11} & 0 & 0 & 0 \\ 0 & 0 & 0 & R_{44} & 0 & 0 \\ 0 & 0 & 0 & 0 & R_{44} & 0 \\ 0 & 0 & 0 & 0 & 0 & R_{44} \end{bmatrix}, \; R_{44} = \frac{R_{11} - R_{12}}{2}$$

$$(3.6)$$

Let us assume ,without loss of generality, that the electric field $E = (E_1, E_2, E_3)$ is applied along the z-direction ($E_1 = 0, E_2 = 0$). In order to determine the electro-optic effects, the ellipsoid can be rewritten using the modified impermeability ($\eta_{ij}(E) = \eta_{ij}(0) + \Delta\eta_{ij}$), with $\eta_{ij}(0)$ being a diagonal matrix whose elements are $1/\bar{n}_1^2, 1/\bar{n}_2^2, 1/\bar{n}_3^2$. Due to the fact that the GaAs crystal is isotropic, the principal refractive indices are equal: $\bar{n}_1 = \bar{n}_2 = \bar{n}_3 = \bar{n}$.

Pockels effect (LEO effect):

In order to extract the expression for the Pockels effect we consider only the first order of the Taylor series in equation 3.5 with the coefficients ($\bar{r}_{ij,k} = \frac{\partial \eta_{ij}}{\partial E_k}|_{E=0}$):

$$\eta_{ij}\left(\boldsymbol{E}\right) = \eta_{ij}\left(\boldsymbol{0}\right) + \sum_{ij} \bar{r}_{ij,k} E_k, \quad i, j, k = 1, 2, 3 \tag{3.7}$$

By inserting equations 3.6 and 3.7 in 3.4, the modified ellipsoid for the Pockels effect (LEO effect) can be written as [37]:

$$\frac{x_1^2 + x_2^2 + x_3^2}{\bar{n}^2} + 2\bar{r}_{41} \cdot E_3 \cdot x_1 x_2 = 1 \tag{3.8}$$

Let us now consider the modified coordinates $v_1 = \frac{x_1 - x_2}{\sqrt{2}}$, $v_2 = \frac{x_1 + x_2}{\sqrt{2}}$, and $v_1 = x_3$. By taking into account that $2 \cdot x_1 x_2 = v_2^2 - v_1^2$, equation 3.8 yields:

$$\frac{1}{\bar{n}_1^2(E)} \cdot v_1^2 + \frac{1}{\bar{n}_2^2(E)} \cdot v_2^2 + \frac{1}{\bar{n}_3^2(E)} \cdot v_3^2 = 1 \tag{3.9}$$

where:

$$\frac{1}{\bar{n}_1^2(E)} = \left(\frac{1}{\bar{n}^2} + \bar{r}_{41} \cdot E\right)$$
$$\frac{1}{\bar{n}_2^2(E)} = \left(\frac{1}{\bar{n}^2} - \bar{r}_{41} \cdot E\right) \tag{3.10}$$
$$\frac{1}{\bar{n}_3^2(E)} = \frac{1}{\bar{n}^2}$$

Equations 3.9 and 3.10 shows that the modified principal axes correspond to v_1, v_2, v_3 which are rotated by 45° with respect to the original coordinates x_1, x_2, x_3. The modified ellipsoid is now given in the new coordinate system (v_1, v_2, v_3) and the final step is to extract the associated refractive index change due the LEO effect. This follows from equation 3.10 by using the approximation $1/\sqrt{1 + \delta} \approx 1 - \frac{1}{2}\delta$ which leads to:

$$\bar{n}_1\left(E\right) \approx \bar{n} - \frac{1}{2}\bar{n}^3\bar{r}_{41} \cdot E_3$$
$$\bar{n}_2\left(E\right) \approx \bar{n} + \frac{1}{2}\bar{n}^3\bar{r}_{41} \cdot E_3 \tag{3.11}$$
$$\bar{n}_3\left(E\right) = \bar{n}$$

The previous discussion yields the following: for the GaAs crystal with the principal axes $x = x_1$ and $y = x_2$ matched to the [100] and [010] crystallographic directions, the modified ellipsoid due LEO effect is rotated with respect to the principal axes by 45°. Which means that the corresponding modified v_1, v_2 coordinates v_1, v_2 are then oriented to the [110] and [1$\bar{1}$0] crystallographic directions, respectively. A plane wave that is propagating in the xy-plane (parallel to the principal plane (001), see figure 3.1 (right)) can observe the modification of the refractive index by the LEO effect as long as the oscillation of its electric field in also parallel to the xy-plane, which is the case of a TE polarized wave. If the propagation vector $\mathbf{k}$ of the TE wave is chosen to be parallel to the [110] crystallographic direction (waveguide along the v_1 access), the modification of the refractive index by the LEO effect corresponds to $\bar{n}_1$ in equation 3.11. For propagation in the [1$\bar{1}$0] direction, the modification of the refractive index by the LEO effect corresponds then to $\bar{n}_2$ in equation 3.11. If the plane wave is on the other hand TM polarized, with the oscillation of the electric field perpendicular to the xy-plane, no contribution of the LEO effect is observed according to $\bar{n}_3$ in equation 3.11.

Kerr effect (QEO effect):

Following a discussion similar to what was described for the LEO effect, we drop this time the first derivative (linear coefficient) which reduces equation 3.5 to:

$$\eta_{ij}(\boldsymbol{E}) = \eta_{ij}(\boldsymbol{0}) + \sum_{ij} \bar{R}_{ij,kl} E_k E_l, \quad i,j,k,l = 1, 2, 3 \tag{3.12}$$

By inserting equations 3.6 and 3.12 in 3.4, the modified ellipsoid for the Kerr effect (QEO effect) can be written as [37]:

$$\left(\frac{1}{\bar{n}^2} + \bar{R}_{12} \cdot E_3{}^2\right)(x_1^2 + x_2^2) + \left(\frac{1}{\bar{n}^2} + \bar{R}_{11} \cdot E_3{}^2\right) x_3^2 = 1 \tag{3.13}$$

Equation 3.13 shows that the Kerr effect corresponds to an equal modification of the ellipsoid in the principal xy-plane and another, different modification in the principal z-direction.

The resulting refractive index change due to the QEO effect (using the approximation $1/\sqrt{1+\delta} \approx 1 - \frac{1}{2}\delta$) is:

$$\begin{aligned}
\bar{n}_{\acute{a}} &= \bar{n}_{1,2}(E) \approx \bar{n} - \frac{1}{2}\bar{n}^3 \bar{R}_{12} \cdot E_3^2 \\
\bar{n}_{\acute{b}} &= \bar{n}_3(E) \approx \bar{n} - \frac{1}{2}\bar{n}^3 \bar{R}_{11} \cdot E_3^2
\end{aligned} \tag{3.14}$$

here $\bar{n}_{\acute{a}}$ and $\bar{n}_{\acute{b}}$, are the modified refractive indices of the normal modes in the xy-principal plane and in the z-axis, respectively.

Hence, for a plane wave that is propagating in the xy-plane (parallel to the principal plane (001)), the QEO effect has no orientation dependence on the crystallographic direction of the waveguide. The first and second terms in equation 3.14 correspond to the contribution to phase modulation of the TE mode (with the QEO coefficient $\bar{R}_{12}$), and the TM mode (with the QEO coefficient $\bar{R}_{11}$), respectively.

LEO and QEO effects in GaAs-based waveguides

The previous discussion of the LEO and QEO effects yields the following: in a GaAs-based phase modulator waveguide that is realized on a (001) GaAs substrate with the electric field perpendicular to the multi-layer, the waveguide (the propagation direction) should be realized parallel to the [110] or [1$\bar{1}$0] directions to use the LEO effect. The following two equations describe the refractive index modification by the LEO and QEO effects depending on the modal excitation (TE or TM) [23], [19]:

For the TE mode:

$$\Delta\bar{n} = \pm\frac{\bar{n}^3}{2}\bar{r}_{41} \cdot E - \frac{\bar{n}^3}{2}\bar{R}_{12} \cdot E^2 \tag{3.15}$$

and for the TM mode:

$$\Delta \bar{n} = -\frac{\bar{n}^3}{2} \bar{R}_{11} \cdot E^2 \qquad (3.16)$$

The positive and negative signs in the first term of 3.15 correspond to light propagation in the $[1\bar{1}0]$ and $[110]$ directions, respectively.

3.2   Free carrier effects (carrier density-related effects)

Free carriers in GaAs which are introduced by doping or injection reduce the refractive index [23], [30]. This change of the refractive index is attributed to a modification of the absorption in two regions of the spectrum, namely, in the mid-infrared and at the absorption edge. In the mid-infrared region, the refractive index changes due to the plasma and intervalence-band absorption. At the absorption edge the band-filling effect and the many-body effect modify the refractive index. In [23], J. Faist and F.-K. Reinhart found that the overall contribution of the free carrier effects is proportional to the free carrier concentration and independent of the effective mass of the free carriers. They were able to give an analytic formula for the free carrier effects in GaAs. Accordingly, the modification of the refractive index by free carriers is given by [23]:

for holes:

$$\Delta \bar{n} = -\left(\frac{8 \times 10^{-22}}{E_{ph}^2} + \frac{1.46 \times 10^{-21}}{(E_g + kT)^2 - E_{ph}^2} \right) \cdot n_h \qquad (3.17)$$

and for electrons:

$$\Delta \bar{n} = -\left(\frac{2.8 \times 10^{-21}}{E_{ph}^2} + \frac{1.99 \times 10^{-21}}{(E_g + kT)^2 - E_{ph}^2} \right) \cdot n_e \qquad (3.18)$$

where n_h and n_e are the holes and electrons densities in $[cm^{-3}]$ unit, respectively, E_g is the bandgap energy (in [eV]), and E_{ph} is the photon energy (in [eV]). kT is the thermal energy (also in [eV] with k being Boltzmann constant and T the temperature.

GaAs-based electro-based phase modulators use both, the electro-optic effects and the free carriers effects. The phase modulator waveguides are realized in double heterostructures for optical field confinement with intentionally doped (or undoped) layers for electric field and carrier confinement as discussed in the following sections.

3.3   GaAs-based double heterostructures

GaAs is one of a few binary semiconductors that can exist as a high-quality substrate. It can also be mixed with atoms from the same groups of the periodic system to form ternary or quaternary compound semiconductors such as $Al_xGa_{1-x}As$ and $(Al_xGa_{1-x})_yIn_{1-y}As$, with $0 < x < 1$ and $0 < y < 1$. Mixed compound semiconductors from the III-V groups are very attractive for the realization of photonic integrated circuits. They can be grown in thin layers which are called *epitaxial layers*. As a rule of thumb, within a system of multiple epitaxial layers with different compound semiconductors, the material with the lower bandgap has a larger refractive index. This is a key for defining the functionality of photonic devices such as laser diodes and waveguides. For example, in the planar waveguide in figure 2.2, the $Al_xGa_{1-x}As$ with $0 < x < 1$ has a larger bandgap than GaAs. Thus for the purpose of wave guiding, the GaAs is used as a core material and the cover is made of $Al_xGa_{1-x}As$ with $0 < x < 1$. The waveguide is realized using $GaAs/Al_xGa_{1-x}As$ multi-layers. The entire waveguide is grown on a GaAs substrate. Further, in GaAs-based electro-optic devices, the multi-layers are doped with negative (n-type) free electrons or positive (p-type) free holes in order to form heterojunctions for electric field confinement.

3.3.1 The p-n junction and the heterojunctions

The p-n junction occurs between *p*-type and *n*-type regions of the same semiconductor material. When the *p*- and *n*-type regions are brought in contact the electrons diffuse from the *n*-region into the *p*-region where they then recombine with excess holes. In a similar way, the holes diffuse from the *p*-region into the *n*-region and recombine with excess electrons. The diffusing electrons leave positively charged ionized *doner* atoms whereas the diffusing holes leave negatively charged ionized *acceptor* atoms. This diffusion on both sides of the junction leaves a narrow area at both sides of the junction which is totally empty of free carriers and called the *depletion region* [24]. The tension that is created due to this situation creates a so-called *built-in* electric field. Applying a reverse biased voltage to the p-n junction will drive the holes in the p-side of the junction and the electrons in the n-side further away from the junction which increases the depletion width.

In double heterostructures, the junction can be created between different semiconductor materials (for example between GaAs and $Al_xGa_{1-x}As$, or between $Al_{x_1}Ga_{1-x_1}As$ and $Al_{x_2}Ga_{1-x_2}As$ with $x_1 \neq x_2$) with different doping types, and is therefore called a heterojunction. The energy band-diagram of the heterojunction suffers a local discontinuity at the junction. This creates a barrier that can be used for example to create prevented zones for selected carriers (carrier confinement in desired regions of space). This property is used in GaAs-based double heterostructures for the design of diode lasers, photodiodes, and for phase modulators as we will show in the following section.

3.3.2 GaAs/AlGaAs double heterostructures phase modulators

GaAs-based phase modulators use GaAs/AlGaAs double heterostructures to enforce index guiding of the optical field confinement. Appropriate free carrier injection into the different multi-layers is applied to create a p-n heterojunction in the waveguide with a depletion area for electric field confinement.

Let us consider for example the multilayer in figure 3.2. The GaAs core with the lower band-gap is sandwiched between the $Al_xGa_{1-x}As$ cladding layers to form a double heterostructure. The layers are doped as follows: upper cladding p-doped(P-$Al_xGa_{1-x}As$), core p-doped (p-GaAs), lower cladding n-doped (N-$Al_xGa_{1-x}As$). Such a doping profile is called: P-p-N. The device is assumed to be grown on a n^+-GaAs (n-type highly doped) substrate that forms the n-contact layer and an additional p^+-GaAs (p-type highly doped) upper layer forms the p-contact layer. We further

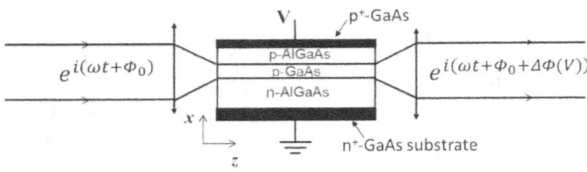

Figure 3.2: Concept of a double heterostructure phase modulator. Light beam is focused into the guiding layer. The application of reverse-biased voltage changes the electric field and carrier density in the junction which modifies the refractive index. $\Delta\Phi(V)$ is the phase shift due to applied reversed bias voltage V.

assume that the concentration of the free carriers in the core layer is much lower than their concentration in the cover layers. In the absence of external electric field (corresponding to a reverse biase voltage $V = V_0 = 0$) a depletion region is formed due to the built-in voltage (V_D). This region has one side in the p-GaAs core layer and one side in the N-Al$_x$Ga$_{1-x}$As cladding layer. Free carriers are pushed on the sides of this region. The depletion widths into the p-side (x_p) and into the N-side (x_N) are given from the Poisson's equations by [13]:

$$x_p = \sqrt{\frac{2\epsilon_p\epsilon_N}{q} \cdot \frac{N_N}{n_p} \cdot \frac{V_D - V}{\epsilon_N \cdot N_N - \epsilon_p \cdot n_p}}$$

$$x_N = \sqrt{\frac{2\epsilon_p\epsilon_N}{q} \cdot \frac{n_p}{N_N} \cdot \frac{V_D - V}{\epsilon_p \cdot n_p - \epsilon_N \cdot N_N}}$$

(3.19)

where ϵ_p and ϵ_N are the dielectric constants of GaAs and Al$_x$Ga$_{1-x}$As, respectively, q is the elementary charge, n_p the doping in the p-GaAs core, N_N the doping in the N-Al$_x$Ga$_{1-x}$As cladding. Please note that equation 3.19 is only valid for the case when x_p does not exceed the total thickness of the p-GaAs core d. For the cases when x_p extends beyond d, a different equation (without loss of generality) arises from solving the Poisson's equations in the three regions (upper-cladding, core, lower-cladding), see [13].

Since $n_p \ll N_N$ in equation 3.19, the depletion region extends more into the p-side of the junction, hence $x_p > x_N$. The built-in electric field covers the entire depletion region with the width $x_p + x_N$. If a reverse bias voltage $V = V_1 < 0$ is applied to the heterojunction, the width of the depletion region expands and the free carrier density is pushed to its edges. As a result the local refractive index is changed due to both, the electro-optic effects, and the free carriers effects as we previously explained.

3.3.3 Phase modulation efficiency in double heterostructures

Phase modulation is attributed to the overlap of the optical field with the change of the refractive index due to electro-optic effects (LEO and QEO effects) and due to the depletion of the carrier density by electric field (carrier density-related effects). The electric field is present inside the depletion region of the modulator which is assumed to overlap with the guiding region for the optical field whereas the free carriers density is pushed to the sides of the depletion region. Therefore, the resulting phase modulation due to electro-optic effects and carrier effects can be separately handled. This is the key for designing GaAs/AlGaAs double heterostructure phase modulators. By carefully choosing the doping profiles of the different layers, the contribution of the free carriers effects to phase modulation can be controlled in order to optimize the performance of the phase modulators.

Let $I(x)$ be the intensity distribution (assumed to be uniform in y-direction) of the wave propagating along the modulator in figure 3.2 in the guiding core with the refractive index profile $\bar{n}(x)$. Then the modal refractive index change $\Delta\bar{n}_{eff}$ (not to be confused with the refractive index change $\Delta\bar{n}$) that contributes to the phase shift is given by [19]:

$$\Delta\bar{n}_{eff} = \frac{1}{\bar{n}_{eff}} \cdot \frac{\int_{-\infty}^{+\infty} \bar{n}(x)\Delta\bar{n}(x)I(x)dx}{\int_{-\infty}^{+\infty} I(x)dx} \tag{3.20}$$

where $\bar{n}_{eff}$ is the effective refractive index (the modal refractive index). The overlap integral in equation 3.20 can be used to determine the contribution of each of the three effects individually (LEO, QEO, and carrier effects) to $\Delta\bar{n}_{eff}$, and hence the relevant phase shift in a modulator of length L is given by:

$$\Delta\Phi = \frac{2\pi}{\lambda} \cdot L \cdot \Delta\bar{n}_{eff}. \tag{3.21}$$

Chapter 4

Design of GaAs-based phase modulators

Laser emission at the wavelengths of 780 nm and 1064 nm is realized in the GaAs-based technology using GaAs/AlGaAs double heterostructures [43], [44]. The layer structure of lasers includes a region to provide gain that is usually referred to as active region. This region typically consists of a p-n junction where injected carriers permanently recombine [24]. GaAs/AlGaAs double heterostructures can also be used to realize passive components i.e. components that do not generate (coherent) light such as electro-optic phase modulators [23]. Unlike for active components, for passive components the layer structure does not contain an active region.

This chapter is dedicated for the design of GaAs-based phase modulators. The parameters for the phase modulator double heterostructure multi-layer (material, thicknesses, doping profiles) are calculated and the corresponding electro-optic coefficients for the guiding core at the operation wavelength are estimated. Next, the design of the lateral waveguides (ridge width and etching depth) of the phase modulators is presented.

4.1 Material profile for GaAs-based phase modulators

In the literature, GaAs/AlGaAs double heterostructure phase modulators are typically realized at the wavelength range of 1.05 μm to 1.32 μm, (corresponding to the photon energy range of 1.18 eV to 0.94 eV). The GaAs material is suitable for guiding of optical signals with a photon energy below the bandgap of GaAs (1.43 eV) [29, p. 42-44] which corresponds to wavelengths larger than λ =872 nm (see figure 4.1). This is why GaAs is used for the guiding region of the waveguide of phase modulators at the wavelength range of 1.05 μm to 1.32 μm. The natural choice for the cladding layers is in this case $Al_xGa_{1-x}As$ $(0 < x < 1)$ with a refractive index lower than that of GaAs. However, for applications at photon energies larger than the bandgap of GaAs, i.g. at the wavelength of 780 nm with the photon energy of 1.59 eV, GaAs suffers strong intraband absorption [19]. This is why we chose AlGaAs with the Aluminum concentration $x = 0.35$. The bandgap energy of $Al_{0.35}Ga_{0.65}As$ corresponds to 1.9 eV which is sufficiently larger than the photon energy at the wavelength of 780 nm (1.59 eV) [19]. This is the first time a core material different from GaAs is used in GaAs/AlGaAs double heterostructure phase modulators.

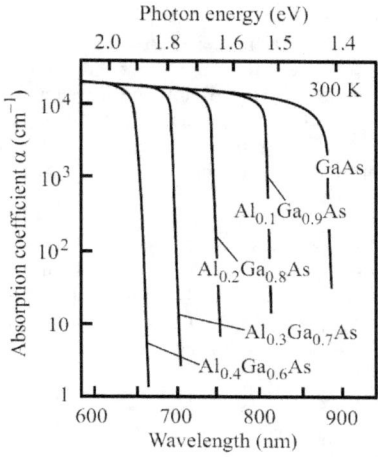

Figure 4.1: Fundamental absorption in GaAs and AlGaAs. Figure taken from [30].

4.2 Design of phase modulators for laser radiation at 780 nm

In this section we present a detailed description of the design of the phase modulator for operation at the wavelength of 780 nm. We calculate the electro-optic coefficients of $Al_{0.35}Ga_{0.65}As$ at 780 nm to determine the contribution of the LEO and QEO effects to phase modulation. Then we present the multi-layer epitaxial structure for optimum wave guiding. Further, the doping profile is carefully selected to use the contribution of the carrier density-related effects to phase modulation in addition to the electro-optic effects (LEO and QEO). Finally, the lateral design of the cross-section of the modulator waveguide that supports single lateral mode operation (single mode ridge waveguide) is presented.

4.2.1 Electro-optic coefficients of $Al_{0.35}Ga_{0.65}As$

Electro-optic effects in GaAs-based double heterostructures are the LEO effect, QEO effect, and the carrier density-related effects (see chapter 3). In the following analysis we consider the case where the phase modulator waveguide is grown on a (001) GaAs substrate and the heterojunction electric field is applied along the [001] principal axis. The modification of the refractive index by the LEO ad QEO effects follows equations 3.15 and 3.16 in chapter 3.

The electro-optic coefficients for $Al_{0.35}Ga_{0.65}As$ are unknown and have to be estimated for the design of the phase modulator. In the following, we suggest a method to estimate the electro-optic coefficients of $Al_{0.35}Ga_{0.65}As$ at the wavelength of 780 nm using the reported values of these coefficients for GaAs. This method has been published in [19]. In the previous works [45], [15], the LEO coefficients for GaAs with the bandgap wavelength $\lambda_{1g} = 0.872\,\mu m$ were reported within the wavelength range of $1.05\,\mu m$ to $1.31\,\mu m$. We assume that for $Al_xGa_{1-x}As$ material with $0 \leq x \leq 1$, the electro-optic coefficients are determined solely by means of the spacing between the desired wavelength and the bandgap wavelength (independently from the Al-content) [19].

For the $Al_{0.35}Ga_{0.65}As$ device, the design wavelength $\lambda_2 = 0.780\,\mu m$ ist $0.129\,\mu m$ below the bandgap wavelength $\lambda_{2g} = 0.651\,\mu m$. We hence assume, that the LEO coefficient of $Al_{0.35}Ga_{0.65}As$ at $0.780\,\mu m$ correspond to the coefficients of a GaAs device operated $0.129\,\mu m$ above its bandgap, i.e. at $\lambda_1 = 1.001\,\mu m$. The final step is to interpolate the value of the LEO coefficient for GaAs at the wavelength λ_1 from the values which are given in [45]. This leads to a value of $\bar{r}_{41}(GaAs, \lambda_1 = 1.001\,\mu m) = 1.84 \times 10^{-12}\,m/V$ which is then assumed to correspond to the requested value of the LEO coefficients:

$$\bar{r}_{41}(Al_{0.35}Ga_{0.65}As, \lambda_2 = 0.780\,\mu m) = 1.84 \times 10^{-12}\,m/V.$$

Next, we determine the QEO coefficient $\bar{R}_{12}$ for $Al_{0.35}Ga_{0.65}As$. In [23], $\bar{R}_{12}$ for GaAs was calculated using the expression:

$$\bar{R}_{12} = \frac{C \cdot E_{ph}^{\,2}}{\bar{n}^4(E_{ph})\left(E_g^2 - E_{ph}^2\right)^2} \tag{4.1}$$

with E_g the gap energy, E_{ph} the photon energy, and C is a constant. Equation 4.1 is valid for $Al_xGa_{1-x}As$, $0 \leq x \leq 1$. Thus, by relating $\bar{R}_{12}$ for $Al_{0.35}Ga_{0.65}As$ at the requested wavelength $\lambda_2 = 0.780\,\mu m$ to $\bar{R}_{12}$ of GaAs at a given wavelength λ_1:

$$\bar{R}_{12}(\lambda_2) = \bar{R}_{12}(\lambda_1) \cdot \left(\frac{\bar{n}^2(\lambda_1) \cdot \lambda_2 \cdot \lambda_{2g}^2 \cdot \left(\lambda_1^2 - \lambda_{1g}^2\right)}{\bar{n}^2(\lambda_2) \cdot \lambda_1 \cdot \lambda_{1g}^2 \cdot \left(\lambda_2^2 - \lambda_{2g}^2\right)}\right)^2 \tag{4.2}$$

The experimental value of $\bar{R}_{12} = -1.7 \times 10^{-20}\,m^2/V^2$ was given for GaAs at the wavelength $\lambda_1 = 1.15\,\mu m$ [23]. The corresponding bandgap wavelength is $\lambda_{1g} = 0.872\,\mu m$. With $\bar{n}(\lambda_1) = 3.4496$ for GaAs and $\bar{n}(\lambda_2) = 3.4265$ for $Al_{0.35}Ga_{0.65}As$. The resulting QEO coefficient is:

$$\bar{R}_{12}(Al_{0.35}Ga_{0.65}As, \lambda_2 = 0.780\,\mu m) = -2.3 \times 10^{-20}\,m^2/V^2.$$

The phase modulator double heterostructure can be modeled using the estimated values of the LEO and QEO coefficients and the contribution from the carrier density-related effects that were presented earlier in chapter 3.

4.2.2 Vertical waveguide at 780 nm

Multi-layer structure for operation at the wavelength 780 nm

For a well-defined phase modulation, the vertical waveguide has to be single mode [23]. Phase modulation in the waveguide double heterostructure is achieved by the electro-optic effects and contributions from the free carriers effect.

The first design criteria of the vertical multi-layer structure of the phase modulator is the phase modulation efficiency. To increase the phase shift due to the electro-optic effects, an optimal overlap between the optical field and the applied external electric field should be achieved [19]. Further, the contribution of the free carriers effect to the phase shift can be increased by increasing the overlap of the optical field with the change of the carrier density. The free carriers effect can be controlled by carefully selecting the doping profile of the different layers in the double heterostructure.

The second design criterium of the vertical waveguide is the propagation loss. In addition to fundamental absorption, losses arise in the vertical waveguide due to free carrier absorption, and by leaky modes in the cladding layers [46]. This has to be taken into consideration when choosing the material, the doping profile, and thickness of the different layers [46].

Let us first consider the most simple vertical planar waveguide which is a 3-layer (cladding-core-cladding) waveguide. In order for the waveguide with core thickness d to support only one guided mode, the so-called *low-index* guiding concept has to be applied. This concept is based on that the difference between the refractive indices of the core and the cladding materials are chosen small enough such that only one mode, the fundamental mode, is guided [37, p. 252]. For example for the $Al_{0.35}Ga_{0.65}As$-based waveguide with the core thickness $d = 2\,\mu m$ the refractive index of the core corresponds to $\bar{n}_{core} = 3.426$. To support single mode operation at 780 nm, the refractive index $\bar{n}_{cladd}$ has to be $\bar{n}_{cladd} > 3.421$. The corresponding refractive index difference is $\Delta\bar{n} < 0.01$ which means that a significant fraction of the guided mode will be propagating outside the core, i.e. inside the cladding [29, p. 19-47]. If, for example, the modulating electric field was selected to be well-confined within the guiding core, inefficient phase modulation can be expected due to the small overlap between optical and electrical fields.

Thus, to fulfill first design criterium, the vertical waveguide has to support a single guided mode who's optical field is well confined within the waveguide core. To enforce this, we add a thin intermediate confinement layer between the core and each of the cladding layers to create a 5-layer vertical structure. In order for this multi-layer to support only the guided fundamental mode, the refractive index difference between the core and cladding has to be chosen small enough (on the order of 10^{-2}) in order to fulfill the low-index guiding requirement. Further, the additional thin confinement layer should have a much lower refractive index than the cladding layer. This confinement layer serves as a mode filter [46]. This is because the fundamental mode is confined inside the core region whereas the higher order modes leak through this layer into the substrate [46]. The resulting refractive index profile is also referred to as a *W-shape* multi-layer.

Further, suppose the refractive indices of the core, confinement, and cladding layers are $\bar{n}_{core}$, $\bar{n}_{conf}$, and $\bar{n}_{cladd}$, respectively. Then the following two conditions must be met [46]:

$$\bar{n}_{eff_1} < \bar{n}_{cladd} < \bar{n}_{eff_0} \ , \quad \bar{n}_{conf} < \bar{n}_{cladd} < \bar{n}_{core} \tag{4.3}$$

with $\bar{n}_{eff_0}$ and $\bar{n}_{eff_1}$ in equation 4.3 are the effective refractive indices of the fundamental mode and the first higher order mode, respectively.

The first (left) condition in equation 4.3 describes the single mode requirement in weakly (low-index) guiding structures and the second (right) condition in equation 4.3 implies mode confinement in the W-shape multi-layer.

Table 4.1: Multi-layer structure of the phase modulator waveguide at the wavelength of 780 nm.

index	function	Material	Thickness [nm]
1	upper cladding	$Al_{0.37}Ga_{0.63}As$	1000
2	confinement	$Al_{0.7}Ga_{0.3}As$	150
3	core	$Al_{0.35}Ga_{0.65}As$	1900
4	confinement	$Al_{0.7}Ga_{0.3}As$	150
5	lower cladding	$Al_{0.37}Ga_{0.63}As$	1500

The waveguide multi-layer for operation at 780 nm is described in table 4.1. The Al-contents in the materials for the core, confinement, and cladding layers are ($x = 0.35$), ($x = 0.7$), and ($x = 0.37$), respectively. This corresponds to the refractive indices $\bar{n}_{core} = 3.426$, $\bar{n}_{conf} = 3.193$, and $\bar{n}_{cladd} = 3.413$, respectively, which satisfies the second condition in equation 4.3. The thickness of the 5 layers has been selected such that

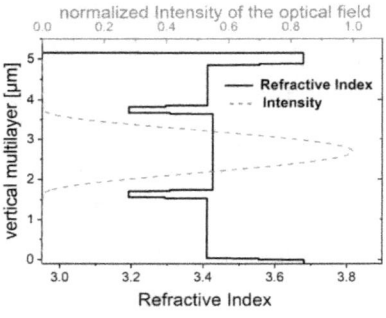

Figure 4.2: Refractive index profile (W-shape) of the vertical multilayer structure described in table 4.2 and the intensity profile of the fundamental TE mode. Adapted/Reprinted with permission from Ref [19], [Springer Nature].

the effective refractive indices of the TE (vertical) modes are $\bar{n}_{eff_0} = 3.421$ for the fundamental TE mode, and $\bar{n}_{eff_1} = 3.407$ for the first higher order (leaky) TE mode. This satisfies the first condition in equation 4.3. In figure 4.2 (which corresponds to the vertical structure in table 4.2), the W-shape refractive index profile can be clearly seen. Please note that the minor steps in the index profile correspond to additional thin AlGaAs layers with a suitable Al-content to introduce an intermediate refractive index step between the main layers. The optical field profile of the fundamental TE mode in figure 4.2 and the effective refractive indices $\bar{n}_{eff_0}$ and $\bar{n}_{eff_1}$ were calculated using a commercial software tool that utilizes a finite element method (FEM) [47].

It can be seen in figure 4.2 that the optical field intensity profile is well confined inside the core region. The full width at half maximum (FWHM) of the intensity profile of the far field is 22.5° which satisfies well the requirements for integration of the phase modulator into hybrid laser modules with other passive/active optical elements.

Table 4.2: Double heterostructure of a phase modulator at 780 nm with a p-i-n doping profile of the waveguide core. Adapted/Reprinted with permission from Ref [19], [Springer Nature].

Layer	Material	Thickness [nm]	Doping [cm^{-3}]
contact	p-GaAs	270	2×10^{19}
cladding	p-Al$_{0.37}$Ga$_{0.63}$As	1000	2×10^{18}
confinement	p-Al$_{0.7}$Ga$_{0.3}$As	150	7×10^{17}
p-core	p-Al$_{0.35}$Ga$_{0.65}$As	200	3×10^{17}
intrinsic core	p-Al$_{0.35}$Ga$_{0.65}$As	1500	2×10^{15}
n-core	n-Al$_{0.35}$Ga$_{0.65}$As	200	3×10^{17}
confinement	n-Al$_{0.7}$Ga$_{0.3}$As	150	7×10^{17}
cladding	n-Al$_{0.37}$Ga$_{0.63}$As	1500	2×10^{18}
buffer	n-GaAs	300	2×10^{19}
substrate	n-GaAs	130000	2×10^{19}

Modal losses

In order to create the modulator heterojunction for electric field confinement, free carriers (holes/electrons) are introduced by doping. The doping profile has to consider the free carriers absorption in order to realize a low-loss waveguide. In [48, p. 175], the free carrier absorption α_{fc} in GaAs near the absorption edge has been given by:

$$\alpha_{fc}([\text{cm}^{-1}]) \approx 3 \times 10^{-18} n_e + 7 \times 10^{-18} n_h \qquad (4.4)$$

where n_e and n_h are being the free carrier density for electrons and holes, respectively (both in cm^{-3}]). The constants in equation 4.4 correspond to the electron cross-section (3×10^{-18}cm^2) and to the hole cross-section (7×10^{-18}cm^2).

Based on the waveguide given in table 4.1, the complete vertical multi-layer structure of a phase modulator at the wavelength of 780 nm is given in table 4.2. The central part of the waveguide core is intentionally not doped (intrinsic core), whereas a 200 nm thick region on either side of the core are moderately doped with $n_e = n_h = 3 \times 10^{17}$ cm^{-3}. The low index (confinement) and cladding layers are strongly doped in order to enforce a large overlap between the electric field and the optical field inside the core which accounts to modal losses amount of only $\alpha_{mod} = 0.1$ cm^{-1}.

Optimization of the phase modulation efficiency

In order to determine the phase modulation efficiency of the double heterostructure one has to calculate the electric field and free carriers density for different modulating voltage signals. Let us compare the electric field and free carrier density for the phase modulator of table 4.2 for two different settings of the modulating reverse-bias voltage, for example at $V_0 = 5$ V and at $V_1 = 15$ V. We determine the dependence of the distribution of the electric field on the voltage by using the drift-diffusion equations. The equations are solved using an in-house software that takes into account

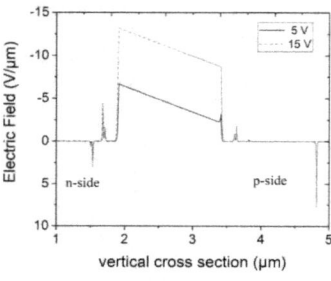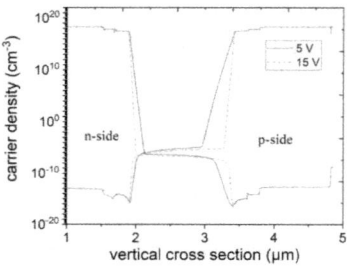

Figure 4.3: Simulation of the modification of the electric field and carrier density (holes+electrons) inside the modulator heterojunction of table 4.2 when the reverse bias voltages $V_0 = 5\,\text{V}$ and $V_1 = 15\,\text{V}$ are applied.

the Fermi statistics and the hetero-boundaries of the double heterostructure. As we explained earlier in the previous chapter, in the absence of an external electric field (at $V = V_0$), the free carriers deplete and a built-in electric field is confined inside the depletion region. When the reverse-bias voltage is applied ($V = V_1$), the width of the depletion region increases and the free carriers are pushed to it's boundaries. The resulting electric field is larger than the built-in electric field as shown in figure 4.3. The dependence of the distribution of the electric fields on the voltage was determined by solving the drift-diffusion equations by taking into account Fermi statistics and the hetero-boundaries. The phase shift can be determined from the modification of the modal refractive index $\Delta\bar{n}_{eff}$ and the overlap integral that was previously given in equation 3.20.

The doping profile of the double heterostructure multi-layer can be further optimized in order to increase phase modulation efficiency. To better understand the effect of the doping profile on the phase modulation efficiency, we compare the P-p-i-n-N double heterostructure of table 4.2 with another double heterostructure with identical multi-layer and a slightly different doping profile.
Instead of the p-i-n doping profile, the core in the second double heterostructure has a symmetric p-n (p-n core) doping profile. The doping profiles of the cladding layers and the substrate remain unchanged. This new multi-layer structure is given in table 4.3. We refer to the new doping profile as P-p-n-N.

The comparison between the two double heterostructures is shown in figure 4.4. The modification of the electric field and carrier density is plotted together with the corresponding intensity profile of the TE mode in order to demonstrate the difference of the overlap between optical and electrical fields for both double heterostructures. The blue curve corresponds to the change of the electric field inside the heterojunction and the red curve is related to the modification of the electrons and holes (carrier) density.
The evaluation of figure 4.4 leads to the following conclusions:

Table 4.3: Vertical multi-layer structure of a phase modulator at 780 nm with a p-n doping profile of the waveguide core.

Layer	Material	Thickness [nm]	Doping [cm^{-3}]
contact	p-GaAs	270	2×10^{19}
cladding	p-Al$_{0.37}$Ga$_{0.63}$As	1000	2×10^{18}
low index	p-Al$_{0.7}$Ga$_{0.3}$As	150	7×10^{17}
p-core	p-Al$_{0.35}$Ga$_{0.65}$As	450	3×10^{17}
p-core	p-Al$_{0.35}$Ga$_{0.65}$As	500	3×10^{16}
n-core	n-Al$_{0.35}$Ga$_{0.65}$As	500	3×10^{16}
n-core	n-Al$_{0.35}$Ga$_{0.65}$As	450	3×10^{17}
low index	n-Al$_{0.7}$Ga$_{0.3}$As	150	7×10^{17}
cladding	n-Al$_{0.37}$Ga$_{0.63}$As	1500	2×10^{18}
buffer	n-GaAs	300	2×10^{19}
substrate	n-GaAs	130000	2×10^{19}

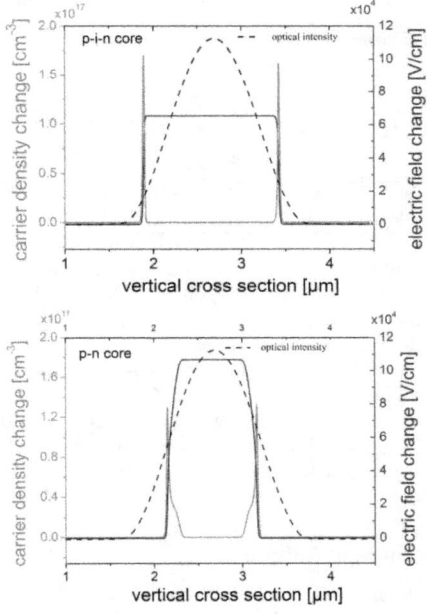

Figure 4.4: Modification of the electric field and carrier density of two modulators hetero-junctions when the reversed bias voltage changes from 5 V to 15 V. (top) the phase modulator with p-i-n core from table 4.2. (bottom) the phase modulator wih p-n core (table 4.3).

p-i-n double heterostructure (table 4.2): the core is almost fully depleted. The modification of the free carriers density occurs at the limits of the guiding core whereas the optical field is well-confined inside the core. As a result of the minor overlap between the optical field and carrier density, phase modulation due the free carrier effects is expected to show a very low efficiency. Nevertheless, the modification of the electric field, on the other hand, overlaps very well with the optical field. The EO effects (LEO and QEO) are therefore expected to be the dominant effects to phase modulation for the p-i-n double heterostructure.

p-n double heterostructure (table 4.3): the contribution of the free carriers effect to phase modulation is expected to increase due to the larger overlap of carrier density with the optical field.

The individual contribution of the LEO and QEO effects to phase modulation can be calculated from equations 3.15, 3.16 and the overlap integral in equation 3.20. For the carrier effects, the local refractive index change can first be calculated using equations 3.17 and 3.18, then the overlap integral in (3.20) can be used. The resulting values of the phase modulation efficiency for each of the three effects is given in table 4.4 for both double heterostructures. The enhancement in the carrier effect in the p-n

Table 4.4: Modulation efficiency of phase modulators at 780 nm with different doping profiles from tables 4.2, 4.3.

λ [nm]	structure	linear effects [deg/(V $\cdot$ mm)]			quadratic effects [deg/(V^2 $\cdot$ mm)]
		Pockels	carrier	total	Kerr
780	table 4.2	8.41	0.17	8.58	0.96
780	table 4.3	10.73	0.63	11.36	1.13

double heterostructure increases the modulation efficiency in comparison to the p-i-n double heterostructure. The p-i-n structure, on the other hand, has a smaller junction capacitance, which is more suitable for high speed operation. In both structures the QEO effect is very small due to the large difference between the photon energy and the band gap energy of the core layer [19]. If one decreases the spacing between the band gap energy and photon energy (by reducing the Al-content of the guiding layer), the QEO effect can be increased [19]. Another way to increase the QEO effect requires the employment of quantum wells [22] in the guiding region. However, the use of quantum well structures is beyond the scope of this work but is certainly interesting for the future.

4.2.3 Lateral waveguide at 780 nm

The lateral confinement can be provided by means of the ridge waveguide (RW). The ridge waveguide shall only support the fundamental lateral guided mode in order to ensure a well-defined phase shift [19]. We use the finite element method [47] to pose the conditions for lateral single modes in the RW. The cutoff condition between the multi-mode and single mode regimes as a function of the ridge width and the etching depth is given in figure 4.5. For example, if the ridge width is set to 3 µm, the etching depth should be less than 1.6 µm in order for the ridge to guide only the fundamental

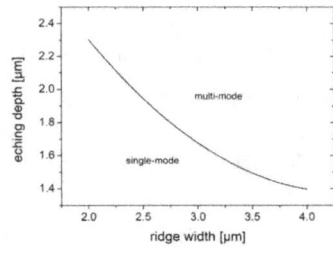 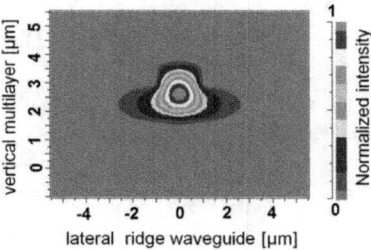

Figure 4.5: (left): Simulated single mode propagation condition at the wavelength 780 nm for the vertical structure in table 4.2. The region over the solid line corresponds to the multi-mode regime, and the region under the ridge represents the single mode regime. (right) fundamental TE mode with the ridge width 2 μm and etch depth 1.9 μm. Adapted/Reprinted with permission from Ref [19], [Springer Nature].

TE mode. To ease coupling of a laser beam into the phase modulator, a wider RW may however be recommended. This implies a smaller etching depth which reduces the effective index step of the lateral waveguide. The small effective refractive index step should not be problematic for phase modulators with straight or tilted waveguides. However, waveguides that feature a small step of the effective refractive index may be problematic for the design of more complex photonic circuits. The smaller the step, the less the wave is confined so that in more complex PICs, where bent waveguides have to be implemented, significant radiation loss may occur. This requirement has been taken into consideration for the design of the bent waveguides for the couplers in the next chapter.

4.3 Design of phase modulators for laser radiation at 1064 nm

4.3.1 Electro-optic coefficients of GaAs at 1064 nm

As earlier discussed in section 4.1, the GaAs is a suitable material for the waveguide core of the phase modulator at 1064 nm. The corresponding LEO coefficient for GaAs at 1064 nm follows directly from the linear interpolation in [45]:

$$\bar{r}_{41}(\text{GaAs}, \ \lambda = 1.064 \, \mu\text{m}) = 1.77 \times 10^{-12} \, \text{m/V}.$$

To determine the QEO coefficient we use equation 4.1 for GaAs at 1064 nm with the photon energy of 1.156 eV, bandgap energy 1.424 eV, the refractive index $\bar{n} = 3.4805$, and $C = 8.5 \times 10^{-15} \, (\text{eV})^2 \text{cm}^2/\text{V}^2$ [23]:

$$\bar{R}_{12}(\text{GaAs}, \ \lambda = 1.064 \, \mu\text{m}) = -1.95 \times 10^{-20} \, \text{m}^2/\text{V}^2.$$

The design of the phase modulator at 1064 nm follows in similar lines to the procedure that was earlier presented for phase modulators at 780 nm. First, the vertical multi-layer structure is optimized for low propagation losses and efficient phase modulation, then a single mode lateral waveguide is designed.

4.3.2 Vertical waveguide at 1064 nm

Two vertical layer structures of phase modulators at the wavelength of 1064 nm with GaAs core and AlGaAs cladding lasers is given in table 4.5 and in table 4.6.   The

Table 4.5: Vertical layer structure of a phase modulator for operation at the wavelength of 1064 nm with a p-p-n-n guiding core.

Layer	Material	Thickness [nm]	Doping [cm^{-3}]
contact	p-GaAs	270	2×10^{19}
cladding	p-Al$_{0.05}$Ga$_{0.95}$As	1300	2×10^{18}
low index	p-Al$_{0.4}$Ga$_{0.6}$As	180	7×10^{17}
p-core	p-GaAs	600	3×10^{17}
p-core	p-GaAs	600	3×10^{16}
n-core	n-GaAs	600	3×10^{16}
n-core	n-GaAs	600	3×10^{17}
low index	n-Al$_{0.4}$Ga$_{0.6}$As	180	7×10^{17}
cladding	n-Al$_{0.05}$Ga$_{0.95}$As	1800	2×10^{18}
buffer	n-GaAs	300	2×10^{19}
substrate	n-GaAs	130000	2×10^{19}

Table 4.6: Vertical layer structure of a phase modulator for operation at the wavelength of 1064 nm with a p-n guiding core.

Layer	Material	Thickness [nm]	Doping [cm^{-3}]
contact	p-GaAs	270	2×10^{19}
cladding	p-Al$_{0.05}$Ga$_{0.95}$As	1300	2×10^{18}
low index	p-Al$_{0.4}$Ga$_{0.6}$As	180	7×10^{17}
p-core	p-GaAs	1200	5×10^{16}
n-core	n-GaAs	1200	5×10^{16}
low index	n-Al$_{0.4}$Ga$_{0.6}$As	180	7×10^{17}
cladding	n-Al$_{0.05}$Ga$_{0.95}$As	1800	2×10^{18}
buffer	n-GaAs	300	2×10^{19}
substrate	n-GaAs	130000	2×10^{19}

layers thicknesses and doping profile were optimized in similar lines to the modulators at 780 nm. The modal losses of the structure in table 4.5 amount to $\alpha_{mod} = 0.59 \, \text{cm}^{-1}$. The structure in table 4.6 has lower modal losses $\alpha_{mod} = 0.28 \, \text{cm}^{-1}$. Figure 4.6 shows for the modulator structure in table 4.5 the simulated modification of the electric field and carrier density when the applied modulation reverse-bias voltage is changed from 5 V to 15 V.

The phase modulation efficiency is calculated from the overlap integrals of the optical field with the electric field and the free carrier density. The calculated phase modulation due to the LEO effect, the QEO effect, and the carrier density-related effects are given in table 4.7.

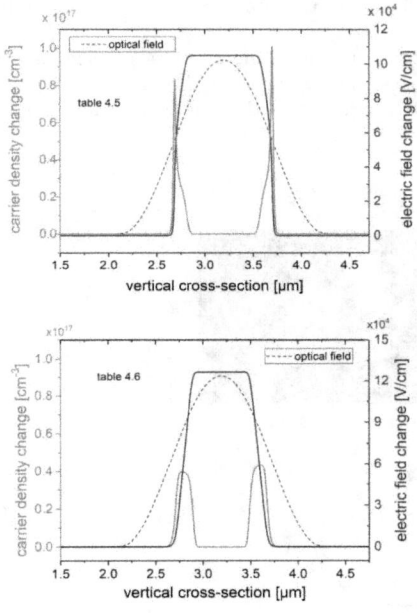

Figure 4.6: Modification of the electric field and carrier density of the modulator heterojunctionS at the wavelength of 1046 nm in table 4.5 (top), and in table 4.6 (buttom) when the reversed bias voltage changes from 5 V to 15 V.

Table 4.7: Modulation efficiency of phase modulator at the wavelength of 1046 nm with the layer structure in table 4.5.

λ [nm]	structure	linear effects [deg/(V · mm)]			quadratic effects [deg/(V² · mm²)]
		Pockels	carrier	total	Kerr
1064	table 4.5	8.46	1.41	10.27	0.88
1064	table 4.6	8.88	2.03	10.91	1.18

4.3.3 Lateral waveguide at 1064 nm

The lateral waveguide has been designed to support only the fundamental guided TE mode. The ridge width was set to 3 μm. The corresponding etching depth was set to 2 μm.

The simulated intensity profile (using the Fimmwave mode solver) of the single guided TE mode with the corresponding vertical and horizontal cross-sections are shown in figure 4.7. The FWHM lateral and vertical far field angles corresponds to 16.5 deg and 26.5 deg, respectively.

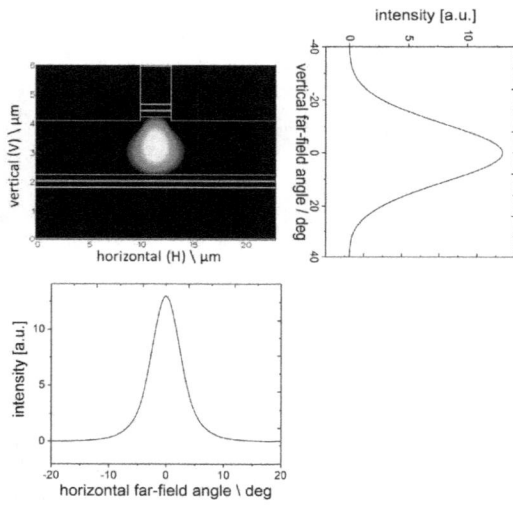

Figure 4.7: Simulated intensity profile (using a commercial software tool that uses a film mode matching method (https://www.photond.com/products/fimmwave/fimmwave_features_21.htm) of the fundamental guided TE mode in the modulator waveguide at the wavelength of 1.064 nm. Ridge width is 3 μm. Etching depth is 2 μm.

Later on, in chapter 7, phase modulators based on the two multi-layers structures in table 4.2, table 4.3 at 780 nm, and on table 4.5, and table 4.6 at 1064 nm are realized in the GaAs technology.

Chapter 5

Design of GaAs-based waveguide couplers

GaAs-based couplers are realized in this work based on the GaAs/AlGaAs double heterostructure of the phase modulators at the wavelength of 780 nm. For this purpose, two different coupling concepts are realized. The MMI coupler and the directional coupler. MMI couplers are based on the self-imaging principle. Directional couplers are based on evanescent mode coupling between two ridge waveguides. Please refer to chapter 2 for the description of these two couplers.

5.1 General remarks on multi-mode interference couplers

The first step towards the design of an MMI coupler is to select the lateral parameters of the input and output waveguides of the MMI coupler which we refer to as *access waveguides*. The fundamental mode of the access waveguides is considered to be the input mode of the MMI coupler and is launched into the multi-mode waveguide (multi-mode waveguide) to excite higher order modes. The interference mechanism of these modes generates the self-imaging effect. For an MMI coupler with N output ports, the multi-mode waveguide has to support at least $m \geq N + 1$ guided modes which can be set by the lateral parameters of the waveguide (width and etching depth of the multi-mode waveguide). The longitudinal parameter of the multi-mode waveguide (length L_N) corresponds to the length at which N fold-images are created [26]. The length depends directly on the lateral position y of the exciting field at the input side of the multi-mode waveguide as earlier described in section 2.2.2 in chapter 2. The design of MMI couplers should consider the following requirements:

- vertical structure: the same vertical structure for phase modulators in order to enable integration of the couplers and phase modulators to realize a MZI modulator.

- access waveguides: the lateral parameters of the access waveguide (ridge width and etching depth) can be set using the single-mode condition that was given in figure 4.5.

- etching depth: in a multi-mode waveguide, the beat length is given by $L_\pi = \lambda / (2 \cdot \Delta \bar{n}_{eff})$ (equation 2.42 in chapter 2) with $\Delta \bar{n}_{eff} = \bar{n}_{eff_0} - \bar{n}_{eff_1}$ denoting

51

the difference between the effective refractive indices of the guided fundamental and first higher order modes in the multi-mode waveguide, respectively. For shorter multi-mode waveguides, the etching depth should be increased to increase $\Delta \bar{n}_{eff}$. However, the etching depth must not exceed the value for the single-mode cut-off condition of the access waveguide (see figure 4.5).

- width of the multi-mode waveguide: the design of some types of MMI couplers requires to increase the number of guided modes inside the multi-mode waveguide as we will explain in the following sections. This increases the width of the multi-mode waveguide. As a rule of thumb, L_π increases quadratically with W_m (see equation 2.37 and 2.42 in chapter 2), which then accounts for longer MMI coupler devices.

In figure 5.1, two types of MMI couplers are simulated as the etching depth is varied. A 1×2 MMI coupler with $W_m = 15\,\mu m$, and a 2×2 MMI 3dB coupler with $W_m = 20\,\mu m$. The lengths of the muli-mode waveguides are calculated from equations 2.45 and 2.46 for $N = 2$. The simulation shows that the increment of the etching depth by $0.5\,\mu m$ from $1.7\,\mu m$ to $2.2\,\mu m$ reduces the length of the multi-mode waveguide of the 1×2 devices from $624\,\mu m$ to about $524\,\mu m$. Further, the increment of the etching depth of the 2×2 MMI 3-dB coupler by $0.5\,\mu m$ from $1.8\,\mu m$ to $2.3\,\mu m$ reduces the length of the multi-mode waveguide from $1370\,\mu m$ to about $1230\,\mu m$.

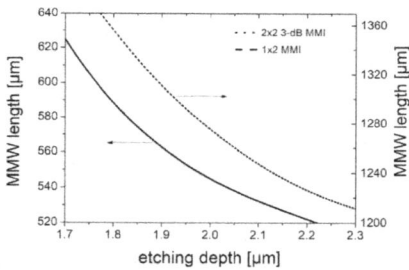

Figure 5.1: The calculated length of the multi-mode waveguide from the beat length of 1×2 MMI coupler ($W_m = 15\,\mu m$) and 2×2 MMI 3-dB coupler ($W_m = 20\,\mu m$) as a function of the etching depth.

5.2 Design rules of the multi-mode interference couplers

As a result of the foregoing discussion in the previous section, the design of the MMI coupler has to go through five steps that are ordered as follows:

1. set the lateral parameters (ridge width and etching depth) of access waveguides to define the input mode into the multi-mode waveguide.

2. select a width of the multi-mode waveguide that allows a sufficient number of guided modes and calculate the guided modes inside the multi-mode waveguide.

3. the beat length can be calculated from the propagation constants of the fundamental mode and the first higher order mode, β_0, and β_1, respectively, using $L_\pi = \pi/(\beta_0 - \beta_1)$.

4. depending on the number of input and output ports, the device length can be calculated from the beat length as we explained above.

5. run numerical simulation to find the optimum length of the multi-mode waveguide.

5.3   Numerical methods for simulation of waveguide couplers

The beam propagation method is recommended for simulation of light propagation along couplers that are based on ridge waveguides [50]. We used a commercial software tool (RsoftCAD) which allows to model the full 3D structure of the coupler device (2D cross-section of the ridge waveguide, and one longitudinal dimension). The simulation of the 3D structure is accurate but computationally intensive. An effective way to reduce the computing time is to downsize the 3D structure into a two-dimensional (2D) structure. This is achieved by reducing the 2D cross section (the ridge waveguide) into one dimension using the effective index method [32]. As earlier described in chapter 2 in this method (see figure 5.2), every multilayer section of the lateral waveguide structure is attributed to a characteristic parameter, the effective index of the fundamental guided mode of a corresponding slab waveguide. This slab waveguide

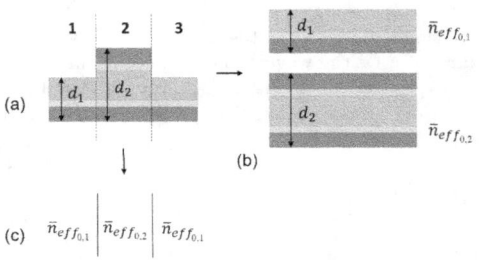

Figure 5.2: Effective refractive index method. (a) 5-layers ridge cross section, (b) two slab multi-layers waveguides, (c) corresponding effective refractive indices $\bar{n}_{eff_{0,1}}, \bar{n}_{eff_{0,2}}$, of the regions 1 and 2, respectively.

is considered to feature the same vertical multilayer structure and is assumed to extend infinitely in the lateral direction. The reduction of the structure by means of the effective index method significantly reduces the computing time.

5.4 Design of MMI couplers for applications at 780 nm

5.4.1 Access waveguides

We consider the multi-layer structure in table 4.2. We set the ridge width to $W_r = 2.2\,\mu m$, the etching depth of $d_e = 2.15\,\mu m$. The resulting access waveguide is single-mode (see figure 4.5). It also ensures a sufficiently large effective refractive index step for a good image quality [26]. Further, the etching depth is large enough so that s-bends without significant radiation losses can be realized as will be shown in this section and demonstrated later in the experiment. The FWHM vertical and lateral far field angles of 23.5° and 13.2°, respectively, satisfy the requirements defined by hybrid integration technologies for micro-integration of laser chips with optics and PICs [19]. In fact, the simulation of the beam collimation using WinABCD-3D[1] shows that even with one round aspheric lens ($f = 1.45\,mm$) the horizontal and vertical beam diameters correspond to $623\,\mu m$ and $718\,\mu m$, respectively, which is close to the optimal value of $600\,\mu m$ [24] and should account for a high coupling efficiency into a single mode optical fiber.

5.4.2 Geometry of the multi-mode waveguide

Now that the input mode of the MMI coupler is defined, the next step is to set the width of the multi-mode waveguide. The number of guided modes m in a multi-mode waveguide of a width W_m is calculated using numerical simulations (a finite-element method [47]).

Figure 5.3 shows the intensity profiles of the highest order guided modes for three different values of the ridge width W_m of the multi-mode waveguide. At a ridge width of $W_m = 5\,\mu m$ (Figure 5.3 (a)) the waveguide supports 3 guided modes. 8 modes are supported at $W_m = 15\,\mu m$ (figure 5.3 (b)). As a rule of thumb, the more the mode is confined under the ridge, the more efficient it may contribute to the self-imaging mechanism and hence, to the quality of the images. For example, one may expect that in a multi-mode waveguide with $W_m = 20\,\mu m$ that supports 11 guided modes (figure 5.3 (c)), the 11th (or the 10th highest order) guided mode may contribute less efficiently to self-imaging in comparison to the 10th (or the 9th higher order) guided mode (figure 5.3 (d)) that has a better confinement under the ridge.

In table 5.1, the number of guided modes m is given with the confinement factors (under the ridge) of the two highest order guided modes Γ_n, $n = m - 1\,m - 2$ under the ridge. Starting with the ridge width of the access waveguide ($W_r = 2.2\,\mu m$), only the fundamental mode is guided with a confinement factor of $\Gamma_0 = 0.93$ under the ridge. At a ridge width of $3\,\mu m$, the first higher order TE mode is supported and has a confinement factor of $\Gamma_1 = 0.57$. Three modes are supported at a ridge width of $5\,\mu m$. The confinement factor of the first two higher order modes are $\Gamma_2 = 0.68$, and $\Gamma_2 = 0.94$.

1×2 MMI coupler: For the design of an MMI coupler with the number of output ports $N = 2$, at least $m = N + 1$ modes should contribute to the self-imaging in

---

[1]software product from the FBH, see for example: https://application.wiley-vch.de/berlin/journals/op/08-02/OP0802_S48-S51.pdf

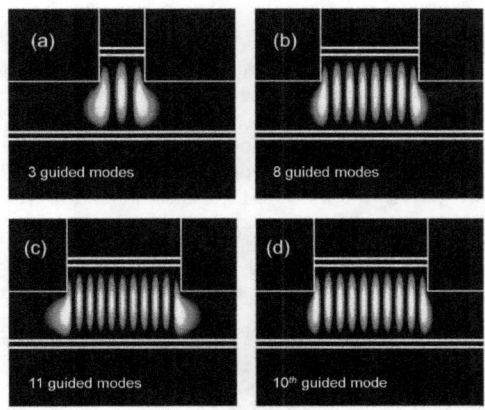

Figure 5.3: TE guided modes in a mutli-mode ridge waveguide from the structure in table 4.2 at the etching depth $d_e = 2.15\,\mu\text{m}$. (a), (b), and (c) the intensity profiles of the higher order guided modes for the ridge width of the multi-mode waveguide $W_m = 5\,\mu\text{m}$, $W_m = 15\,\mu\text{m}$, and $W_m = 20\,\mu\text{m}$, respectively. (d) the 10th (or the 9th higher order) guided mode at a ridge width of $W_m = 20\,\mu\text{m}$.

Table 5.1: Number of the guided modes m with respect to the ridge width with the confinement factor of the two higher order guided modes. Ridge etching depth is $d_e = 2.15\,\mu\text{m}$. Vertical waveguide structure in table 4.2. Simulated using a commercial software tool that uses a film mode matching method.

ridge width [μm]	m	Γ_{m-1}	Γ_{m-2}
2.2	1	0.93	–
3	2	0.57	0.96
5	3	0.68	0.94
7	4	0.75	0.94
9	5	0.78	0.93
11	6	0.81	0.93
13	7	0.84	0.94
15	8	0.86	0.94
17	9	0.87	0.94
19	10	0.88	0.94
20	11	0.75	0.93

order to achieve a good image quality [26]. For example, for a 1×2 splitter, at least 3 guided modes are required to contribute to the images. In this case, if the coupler is realized using the symmetric interference mechanism, the multi-mode waveguide must support at least 5 guided modes (modes 0, 1, 2, 3, 4) since the modes 1 and 3 are not excited. In order for the contributing guided modes to self-imaging to be well-confined under the ridge, the width of the multi-mode waveguide has to be $W_m \geq 10\,\mu m$ as can be seen in table 5.1. If the width is further increased to support more guided modes, the image resolution increases which is preferred for beam splitting applications [51]. This is why for the design of the 1×2 MMI splitter, the width of the multi-mode waveguide has been set to 15 μm, for which 4 guided modes are excited.

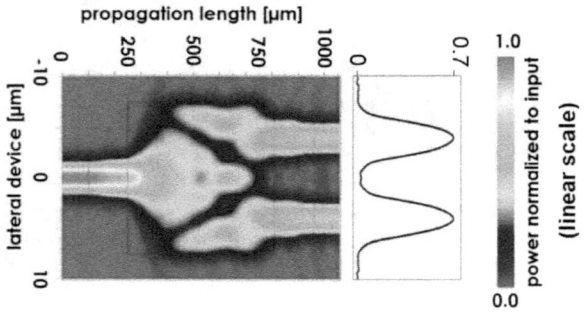

Figure 5.4: 2-D simulation of optical signal propagation along a 1 × 2 MMI coupler with the corresponding electric field at the end of the multi-mode waveguide section. $L_{MMW} = 520\,\mu m$, $W_m = 15\,\mu m$.

The effective refractive indices of the first two guided modes are $\bar{n}_{eff_0} = 3.42103$, $\bar{n}_{eff_1} = 3.42077$. The corresponding beat length is $L_\pi = 1500\,\mu m$. Due to the symmetric interference mechanism, the expected length of the multi-mode waveguide for TE operation should be $L = 3L_\pi/8 = 562\,\mu m$.

Figure 5.4 shows for example the intensity distribution along the different sections of a 1 × 2 MMI coupler using a 2D beam propagation [2] simulation. It can be clearly seen in figure 5.4 that the positions of the two images at the output are well-matched to the output ports at the end of the multi-mode waveguide. The distance between the center of the output ports is $W_m/2 = 7.5\,\mu m$. For practical reasons, for example, later for the realization of MZI modulators, a sufficient lateral distance is required between the two outputs of the MMI coupler in order to incorporate contacts for the active arms of the MZI modulator. This is why S-bends are required to be added. The complete 1 × 2 MMI coupler with S-bends is shown by figure 5.5.

2×2 MMI coupler: For the 2 × 2 MMI couplers, the first excited three modes are mode 0, 1, 3 (due to paired interference mechanism). Thus, the minimum width

---

[2] https://www.synopsys.com/optical-solutions/rsoft/passive-device-beamprop.html

of the multi-mode waveguide should be $W_m > 6\,\mu m$. In this work, the width of the multi-mode waveguide was set to $W_m = 20\,\mu m$ which supports a total number of 11 of guided modes as given by table 5.1. Only 8 of these modes shall then contribute to self-imaging imaging due to the paired interference mechanism. In the simulation, the TE input field was injected at lateral position $y = +W_m/6$. The corresponding beat length amounts to $L_\pi = 2480\,\mu m$ which is the length of the multi-mode waveguide of a cross coupler. The corresponding length of the multi-mode waveguide of a 3dB coupler is therefore $L_\pi/2 = 1240\,\mu m$.

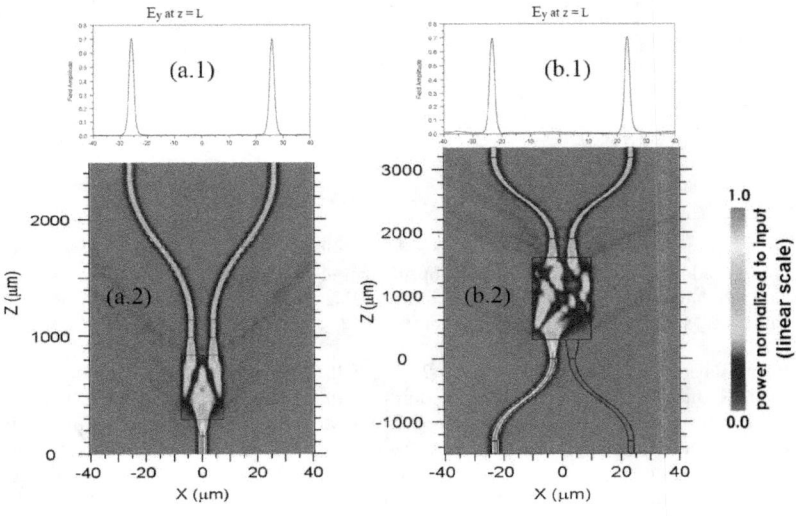

Figure 5.5: 2D simulation of beam propagation in complete 1×2 MMI coupler and 2×2 MMI 3dB coupler, respectively, with S-bends to separate the output waveguides. (a.1), (b.1) TE electric field at the outputs of the 1×2 MMI coupler and the 2×2 MMI 3dB coupler, respectively. L is the total length of the device.

Any modification in the geometry of the multi-mode waveguide should modify the performance of the MMI coupler. The performance is characterized by the splitting ratio of the input power into the output ports (imbalance, see equation 2.48 in chapter 2), and by the excess loss (equation 2.47 in chapter 2). In figure 5.6, the length of the multi-mode waveguide of a 1×2 MMI coupler and a 2×2 3dB MMI coupler was first optimized (using a 2D simulation) for the lowest excess loss. Then, the effect of the deviation of the width of the multi-mode waveguide on the device performance was simulated. Here we assumed a symmetric modification of the width of the multi-mode waveguide. As a result, the excess loss of the 1×2 MMI coupler increases at a slower rate (about factor 2) than in the case of the 2×2 3dB MMI coupler when the multi-mode waveguide deviates from the nominal value by ΔW_m. The imbalance of the 1×2 MMI coupler does not depend on ΔW_m due to the symmetric interference mechanism [26]. As for the 2×2 3dB MMI coupler, the imbalance changes with ΔW_m which was predicted in [26] for paired interference devices.

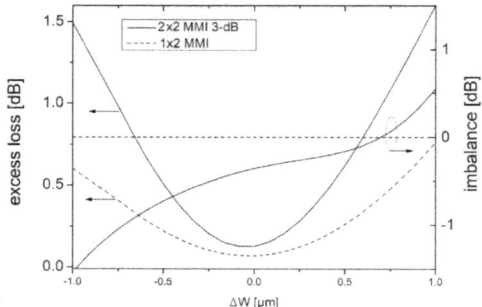

Figure 5.6: Simulated (2D structure) excess loss and imbalance vs. deviation of the width of the multi-mode waveguide ΔW_m from its optimal value W_m using a 2D beam propagation method. Nominal multi-mode waveguide width is $W_m = 15 \, \mu m$ (optimum length 546 µm) for the 1×2 MMI coupler and $W_m = 20 \, \mu m$ for the 2×2 MMI 3dB coupler.

The simulation also shows that for the 2×2 MMI 3dB coupler, the minimum of the excess loss and the minimum imbalance don't occur simultaneously. In fact, only one of these two parameters can be optimized if the width of the multi-mode waveguide is fixed. If the 3dB coupler is used in a switch or a Mach-Zehnder modulator, the imbalance directly translates into extinction ratio [26]. Please note that the minimum excess loss does not equal 0 dB due to radiation losses at the interfaces between the multi-mode waveguide and the access waveguides.

The numerical simulation (beam propagation in a 2D model then a 3D model) of the MMI coupler deliver values of the multi-mode waveguide length which slightly differ from the that predicted by the simple approach (using the beat length) as shown by table 5.2. Table 5.2 also shows that the error of the optimum length between the re-

Table 5.2: Simulated optimum multi-mode waveguide length of a 2×2 3dB MMI coupler using 2D and 3D beam propagation methods with the corresponding length calculated from the beat length ($W_m =$20 µm).

etching depth [µm]	multi-mode waveguide length [µm]		
	$L_\pi/2$	2D BPM	3D BPM
2.0	1273	1320	1290
2.15	1240	1280	1265
2.3	1210	1240	1235

sults of the 2D and the 3D simulations decreases with increasing etching depth. This is attributed to the fact that, with increasing etching depth, the guided modes of the multi-mode waveguide become more confined under the ridge region, which then increases the accuracy of the refractive index approximation in the 2D method [32].

However, despite being efficient, the 2D model may not fully reflect the real 3D structure due to the effective index approximation. Please note that the 2D simulation considers the guided mode of a slab waveguide that does not take the modal losses of the actual input mode into consideration. Thus, the actual values of the excess loss are expected to be larger than the values depicted in figure 5.6. A 3D model that considers the boundary conditions of the ridge waveguide and the lateral guided modes instead of the slab modes of the effective waveguide should deliver an estimation of the actual excess loss and imbalance in the MMI couplers. These are given in table 5.3 for one value of the etching depth $2.15\,\mu m$.

Table 5.3: Simulated excess loss and imbalance of a 2×2 3dB MMI coupler using 2D and 3D beam propagation methods ($W_m =20\,\mu m$, $d_e =2.15\,\mu m$).

model	excess loss [dB]	imbalance [dB]
2D-BPM	0.17	0.3
3D-BPM	0.74	0.3

5.4.3 Interfaces of the multi-mode waveguide to access waveguides

The output ports of the MMI coupler are realized at the end of the multi-mode waveguide where the images of the input field are formed. In order to avoid reflections at

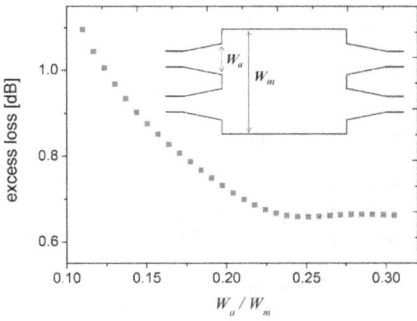

Figure 5.7: Simulated excess loss vs. normalized access waveguide width W_a/W_m of a 2×2 MMI 3dB coupler. $W_m = 20\,\mu m$, $d_e = 2\,\mu m$.

the interface between the access waveguides and the multi-mode waveguide and to efficiently collect all the light at the end of the multi-mode waveguide [40], the width of the access waveguides is linearly tapered from W_r to $W_a > W_r$ at the input ports and from W_a to W_r at the output ports. Such a procedure, modifies the excess loss of the device. Thus in order to find an optimum value of W_a we calculated the excess loss as a function of the normalized width W_a/W_m as shown by figure 5.7. Minimum loss is attained with $W_a/W_m \geq 0.25$ with W_a is the taper width of the (adiabatic) access waveguide. With the width of the multi-mode waveguide $W_m = 20\,\mu\text{m}$, which corresponds to minimum taper width of $W_a = 5\,\mu\text{m}$.

5.4.4 S-bends

S-bends are used at the output of the MMI coupler (see figure 5.4 (right)) to increase the spacial distance between the output ports.

In comparison to straight waveguides, radiative losses in S-bends may not be neglected in comparison to absorption or scattering losses. These additional losses occur due to optical mode radiation at the bends and to transition losses at the interface between the straight and the curved sections of the S-bend [52, p. 328], [36]. For the MMI couplers with the ridge waveguide of the access waveguides selected above ($W_r = 2.2\,\mu\text{m}$, $d_e = 2.15\,\mu\text{m}$), the lateral effective refractive index contrast is $\Delta\bar{n}_{eff} = 6.6 \times 10^{-3}$ for which the confinement factor of the guided optical TE mode under the ridge is 0.93 (see figure 5.8 in the following section). Thus, the amount of radiative losses depends on the curvature of the bent waveguide [53] (the bend radius and the bend angle).

A widely used S-bend profile for low lateral confinement structures is the *cosine* profile. The equation for the cosine S-bend with a propagation length l along the z-direction and a lateral offset W_S is given by:

$$y(z) = \frac{W_S}{\pi} \cdot \sin\left(\frac{2\pi z}{l}\right) + W_S \cdot \left(1 - \frac{2 \cdot z}{l}\right) + W_S \tag{5.1}$$

Using this equation, we designed S-bends with $l = 700\,\mu\text{m}$, $W_S = 40\,\mu\text{m}$, and $W_S = 20\,\mu\text{m}$, respectively. This corresponds to a large bend curvature in order to limit the effect of radiative losses at the bend.

5.5 Design of directional couplers

In this section only one configuration of directional couplers is considered. Operation wavelength is 780 nm and the input field is assumed to be TE polarized. The ridge waveguide of the access waveguides ($W_r = 2.2\,\mu\text{m}$, $d_e = 2.15\,\mu\text{m}$) is selected for both, the input waveguide, and the coupling waveguide of the directional coupler. The distance between the ridges is set to $d_C = 500\,\text{nm}$. Due to the well-defined ridge etching depth, only a small fraction of the input field expands towards the coupling waveguide. A small overlap of both fields is expected.

The simulated optical fields for this configuration are shown in figure 5.8. The values of the effective refractive indices for the calculation of the coupling coefficient Γ_C (equation 2.33 in chapter 2) correspond to $\bar{n}_{eff} = 3.4182$ (the effective index of the guided TE fundamental mode which is equal for both input and coupled fields), and $\bar{n}_c = 3.4116$ (the effective refractive index of the region at the sides of the ridges). The resulting transfer distance (using a 3D model) is given by $L_0 = \pi/(2\Gamma_C) = 508\,\mu\text{m}$ which corresponds to a cross coupler. A 3-dB coupler is then expected at $L_C = 254\,\mu\text{m}$.

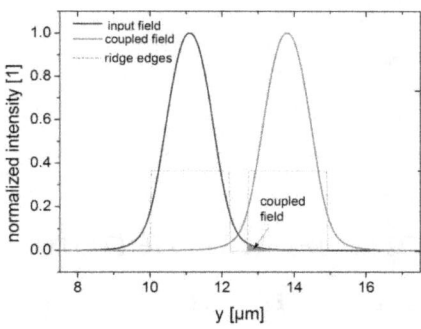

Figure 5.8: Overlap of the input optical field with the coupling waveguide in a directional coupler. (Vertical structure from table 4.2 in chapter 4).

5.6   Conclusions

In this chapter the multi-layer structure of the phase modulators at the wavelength of 780 nm has been used to design waveguide couplers. The lateral design of 1×2 MMI couplers and 2×2 MMI couplers was first estimated using the self-imaging properties of a multi-mode waveguide. Then the design was optimized by using a numerical 2D model that uses a finite difference beam propagation method. The simulation has shown that the 1×2 MMI couplers can provide a 0 dB imbalance due to the symmetric interference. For the 2×2 MMI couplers using the paired interference mechanism, it seems possible to optimize the lateral geometry of the multi-mode waveguide for low imbalance and reasonably low excess losses. The actual excess loss and imbalance were then estimated using a 3D model of the MMI couplers. Further, the lateral structure of a directional coupler of the same length scales of the MMI couplers has been considered. The ridge parameters of the directional coupler are identical to the ridge parameters of the access waveguides of the MMI couplers. Hence, the directional coupler serves as a reference to evaluate the performance of the 2×2 MMI couplers.

Chapter 6

Application: Mach-Zehnder intensity modulator

The integration properties of the designed phase modulators, bend waveguides, and MMI couplers can be demonstrated through a MZI modulator which is one of the simplest PICs for applications at the wavelength of 780 nm.

MZI modulators in III-V compound semiconductors (InP-based) that use MMI couplers have already been reported in the literature, see [28]. In [25] and in [27] integrated MZI modulators based on GaAs/AlGaAs double heterostructures and Y-couplers were reported. The MZI modulators in this work are designed using MMI couplers. The

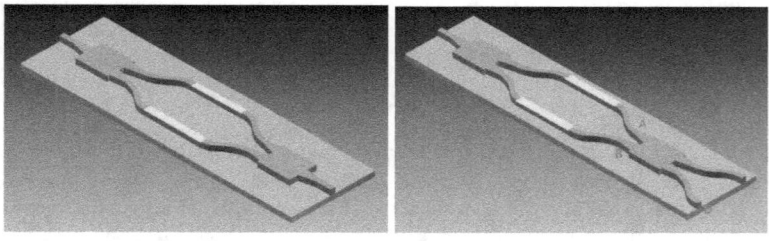

Figure 6.1: Schematic of MZI modulators. (left) MZI with 1x2 input and output MMI couplers. (right) MZI with 2 × 2 MMI 3dB coupler at the output (with input ports A and B and output ports C and D). The p-contact of the sections with the phase modulators are marked with the golden color.

schematic description of both devices is shown in figure 6.1. The first MZI modulator uses two identical 1×2 MMI couplers, one 1×2 MMI (splitter) at the input and one 1×2 MMI (combiner) at the output. The input field is (equally) split between the two phase modulators (arms of the MZI). A modulation voltage signal can be applied on one or both arms to modify the phase difference between the optical signals propagating in the two arms. The optical signals are then fed into the output MMI coupler. Signals which are in-phase fulfill the conditions for a single image with a maximum intensity at the output waveguide of the MZI. If the signals (nominally with identical amplitudes) were out of phase (phase difference is π rad), then the interfere destructively at the output waveguide and the transmitted power is minimum. Thus, phase difference is converted into intensity modulation.

The second MZI modulator uses a 1×2 MMI splitter at the input and a 2×2 MMI 3dB coupler (combiner) at the output. Each of the inputs ports of the output MMI coupler generates two images at the two output ports with a relevant phase shift of $\pi/2$ [26] between the two images. Here we assume a perfect 3dB coupler (imbalance of 0 dB) and equal amplitudes of the signals at the input ports of the 2×2 MMI 3dB coupler. Let the initial phases of the signals at the input ports A and B of the 2×2 MMI coupler be Φ_{A0} and Φ_{B0}. The relevant phases (in radian) of the images at the output ports C and D resulting from the input at port A can be -without loss of generality- written as: $\Phi_{AC} = \Phi_{A0}$ and $\Phi_{AD} = \Phi_{A0} + \pi/2$, respectively. And for the input from port B, the relevant phases of the images at the output ports C and D can be -without loss of generality- written as: $\Phi_{BC} = \Phi_{B0} + \pi/2$ and $\Phi_{AD} = \Phi_{B0}$, respectively. At each output port, the resulting image is then a super-position of two images, one from each input port. The phase difference between these two images corresponds to $\Phi_C = \Phi_0 - \pi/2$ and $\Phi_D = \Phi_0 + \pi/2$, where $\Phi_0 = \Phi_{A0} - \Phi_{B0}$ is the initial phase difference. Hence, if $\Phi_0 = p \cdot 2\pi + \pi/2$ rad (p integer), then the two images at port C are in-phase while they are out of phase at port D. As a result the transmitted power is maximum at port C and minimum at port D. If on the other hand $\Phi_0 = p \cdot 2\pi + 3\pi/2$ rad, the situation is reversed. Thus, for this type of MZI modulator, if a modulating signal is applied on one arm, the voltage required between a maximum and a minimum of the transmitted power corresponds to a phase shift of π rad at the phase modulator arm.

The performance of an MZI modulator in this work is characterized by its excess loss and its extinction ratio. Both device types should feature low excess loss due to the low losses of the phase modulators, the S-bends, and the MMI couplers.

According to [25], the transmission of the MZI modulator with a low extinction ratio follows the expression:

$$P/P_{max} = (1 - P_{min}/P_{max}) \cos^2\left(\frac{\pi V}{2V_\pi} + \Phi_0\right) + P_{min}/P_{max} \qquad (6.1)$$

where P_{max} and P_{min} are the maximum and the minimum transmitted powers, respectively, V is the applied voltage, and V_π is the half-wave voltage.

The extinction ratio at an output port of the MZI modulator is then given by:

$$extinction\,ratio\,[\mathrm{dB}] = 10 \times \log \frac{P_{max}}{P_{min}} \qquad (6.2)$$

Chapter 7

Fabrication of GaAs-based passive components

In this chapter an overview of the semiconductor-technology related aspects of the GaAs-based passive components is presented. The devices were exclusively fabricated in-house. The fabrication was carried out by colleges of the material technology department and of the optoelectronic department.

During the different stages of this work, four technology process runs of GaAs-based passive components have been carried out. Three of these processes runs were to manufacture the basic photonic components (phase modulators, S-bends, couplers, and MZI modulators) for operation at 780 nm. The fourth process was dedicated only to phase modulators operating at a the wavelength of $\lambda = 1064$ nm.

Following the material growth that defines the vertical layout of the devices, lithography was used to implement lateral structuring that defines the lateral waveguide sections for the phase modulators, couplers, and MZI modulators. The realization of the couplers and MZI modulators was restricted to the wavelength of 780 nm.

7.1   Material growth

The epitaxial layers of the four different processes were grown on 3-inch (001) n-GaAs substrates (wafers). Table 7.1 gives an overview of the different process runs with the corresponding wafers, application wavelength, and the types of devices that have been realized. Each process is designated by a unique number (Z1 xxxx). As shown in table 7.1, a unique identifier (I through IV) is assigned to each of the four processes and will be used to refer to the corresponding process in the following parts of the thesis.

In the process run I (or Z1 6105) the multi-layer structure was fabricated that delivered the P-p-i-n-N double heterostructure phase modulator from table 4.2 (see chapter 4). The structure was grown on the GaAs substrate using metal-organic vapor phase epitaxy (MOVPE). Si and C were used as n- and p-type dopants, respectively. In process run II (Z1 6520), the multi-layer structure of a P-p-n-N double heterostructure phase modulator from table 4.3 has been realized. The doping profile of the P-p-n-N structure in process II is intended to increase the phase modulation efficiency when compared to the structure of process I. The comparison of the two structures from process runs I and II have already been presented in chapter 4 (see figure 4.4).

The multi-layer structure realized in process run III (or Z1 7471) is a repetition of the layer structure of the process I. Here the lateral layout has been modified as explained in the next section. In process run IV (Z1 6894), the multi-layer structures of phase modulators for operation at the wavelength of 1064 nm (tables 4.5 and 4.6) were realized.

Table 7.1: Fabrication plan of GaAs-based photonic components. PMod: phase modulator, D. coupl.: directional coupler, MZI (a): layout with only 1×2 MMI couplers, MZI (b): layout with input 1×2 MMI couplers and output 2×2 MMI couplers.

ID	Process #	Wafer	λ[nm]	PMod	bend	D. coupl.	MMI	MZI
I	Z1 6105	D2043-2	780	table 4.2	-	-	-	-
		D2043-3	780	table 4.2	-	-	-	-
II	Z1 6520	D2231-3	780	table 4.3	✓	-	1x2	(a)
		D2231-4	780	table 4.3	✓	-	1x2	(a)
III	Z17471	D2230-3	780	table 4.2	✓	✓	1x2, 2x2	(b)
		D2904-4	780	table 4.2	✓	✓	1x2, 2x2	(b)
IV	Z1 6894	C3059-3	1064	table 4.5	-	-	-	-
		C3062-3	1064	table 4.6	-	-	-	-

7.2 Lithography

For the phase modulators on all wafers, a standard ridge waveguide process was applied with the orientation of the waveguides parallel to the [1$\bar{1}$0] crystallographic direction in order to provide access to the linear electro-optic effect (see section 3.1.2 in chapter 3). The ridge waveguides were defined by reactive ion etching (RIE) and encapsulated with a 100 nm thick SiNx layer. The isolation layer was opened on top of the waveguides for lateral carrier confinement. Ti/Pt/Au layers were deposited for p-side contacts and before evaporation of the n-metalization the wafer was thinned to 150 μm.

Coupler devices and MZI modulators were realized in process runs II and III. For wafers of these two process runs, I-line stepper lithography followed by reactive ion etching was applied for the lateral definition of the MMI couplers and the 2.2 μm wide ridges for linear and bent waveguides.

The MZI modulators of process run II were created on a total chip length of 10 mm. The layout has 1×2 MMI couplers at the input and at the output sides of the MZI modulators. Tapered waveguides (at the interface between the multi-mode waveguides and the access waveguides of the MMI couplers) were introduced. The layout of process III includes 1×2 MMI couplers, 2×2 MMI 3dB couplers, 2×2 MMI cross couplers, directional couplers, and MZI modulators. The MZI modulator were realized in two different layouts. Namely, MZIs with 1×2 MMI couplers at the input and at the output, and MZIs with 1×2 MMI couplers at the input and with 2×2 at the output (see figure 6.1) were realized. Devices of process run III were realized on a total length of 10 mm. The lithography steps of process III followed in similar lines to that in process II. Individual details to different devices will be later included in the experiment. Figures 7.1 and 7.2 shows the cross-section scanning electron micrograph (SEM) of some of the fabricated devices.

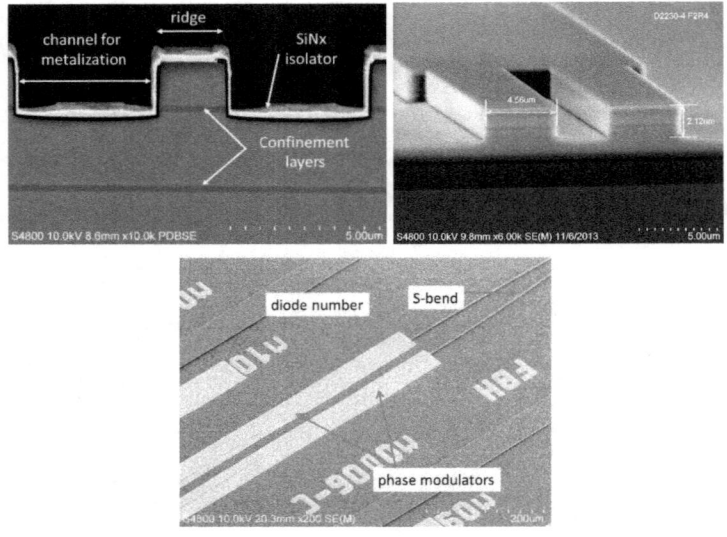

Figure 7.1: SEM image of: (left) fabricated phase modulator at the wavelength 780 nm from process I. (right) output ports of a 1×2 MMI coupler at the wavelength of 780 nm from process II. (down center) part of the MZI modulator from process III showing the phase modulators and S-bends.

Figure 7.2: SEM image of a directional coupler from process run III.

Chapter 8

Electro-optic Performance

Experimental results of the main performance factors of GaAs/AlGaAs double heterostructure phase modulators, directional couplers, MMI couplers, and MZI modulators are presented in this chapter.

8.1 Electro-optic Performance: GaAs-based phase modulators

We apply the well-known Fabry-Pérot (FP) method to determine the phase modulation efficiency of the phase modulators fabricated in process runs I and II (at the wavelength of 780 nm), and IV (at the wavelength of 1064 nm). We also use the FP method to determine the propagation losses in the phase modulator waveguides.

8.1.1 Electrical properties of phase modulators

The phase modulators are operated in the reverse-bias direction in order to apply the electric field necessary to use the electro-optic effects. The total reverse bias voltage must not exceed the break-down voltage of the modulator heterojunction.

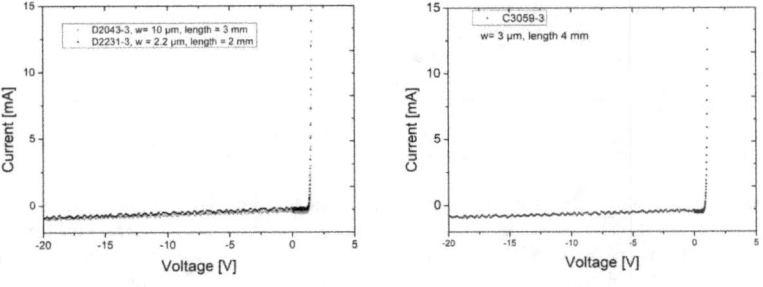

Figure 8.1: Static I-V characteristics of (left) phase modulators from the process runs I and II (Wafer D2043-3:multi-layer in table 4.2, Wafer D2231-3: multi-layer in table 4.3), and (right) phase modulator from the process IV (wafer C3059-3: multi-layer in table 4.5).

To determine the break down voltage, the current through the phase modulator was measured as a function of the applied reverse voltage. As a voltage source we used a power supply (hp 6632b) which provides output ratings of 0-20 V. Figure 8.1 shows for example the result of such a measurement for three phase modulators chips from wafers from process runs I, II and IV. No break through is observed up to reverse voltage of 20 V. i.e. the break-down voltage is larger than 20 V. This result is valid for all the processed wafers in process runs I, II and IV.

The small-signal equivalent circuit of the reverse-biased modulator junction can be well described by the circuit in figure 8.2 , where R_s is the series resistance and C_j the junction depletion capacity [54, p. 98]. An LCR-bridge (hp 4274 LCR meter) was used

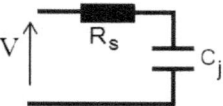

Figure 8.2: Equivalent electrical circuit of a reverse-biased phase modulator junction at low frequencies. C_j is the junction capacity, R_s is the conductance.

to determine the series resistance R_s and the capacity $C_j{}^1$. Phase modulator chips from process run I were mounted on a C-mount. The LCR bridge applies a sinusoidal

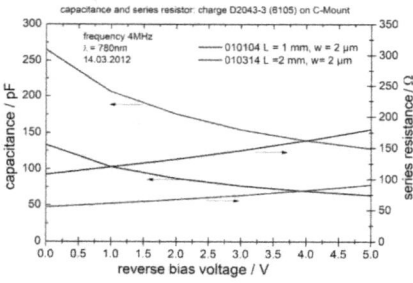

Figure 8.3: Series resistance and capacitance of phase modulator chips on C-mount from process I (multi-layer in table 4.2) measured at different reversed-bias voltages.

modulation signal with a frequency f_m and allows to add a DC voltage (bias voltage). It determines the response (amplitude and phase components of the transfer function) of the load (the phase modulator chips on C-mount), from which R_s and C_j can be determined. A C-mount without a modulator chip was used for calibration. The result of measurements of 1 mm and 2 mm chips are shown in figure 8.3.

The capacitance of a 2 mm long modulator at 0 V is about 250 pF. This limits the 3-dB modulation bandwidth for direct modulation with a 50 Ω source to about

---

[1]The measurements of the Series resistance and capacitance of phase modulator chips on C-mount were carried out by Armin Liero from the Microwave department at FBH.

12.75 MHz (with $R_s = 50\,\Omega$). This value of the modulation bandwidth is sufficient for the generation of the modulation side bands at 8 MHz for Rb spectroscopy as a direct application for the phase modulators from this work.

8.1.2 Phase modulation efficiency

A simple method to estimate the modulation efficiency is the Fabry-Perot (FP) interference method [15], [19]. In this method, the FP cavity is formed by the uncoated facets of the modulator's waveguide. For the generation of the FP fringes a slowly varying sawtooth voltage signal is applied to modify the optical path length of the modulator due to the modification of the effective refractive index. The transmitted power is then recorded. The half-wave voltage is then required between two maxima or two minima of the transmitted power. The experimental realization of this method

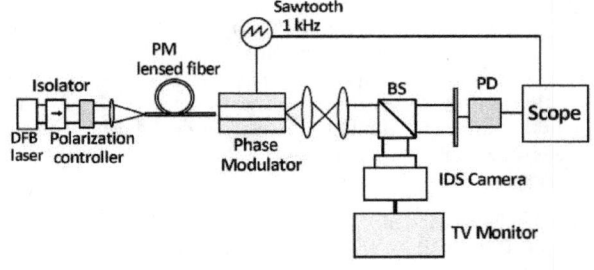

Figure 8.4: Fabry-Perot experimental setup for measurement of phase modulation efficiency and propagation losses of GaAs-based phase modulators.

is shown in figure 8.4. The optical field of a DFB laser at the wavelength of 780 nm (or at 1064 nm) is coupled into the waveguide by means of a polarization maintaining, single mode lensed-fiber. A polarization controller that consists of a zero-order half-wave plate and a polarizing beam splitter selects the TE polarization. The lensed fiber is fixed on a rotation mount (Thorlabs HF R007). The output of the lensed fiber is fed into the waveguide. This setup provides a polarization extinction ratio (PER) of 20 dB and allows for setting the input polarization parallel to TE-polarization to better than 2 deg, corresponding to 29 dB of suppression of the TM-polarization. The PER has been verified experimentally as the output of the lensed fiber was collimated using a round aspheric lens then directed onto a polarizing beam splitter (Linos G335725000) to select the required polarization. To prepare chips for characterization, 1 mm, 2 mm and 4 mm chips were cleaved and mounted on C-mounts. The output signal from the modulator chip was collimated using a coated round aspheric lens and was detected using a photoreceiver. Please refer to Appendix B for the list of measured chips with different lengths and ridge parameters. A 1 kHz sawtooth on top of 10 V DC reverse bias voltage signal is swept from 0 V to −20 V. The voltage V_π corresponding to a phase shift of π along the modulator length L is determined from the reverse-biased voltage required between two maxima (or two minima) of the transmitted power [19]. As an example, figure 8.5 shows the FP fringes of a 2 mm phase modulator chip developed for application at 780 nm, see table 4.2 (process run I).

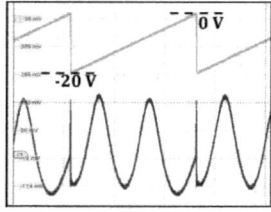

Figure 8.5: The oscilloscope photo of the resulting FP fringes of a 2 mm phase modulator from process run I. The upper curve shows the applied voltage, the lower curve is the corresponding transmitted intensity [19].

The results of the FP measurement are given in table 8.1 and are compared with the theoretical values. The experimental results are to a certain extent consistent with the values expected from the simulation which demonstrates the efficiency of the FP method. The difference between the experimental and the theoretically expected values the calculation may be attributed to deviation of the actual doping profile of the modulator heterojunction from the nominal.

Table 8.1: Phase modulation efficiency of phase modulators from process runs I, II, IV. Experimental values (FP method) vs. theoretical values.

process	Wafer	structure	λ [nm]	measured (FP) [deg/(V·mm)]	theory [deg/(V·mm)]
I	D2043-2	table 4.2	780	10.8	9.54
I	D2043-3	table 4.2	780	8.2	9.54
II	D2231-3	table 4.3	780	13.1	12.49
II	D2231-4	table 4.3	780	15.6	12.49
IV	C3059-3	table 4.5	1064	11.2	10.75
IV	C3062-3	table 4.6	1064	13.2	12.09

8.1.3 Propagation losses

The FP technique is also suitable to perform a loss measurement. For this purpose, the transmission is recorded for different chip lengths. In this way, the propagation loss can be determined from transmission loss measurements carried out on waveguides with different lengths according to [55]:

$$-\ln\left(\left(1 - \sqrt{1 - K^2}\right)/K\right) = \alpha \cdot L - \ln R, \qquad (8.1)$$

where L is the length of the FP cavity (corresponding to the chip length), R is the reflectivity of the uncoated facets of the modulators chips, and K is the contrast of the Fabry-Perot resonances ($K = (P_{max} - P_{min})/(P_{max} + P_{min})$ [55], [56], where P_{max}, P_{min} are the maximum and minimum transmitted powers, respectively.

Propagation losses of phase modulators at 780 nm

In the absence of a modulating electric field, the free carriers density is expected to be largest. Thus, the propagation losses are expected to be largest, when no electric field is applied. In the FP setup in figure 8.4, the application of electric field modifies the carrier density and the electro-absorption associated with the Franz-Keldysh effect (QEO effect) [23]. We therefore modify the FP setup in figure 8.4 in order to optically

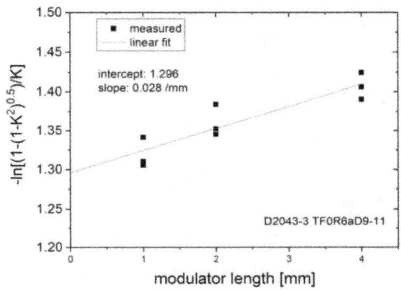

Figure 8.6: Transmission losses: left hand side of equation (8.1) as a function of the length of the modulator cavity. The slope of the linear fit corresponds to the propagation loss coefficient in [1/mm] units [19]. Chips from wafer D2043-3, process run I.

tune the phase as the following: we use a *New Focus* (Velocity 6312) tunable external cavity diode laser (ECDL) instead of the DFB laser. Its wavelength can be tuned within the range 765 nm-781 nm. We tune the wavelength of ECDL by 0.1 nm around the wavelength 780 nm. This fine tuning is sufficient to observe the FP fringes of the intensity profile at the output of the uncoated modulator chip with the smallest cavity length of 1 mm. The measurement is carried out on devices with 3 different lengths: 1 mm, 2 mm, and 4 mm. For each of these lengths three nominally identical chips (process run I) are selected and their transmission profile and I_{max} and I_{min} are measured to calculate the FP contrast K. In figure 8.6 the term on the left hand side of equation (8.1) is plotted as a function of the chip length. The loss coefficient $\alpha = 0.28\,\mathrm{cm}^{-1}$ (which corresponds to 1.2 dB/cm) can be extracted from the slope of the fitted straight line (0.028 mm^{-1}). This value is consistent with the value of 0.1 cm^{-1} calculated in 4.2.2, which only accounts for the free-carrier absorption. The deviation could be attributed to additional losses introduced by the etched planes of the ridge waveguide. The reflectivity of the facets extracted from the interception with the Y-axis is at is R=0.275 which is slightly smaller than the theoretical value of 0.305 [19].

Propagation losses of phase modulators at 1064 nm

For the phase modulators at the wavelength of 1064 nm a tunable laser was not available. Therefore, the FP fringes for the loss measurements were generated by electrically tuning the phase of the optical signal. This assumes the electro-absorption losses associated with the Franz-Keldysh effect to be negligible. In fact this assumption can be verified by investigating the peak levels of the transmission of the phase modulator chips as the modulating voltage is increased. Figure 8.7 shows that the peak levels are almost independent of the modulation voltage which accounts to negligible electro-absorption losses. This agrees very well with the fact that the QEO effect has a

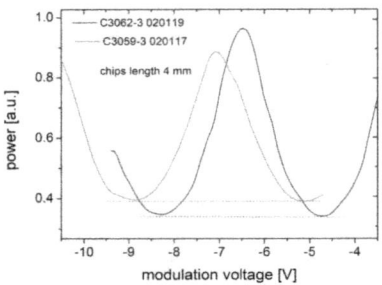

Figure 8.7: The measured power transmission of two uncoated, 4 mm long phase modulators from process run IV as a function of the modulation voltage.

minimum contribution to phase modulation in all the investigated phase modulators. Chips from wafers C3059-3 and C3062-3 of process run IV with lengths of 2 mm and 4 mm were characterized. For each of these lengths 6 nominally identical chips (process run IV) were selected and their transmission profile and P_{max} and P_{min} were measured to calculate the FP contrast K. The resulting values for interception of the

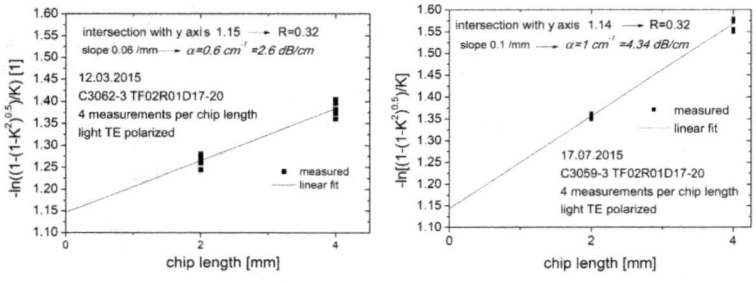

Figure 8.8: Transmission losses: left hand side of equation (8.1) as a function of the length of the modulator cavity of phase modulator chips from wafers from process run IV (C3062-3 from table 4.6 and C3059-3 from table 4.5). The slope of the linear fit corresponds to the propagation loss coefficient α in $[1/mm]$ units.

linear fits with the y-axes which correspond to the facets reflectivity $R \approx 0.32$ are very convenient despite that only 2 different chip lengths were used for the measurements.

The propagation losses amount to 4.34 dB/cm and 2.63 dB/cm for chips from wafers C3059-3, and C3062-3 respectively. The measured propagation losses for the phase modulators at 1064 nm are consistent with the theoretically calculated values, which only accounts for the free-carrier absorption. Any deviation could be attributed to additional losses introduced by the etched planes of the ridge waveguides.

8.1.4 Conclusions

In this section, the main performance factors of phase modulators at 780 nm and 1064 nm were investigated. The break-down voltage for all the devices was found to be larger than -20 V. For a 2 mm phase modulator chip at 780 nm from process I, the total phase modulator capacitance at 0 V was estimated to be 250 pF, limiting direct modulation with a 50 Ω source to 12.75 MHz which is sufficient for the generation of modulation sidebands for rubidium spectroscopy. In the future, the reduction in the modulator capacitance by one to two orders of magnitude seems feasible by adding a benzocyclobutene polymer (BCB) passivation layer between the p-metallization and the upper cladding instead of the thin SiNx layer. This should allow GaAs/AlGaAs-based modulators to provide access to modulation frequencies beyond 1 GHz with direct driving.

The well-known FP method was applied to measure the phase modulation as a function of the reverse-biased voltage for modulator chips from processes I, II, and IV. Phase modulation efficiencies beyond 10 deg/(V·mm) were demonstrated for all the measured modulators. The measured values are consistent with the values expected from the simulation which demonstrates the efficiency of the FP method. Further, using the FP method, the propagation losses of modulators chips from process I and IV were estimated from the transmission loss measurements carried out on waveguides with different lengths. Propagation losses of the waveguides of the phase modulators at 780 nm were found to amount to only 1.2 dB/cm. The propagation losses of the waveguides of modulators at 1064 nm were found to be less than 4.7 dB/cm which is beyond the state-of-the-art for GaAs/AlGaAs double heterostructure phase modulators with a GaAs guiding core.

8.2 Electro-optic Performance: GaAs-based couplers

In this section the electro-optical performance of GaAs-based bent waveguides and waveguide couplers is presented.

8.2.1 Bent waveguides

Relevant parameters for the application of bent waveguides (S-bends) are the radiative loss of the bent waveguides as well as the loss (reflection and scattering) at the interface between bent and straight waveguide section due to different mode sizes (mode mismatch).

In order to determine radiative losses of the S-bends, we included appropriate test structures in the layout of process III. Each of these test structures contains two waveguides: a straight reference waveguide and total of 14 repetitions of a basic bent waveguide structure, which is an S-bend (see equation 5.1). Both waveguides of the test structure are 10 mm long. For the characterization, the test structures were cleaved

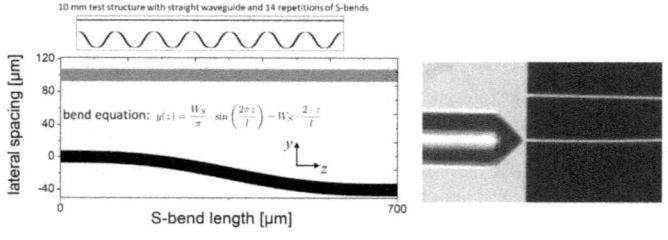

Figure 8.9: (left) Schematic of the layout of the test structure with detailed layout of a section with only one S-bend. (right) Light coupling into the bent waveguide by means of a lensed-fiber.

and the facets were AR-coated to eliminate the FP reflections. The measurement setup is shown in figure 8.10. As a light source we used a DFB laser at the wavelength

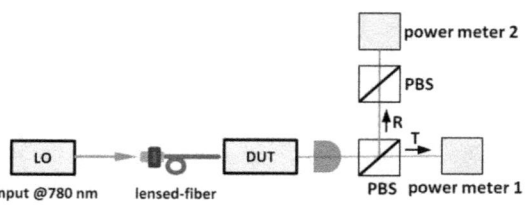

Figure 8.10: Measurement setup for the characterization of S-bends ($W_S = 20\,\mu m$). DUT: device under test, PBS: polarizing beam splitter, T: transmission beam of the PBS, R: reflection beam of the PBS.

of 780 nm. We used a polarization maintaining lensed-fiber to couple the light into the waveguides. To excite one operation mode (TE or TM), the lensed-fiber was fixed on a rotation mount (Thorlabs HF R007). The rotation mount can be manually adjusted to achieve an experimental polarization extinction ratio of 20 dB (see section 8.1.2) at the input of the tested waveguides for both, TE and TM mode operation. The output beam was collimated using a mounted aspheric round lens (f =1.46 mm), then a polarizing beam splitter (PBS) selected the polarization of interest. The transmission signal of the PBS was detected using a powermeter. A second powermeter detected the reflected beam (with the undesired polarization). The second PBS in the way of the reflected beam purifies the TM reflected beam for an accurate measurement of the polarization extinction ratio. Piezo-actuated XYZ-translation stages with 1 nm resolution (Smaract SLC-series) were used to set the position of the lensed-fiber for optimum coupling.

By comparing the power at the transmission (T) (at power meter 1) and reflection (R) (at power meter 2), the polarization extinction ratio of the output signal can be determined. The comparison for both, TE and TM-mode operation has revealed that experimental input PER of 20 dB is maintained by both bent and straight waveguides. In the following, we consider only operation in the TE mode.

The next step is to determine the insertion loss of the bent waveguide which includes the propagation losses and coupling losses. We apply the following procedure: for the input power P_0 delivered by the lensed-fiber, the output power of the reference waveguide P_{ref}, and of the bent waveguide P_b are given by:

$$\begin{aligned} P_{ref} &= \eta_{ref}P_0 \cdot e^{-(\alpha_c \cdot L_{ref})} \\ P_b &= \eta_b P_0 \cdot (1 - \gamma) \cdot e^{-(\alpha_c \cdot L_b)} \end{aligned} \tag{8.2}$$

with η_{ref}, η_b the coupling efficiencies into the reference and into the bent waveguides, respectively, L_{ref} the reference waveguide length (10 mm), L_b the bent waveguide length, α_c the propagation loss, and γ the radiation losses of the bent waveguide. Actually, the reference waveguide suffers also radiative losses at the sides of the ridge. Therefore, γ here is attributed solely to the radiative losses at the bends. Furthermore, the optical path along the waveguide material in the bent waveguide is longer than the length of the straight waveguide L_{ref}. However, the path difference is negligible due to the large curvature radius of the bent waveguide. Therefore we use $L_b \approx L_{ref}$. We assume that $\eta_{ref} = \eta_b$ for the following reasons: both the straight waveguide and the bent waveguide have the same cross-section (at both waveguides facets). In addition, for measurement repetition, we perform the measurement on 4 different chips taken from the same bar. As a result, the radiation losses of the bent waveguide can be directly calculated from the output powers of the bent and the straight waveguides:

$$\gamma = 1 - P_b/P_{ref}$$

The resulting radiation loss of the bent waveguide is $\gamma = 0.04$. The corresponding single S-bend loss is then $\gamma_S = \gamma/14 = 3 \times 10^{-3}$ which is given in dBs by $\gamma_S(\text{dB}) = 0.01\,\text{dB}$. This concludes that the radiation losses of the S-bends can be safely discarded in comparison to the propagation losses (1.2 dB/cm).

In fact, the assumption that $\eta_b = \eta_{ref}$ can be verified by investigating the beam profiles of the bent and straight waveguides. For this purpose, we use a CCD camera instead of powermeter 1 in figure 8.10. The camera detects the collimated beam from each or the reference and bent waveguides. The far field (collimated) profiles for both, the reference waveguide (straight waveguide) and the bent waveguide for operation in the TE mode as imprinted at the CCD camera are shown in figure 8.11. The intensity profiles along the horizontal direction are fitted using a Gaussian function $y = y_0 + \left(A/w\sqrt{\pi/2}\right)\exp\left(-2(x - x_c)^2/w^2\right)$. The comparison of the Gaussian fits for

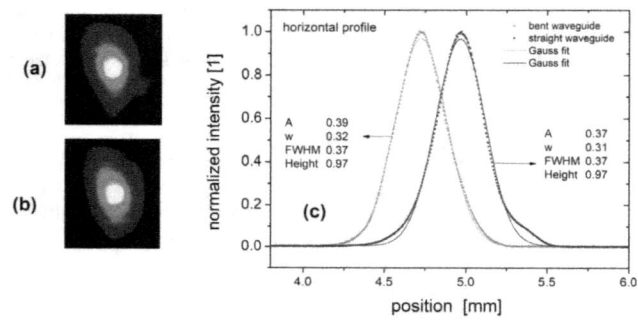

Figure 8.11: (a), (b) Far field profiles of a straight waveguide and a bent waveguide, respectively. (c) The intensity profiles along the horizontal direction. FWHM: full width at half-maximum. Collimation with an aspheric round lens ($f = 1.46\,$mm).

the horizontal profiles in figure 8.11 shows that the output profiles of the reference and bent waveguides are well matched to each other. In the vertical direction, the intensity profiles are expected to be identical since the vertical structures for both, straight and bend waveguides are identical.

Equation 8.2 shows that in order to determine the coupling losses of the reference waveguide η_{ref}, it is sufficient to determine the input power P_0 since α_c is known ($1.2\,$dB/cm). To determine P_0 the beam of the lensed fiber was directly collimated using the aspheric round lens and then detected using the powermeter. The corresponding coupling losses were found to be less than $0.8\,$dB. The well-matched beam spot of the lensed fiber to the guided mode of the reference waveguide and the AR-coating make it feasible to achieve such a high coupling efficiency using the piezo-actuated XYZ-translation stages with 1nm resolution.

8.2.2 Directional couplers

Directional couplers were realized in process (III) together with MZI devices (see figure 7.2 in chapter 7). The waveguide spacing d_C was fixed to 500 nm to allow for spatial overlap of the guided mode of the input waveguide with the coupling mode of the coupling waveguide as previously discussed in section 5.5 in chapter 5.

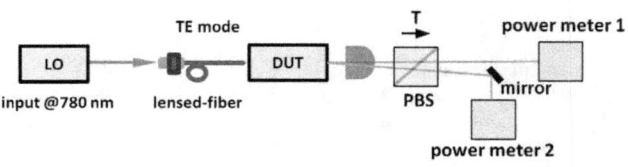

Figure 8.12: Setup for the characterization of directional couplers and MMI couplers. DUT: device under test, PBS: polarizing beam splitter, T: transmission beam of the PBS.

Setup for the characterization of directional couplers

The measurement setup for the characterization of the couplers is shown in figure 8.12. At the input of the DUT, the setup is identical to the setup for the characterization of S-bends in figure 8.10. At the output, the two beams (from the two output ports) are collimated using one aspheric round lens, then a polarizing beam splitter (PBS) allows for the transmission of the TE polarization (the interesting polarization) and reflects the TM polarization. At a sufficient distance from the PBS, the transmitted two beams are separated and detected using power meters 1 and 2 which are equidistant from the chips facets to allow for equal illumination of the sensor of the photodetectors.

Coupling ratio and excess loss of directional couplers

Results of measurements of the coupling ratio and excess loss of coupler devices are given in table 8.2. The values for the coupling length L_C in the table correspond to the nominal length of the straight coupling waveguides. Please note that the layout of directional couplers includes S-bends at the end of the straight coupling waveguides to introduce a smooth lateral separation. The coupling effect is expected to continue in the S-bends. The S-bends were introduced in the couplers layout according to equation 5.1 at a vertical spacing of 40 µm. Hence, the actual coupling length is expected to extend to a few tens of micrometers beyond the straight waveguides.

The experimental results in table 8.2 do not really reflect the expected performance. For example samples 3 and 4 share an exactly identical layout but perform totally different from each other. Sample 3 performs as a 3dB coupler whereas sample 4 has a large imbalance. The same applies to samples 5 and 6. This discrepancy can only be attributed to the fabrication tolerances. During the fabrication process, a well-defined waveguide spacing d_C can be maintained which is not necessarily the case for the etching depth. The actual etching depth may vary from the theoretical value along the coupling length L_C, see figure 8.15. This causes a different lateral confinement of the optical field which changes the coupling efficiency from one waveguide to the other, and hence, modifies the transfer length L_0. In order to compensate for fabrication artifacts, one may vary the coupling length L_C around the theoretical value. However, a reproduction process may not be feasible and the performance is expected to vary from one process to another or even within the same process from one device to the other as the measurement reveals. Additional excess losses in comparison to the theoretical values may be attributed to light scattering at the etched planes of the ridge waveguides.

In conclusion, the performance of GaAs-based directional couplers is limited by the quality of the fabrication process. A different concept that tolerates the fabrication errors, e.g. MMI couplers, is recommended for the realization of ridge waveguide couplers in GaAs-based PICs.

Table 8.2: Performance of directional couplers fabricated in process run III, wafer D2904-4. L_C gives the nominal (design) length of the coupling section according to figure 2.5(b). Total devices length is 10 mm, operation at $\lambda = 780$ nm.

ID	chip TFRRDD	L_C (nom.) µm	port	coupling ratio % theor.	exp.	excess loss dB theor.	exp.
1	060211	180	A-C	65	95	0.1	0.7
			A-D	35	05		
2	060212	180	A-C	65	88	0.1	0.6
			A-D	35	12		
3	060213	280	A-C	45	54	0.1	0.7
			A-D	55	46		
4	060313	280	A-C	45	83	0.1	0.5
			A-D	55	17		
5	060214	380	A-C	25	52	0.1	0.6
			A-D	75	48		
6	060215	380	A-C	25	85	0.1	0.7
			A-D	75	15		
7	060217	580	A-C	12	09	0.1	0.7
			A-D	88	91		
8	060218	580	A-C	12	15	0.1	0.7
			A-D	88	85		

8.2.3 Multi-mode interference couplers

MMI couplers from process runs II and III were fabricated on 3-inch wafers, see figure 8.13. Each wafer consists of a number of test fields. A test field includes a stack of bars, each with a total of 20 chips at a total length of 10 mm. Within the same bar, two of the 20 chips are straight waveguides that can be used as reference devices for insertion loss measurements. The remaining chips include one MZI (10 mm long) based on a 1×2 MMI input and a 1×2 MMI output splitter as well as one MZI based on the same 1×2 MMI coupler and a 2×2 MMI output coupler. The 1×2 MMI coupler is intended to perform as a 50/50 power splitter. The splitting ratio (power at output 1 to power at output 2) is insensitive to process tolerances (length and width of

WG, etch depth). The imbalance of the 2×2 MMI coupler depends on the multi-mode waveguide lateral geometry (width and length of the MMI).

Figure 8.13: Scan electron micrograph (SEM) photo of a 1×2 MMI coupler (left), and a 2×2 MMI coupler (right).

Setup for the measurement of MMI couplers

For the characterization of the MMI couplers, the 10 mm long bars with MZI layout were to be split into two parts such that the input and output waveguides of each input and output coupler of the MZI could be accessed optically (see figure 8.14). The

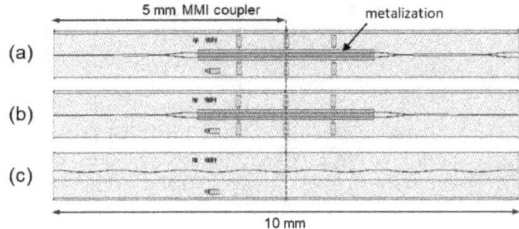

Figure 8.14: The layout of three different chips from the wafers in process run III. (a) an MZI modulator chip with a 1×2 MMI splitter and a 2×2 MMI coupler, (b) an MZI modulator chip with only 1×2 MMI couplers, and (c) chip with a reference straight waveguide and a bent waveguide.

resulting bars at a length of 5 mm were cleaved and were AR-coated to reduce the facets reflectivity. We used a vacuum holder to hold the bars on the test fixture. This kind of measurements of complete bars instead of individual chips has many advantages. For example, it allows to test similar or different devices from the same bar under (almost) identical conditions in order to improve the repetition rate of the measurements. Thanks to the vacuum holder, bars can be easily demounted and replaced by new bars for new experiments. Further, it reduces the costs of the characterization in comparison to the mounting costs of individual chips. However, one disadvantage of this procedure, is that the bars are very fragile and may easily be destroyed if not carefully handled.

The measurement setup for the characterization of the MMI couplers is identical to the setup in figure 8.12 in section 8.2.2. The light signal is fed into one input port of the MMI couplers. The coupling is optimized for maximum power at the output.

Excess loss and imbalance of MMI couplers

The measurement results are summarized in table 8.3. According to equation 2.48, the imbalance is determined from the ratio between the detected powers at powermeters 1 and 2. The excess loss is determined according to equation 2.47

Table 8.3: Performance of the MMI couplers from process runs II and III. Operation in the TE mode. Input port A. X-coupler: cross-coupler.

Process ID	wafer	MMI	chip TFRRDD	W_m [µm]	L_m [µm]	excess loss [dB] theor.	exp.	imbalance [dB] theor.	exp.
III	D2904-4	1×2	080217	15	560	0.3	1.7	0.0	0.2
			080218	15	560	0.3	1.4	0.0	0.2
II	D2231-4	1×2	010604	15	560	0.3	1.5	0.0	0.2
			010605	15	560	0.3	1.4	0.0	0.2
III	D2904-4	2×2	080201	19	1250	1.5	2.7	1.6	1.2
			080301	19	1250	1.5	2.6	1.6	1.2
			080208	20	1250	0.7	1.7	0.1	0.2
		3dB	080308	20	1250	0.7	1.5	0.1	0.3
			070208	20	1250	0.7	1.7	0.1	0.6
			080215	21	1250	1.7	2.7	0.5	1.2
			080315	21	1250	1.7	2.1	0.5	1.0
III	D2904-4	2×2 X-coupler	060203	20	2500	0.8	2.0	30.0	10.8
			060303	20	2500	0.8	1.8	30.0	11.0

Table 8.3 shows that -unlike to directional couplers- the performance of the three types of MMI couplers (splitter, 3dB, and cross-coupler) does not depend on the fabrication tolerances, see figure 8.15.

The 1×2 MMI coupler has the lowest imbalance (0.2 dB). Thus it can be used as the input splitter in an MZI modulator to allow for an experimental extinction ratio of at least 33 dB [26]. The imbalance of the 2×2 MMI 3dB coupler at the optimum width of the multi-mode waveguide ($W_m = 20$ µm) is found to range between 0.2 dB and 0.6 dB. The cross-coupler suffers a low extinction ratio (10 - 11 dB) when compared to the expected value from the theory (30 dB). It is assumed that with increasing length of the multi-mode waveguide, the contribution of leaky modes (only guided modes are considered for the design) may no longer be discarded which may then contribute to the reduction of the extinction ratio of the cross-coupler.

The comparison between table 8.3 and table 8.2 shows that the access loss of the MMI couplers is larger than that of the directional couplers. These additional losses in the MMI devices are attributed to the radiation losses in the multi-mode waveguide.

Nevertheless, the access loss of MMI couplers remains low enough so that MMI couplers remain a more suitable option than directional couplers for the realization of MZI modulators.

Figure 8.15: Two SEM images of the same 1x2 MMI coupler at different lateral longitudinal positions showing different values of the etching depth.

8.2.4 Conclusions

In this section, the performance of GaAs/AlGaAs MMI couplers and directional couplers for applications at the wavelength of 780 nm has been experimentally investigated.

Directional couplers have demonstrated a very low insertion loss (0.7 dB) . However, the investigation of nominally identical couplers has revealed different coupling ratios. This demonstrates the dependence of the performance of the GaAs-based directional couplers on the fabrication tolerances.

MMI couplers have been demonstrated to be an efficient alternative to directional couplers. Unlike to directional couplers, the imbalance and excess loss of a 1×2 MMI coupler and a 2×2 MMI 3dB coupler were found to be almost independent of the transverse structures. The imbalance and excess loss of a 1×2 MMI coupler was found to correspond to 0.2 dB and to 1.7 dB, respectively. The maximum imbalance of an optimum 2×2 MMI 3dB coupler was determined to less than 0.6 dB. The excess loss was estimated to 1.7 dB. Both types of MMI couplers offer an efficient solution for integration with phase modulators to realize an MZI modulator.

8.3   Electro-optic performance: Application

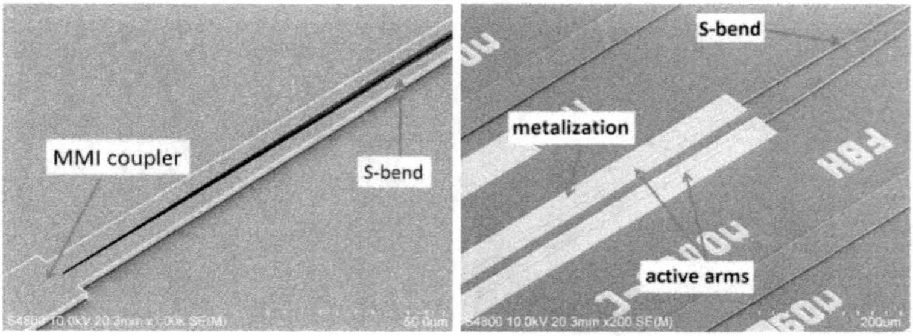

Figure 8.16: SEM photos of parts of an MZI from process III.

In this section, results of MZI modulators as an application of monolithic integration of electro-optic phase modulators and MMI couplers are presented. We investigate the insertion loss measurements and the modulation performance of two different MZI devices. The first MZI modulator from process run II uses 1×2 MMI couplers at both, the input and output sides (see figure 6.1 (left)). The active arm length (length of the sections with electrodes for phase modulation) is 2 mm. The second MZI modulator from process run III has 1×2 MMI coupler at the input and features a 2×2 MMI coupler at the output side (see figure 6.1 (right)). The active arms length is 3.4 mm.

8.3.1   Measurement setup

After fabrication (see chapter 7) the MZI devices were cleaved and AR-coated. The coating process is necessary to reduce the Fabry-Perot resonances which may arise due to self-imaging during the OFF-state of MZIs with two 1×2 MMI couplers [26]. The measurement setup for the characterization of the MZI modulators (figure 8.17) is similar to the setup for the characterization of couplers in figure 8.12. Please note that powermeter 2 is only required in the case of a 2×2 MMI coupler at the output of the MZI modulator. The modulation signal to modify the phase at one of the arms of the MZI modulator is applied using an RF probe needle that can be directly put on the electrical pads on the chip (figure 8.17).

8.3.2   Mach-Zehnder intensity modulator with 1x2 couplers

The schematic of the MZI under test is shown in figure 8.18. In order to determine the excess loss, the transmission of the MZI (without modulation) was compared to that of a reference single mode ridge waveguide. The estimated excess loss is less than 2.5 dB. The insertion loss is about 3.3 dB and includes both, the excess loss and the coupling losses which were found to be about 0.8 dB (see section 8.2.1). This value of the insertion loss is well beyond the excess less of the state-of-the-art GaAs/AlGaAs double heterostructure MZI modulator in [25] which is larger than 8 dB.

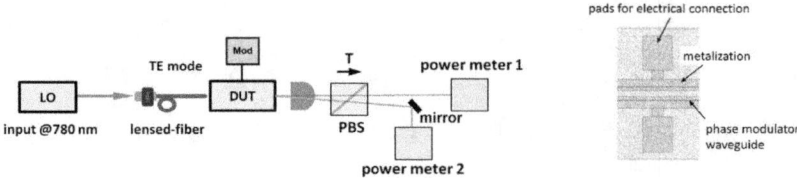

Figure 8.17: (left) Setup for the characterization of MZI modulators. DUT: device under test, Mod: modulating electric signal, PBS: polarizing beam splitter, T: transmission beam of the PBS. (right) part of the CAD layout of an MZI modulator chip showing the electric pads for chip soldering or connection using the RF probe needle.

For the determination of the extinction ratio, a slowly varying sawtooth signal (frequency 1 kHz) is applied to modulate the phase of the optical field at one arm of the MZI. The phase difference is imprinted at the output 1×2 MMI coupler (or the 2 × 1 combiner).

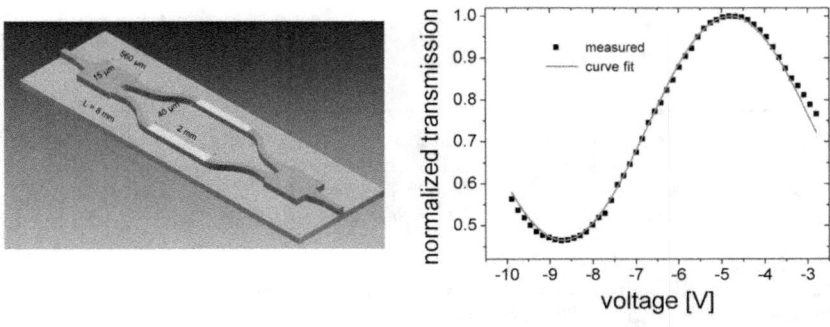

Figure 8.18: (left) Layout of MZI with 1×2 MMI couplers in single-arm operation regime.(right) electro-optic performance of an MZI modulator (process run II, wafer D2231-3, chip 010514), [20] © 2014 IEEE.

The measured transmission of the MZI normalized to the maximum power is shown on the left side of figure 8.18 as a function of the modulating voltage. The transmission is fitted using equation 6.1 and a good agreement is found. For the device the measurement yields a maximum and minimum power of 1.99 mW and 0.93 mW, respectively, which corresponds to the extinction ratio of 3.3 dB which also agrees with the value from the fit. This value is marginally larger than the value of 3.0 dB which was reported in [25].

The half-wave voltage that is calculated from the intensity profile in figure 8.18 is $V_\pi = 3.9\,\text{V}$ which corresponds to a modulation efficiency of $23\,°/\text{V} \cdot \text{mm}$ of the phase modulator at the arm of the MZI. This is so far the largest modulation efficiency reported for a GaAs/AlGaAs electro-optic phase modulator operating at 780 nm.

8.3.3 Mach-Zehnder intensity modulator with 2x2 couplers

The MZI modulators from process run III use 2×2 MMI couplers at the output. This should improve the extinction ratio of the MZI in comparison to MZI modulators with only 1×2 MMI couplers where internal resonances during the OFF-state of the MZI which may not be fully eliminated [26]. The MZI modulators have an active arm

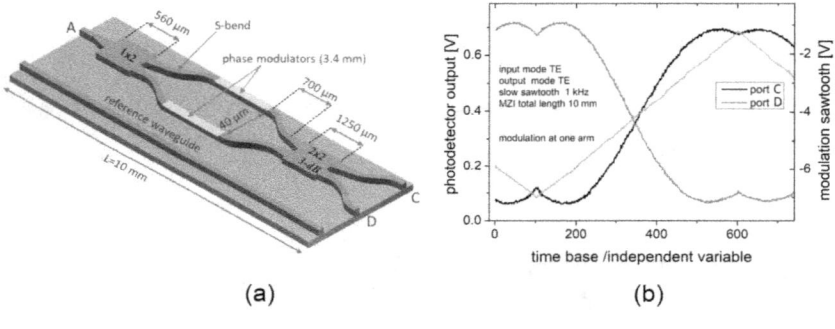

(a)   (b)

Figure 8.19: (a) Layout of an MZI modulator with 1×2 and 2×2 MMI couplers, S-bends, and phase modulators as active arms. (b) Electro-optic performance of the MZI modulator (process run III, wafer D2904-3, chip 080310) in single-arm operation regime with 2×2 MMI coupler at the output. Modulating signal 1 kH sawtooth.

length of 3.4 mm. The layout of the MZI modulator is shown in figure 8.19 (a). the two beams at the output of the 2×2 MMI coupler are separated using a dielectric mirror (see figure 8.17). The powermeters 1 and 2 detect the transmission at both output ports simultaneously.

The excess loss of less than 3 dB of the MZIs has been determined by comparing the output power (sum of the powers at both ports C and D) of the MZI modulator to the output power of reference ridge waveguide that has the same length as the MZI. To the best of our knowledge, the reported values of the excess loss for the MZI modulators in this work are well beyond the state of the art for GaAs-based MZI modulators. In [27], the excess loss of GaAs/AlGaAs double heterostructures modulators was found to be 11.9 dB. Very large losses ($\gg$8 dB) were also found in [25]. Both modulators in [27] and in [25] use Y-couplers which reflects the advantage for using MMI couplers in this work.

A slowly varying sawtooth signal (frequency 1 kHz) is used to modulate the optical field at one arm of the MZI. The result of such a measurement is shown on the left-hand side of figure 8.19.

In order to estimate the extinction ratio, the measurement is fitted using equation 6.1. The normalized transmission (P/P_{max}) at both output ports as a function of the modulating voltage is shown in figure 8.20 for both output ports C and D with the corresponding fit curves. The values of the extinction ratios resulting from the fit correspond to 10.2 dB and 10.8 dB for the output ports C and D, respectively. The corresponding values of the relative initial phase shift Φ_0 of the fit curves in equation 6.1 are -2.43 rad for port C and to -0.79 rad for port D. The difference between the initial phases is $\Delta\Phi = 1.64$ rad $\approx \pi/2$ rad. Please note that the output MMI coupler is a 3dB coupler based on the paired interference mechanism in multi-mode waveguides which explains why the maximum output power at port C occurs alternatively with the minimum output power at port D (see chapter 6).

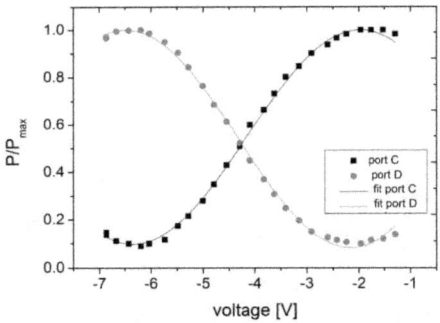

Figure 8.20: The normalized transmission at the two output ports of the MZI modulator in figure 8.19 and its fit using equation 6.1.

8.3.4 Conclusions

In comparison to GaAs-based MZI modulators in the literature, the achieved value of the extinction ratio of 10.8 dB for the MZI modulator in this work is beyond the value of the extinction ratio in [25] which amounts only to 3.0 dB (at 1.550 nm) but less than 23.5 dB that was demonstrated in [27] (at 878 nm). Please notice that the modulator in [27] suffers very large excess losses that were attributed to the losses in the Y-couplers which are undesirable for PICs. The GaAs-based MZI modulators in this work were realized by combining phase modulators and MMI couplers without further adjustment of the waveguides between the phase modulators and MMI couplers or of the semiconductor technology which is beyond the scope of this work. Possible factors that may contribute to the reduction of the extinction ratio in the current design of the MZI modulators are for example, the presence of unmodulated scattered light that is further fed into the output MMI couplers or non-optimal splitting ratios of the input and output MMI couplers. The use of mode transformers was suggested in [25] to filter the unmodulated scattered light and hence reduce its possible contributions to the reduction of the extinction ratio. When applied between the phase modulators and the MMI couplers, mode transformers allow to separately optimize the multi-layers of the phase modulators and the MMI couplers. In this way, the phase modulators may even include multiple quantum wells to deliver high modulation efficiencies. The quantum wells are then etched away in the mode convertor and the MMI couplers can be optimized to improve their extinction ratio which should further improve the performance of the MZI modulator. MZI modulators with mode convertors were successfully demonstrated in the III-V compound semiconductors technology. In [28] an InP-based MZI modulator that incorporates a mode convertor between the phase modulators (with quantum wells) and the MMI couplers features low excess losses (about 3 dB) and the extinction ratio is 24 dB. The adjustment of the technology into the GaAs material system seems to be feasible, so that efficient complex GaAs/AlGaAs double heterostructure PICs can be achieved.

Chapter 9

Heterodyne analysis of GaAs-based phase modulators

Phase modulation in electro-optic phase modulators is accompanied by residual amplitude modulation (RAM) [21], [57]. It is typical for the RAM to cause systematic errors in applications of phase modulators. For example, RAM produces a drifting and systematic frequency offset. This causes a degradation of the frequency stabilization and is therefore a limiting factor, for example, for laser interferometers [57], where the accuracy of the measurements is directly affected by the stability of the frequency locking. In a conventional crystal-based EO phase modulator, the RAM mainly occurs due to birefringence of the crystal [57]. In GaAs-based modulators, the RAM may occur due to spatial inhomogeneities of the electric field of the modulating signal, due to modulated free carriers absorption, by reflections at the modulators facets, by inefficient coupling (excitation of higher order modes), and polarization impurity.

In optical terms, GaAs chip-based phase modulators are designed to operate as a single transverse mode waveguide. Unlike active structures (i.e. laser diodes), the waveguide material in phase modulators is transparent, so that light scattered out of the mode through the chip upon propagation or upon coupling into the modulator chip continues to travel through the transparent material and interferes at the output with the fundamental mode [21]. That is why phase modulation efficiency, non-linearity (phase distortion), and RAM are expected to depend on the design of the waveguide and the mode matching of the injected beam to the wave guide. In electrical terms, GaAs chip-based modulators behave as reversed biased p-n diodes, and hence the modulation efficiency, signal distortion (non-linearities), and RAM are expected to depend on the operating parameters, which are offset bias voltage, TE/TM mode excitation, modulation voltage amplitude, and modulation frequency. Although the first double heterostructure (DH) GaAs-based electro-opitc phase modulators were presented many years ago [23], works since then (to the best of our knowledge) included neither measurements on RAM nor methods to quantify RAM in GaAs-based phase modulators. However, the analysis of non-linearities and RAM dependence on the operation parameters is very essential for the application of GaAs-based phase modulators.

9.1 Novel method for electro-optic characterization of phase modulators

9.1.1 Method description

In [21], we proposed a method that allows to accurately determine phase shifts in GaAs/AlGaAs double heterostructure phase modulators that are less than a degree so that, for example, the modulation efficiency can be determined as a function of the bias voltage or of the modulation voltage. Further, this method allows for an analysis of non-linearities of the modulator device as will be explained in the following sections. Another advantage of this method is that measurement data analysis is carried out in real-time which makes it possible to optimize coupling of the light signal into the modulator waveguide with respect to modulation efficiency and minimum RAM. It should be noted here that this methods can be applied to characterize the electro-optic performance of any kind of phase modulators independent of its physical implementation, i.e. for GaAs-based and for crystal-based phase modulators.

The method is based on the heterodyne interferometer principle as shown in figure 9.1. A single frequency local oscillator (LO) provides the optical field that is injected into the interferometer. The first beam (the reference beam) is frequency shifted (typically by several 10 MHz) by means of an acusto-optical modulator (AOM). The second beam is coupled into the phase modulator waveguide (device under test, DUT) where phase modulation and RAM are imprinted. The output of the DUT then interferes with the reference beam on a fast photoreceiver that generates an RF beat note signal. The I&Q quadrature components of the beat note signal are analyzed to extract the information on the modulation response of the DUT.

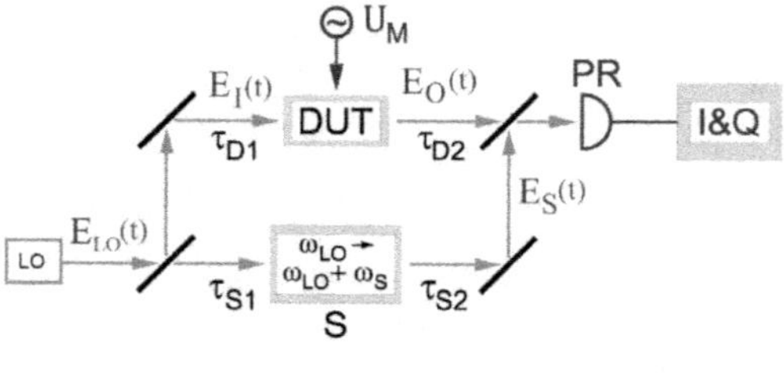

Figure 9.1: schematic description of measurement method. DUT: device under test; S: frequency shifter, U_M : modulation signal applied to the DUT, PR: photoreceiver; I&Q: signal sampling and I&Q demodulation. τ_X denote the group delay for propagation of the optical field from the input beam splitter to the frequency shifter (τ_{S1}) and to the DUT (τ_{D1}), from the frequency shifter to the output beam combiner (τ_{S2}), and from the DUT to the output beam combiner (τ_{D2}).

9.1.2 In-depth analysis of the modulation signal

The LO coherent optical field $E_{LO}(t) \cdot e^{i\varphi_{LO}(t)} + c.c.$ with real-valued amplitude $E_{LO}(t)$ and phase $\varphi_{LO}(t)$ is injected into a Mach-Zehnder-interferometer. To account for amplitude and phase noise of the LO during the measurement time T we write:

$$E_{LO}(t) = \langle E_{LO} \rangle_T (t) \cdot [1 + \delta_{LO}(t)] \tag{9.1}$$

with $\langle \delta_{LO}(t) \rangle_T = 0$ and $\varphi_{LO}(t) = \omega_{LO} \cdot t + \delta\varphi_{LO}(t)$ with $\langle \delta\varphi_{LO}(t) \rangle_T = 0$, i.e. $\delta_{LO}(t)$ and $\delta\varphi_{LO}(t)$ being the relative amplitude noise and phase noise of the LO, respectively. In the special case of small amplitude noise, $|\delta_{LO}(t)| \ll 1$, the relative power noise of the DUT equals twice the relative amplitude noise:

$$\delta P_{LO}(t)/\langle P_{LO}(t) \rangle_T \approx 2 \cdot \delta_{LO}(t) \tag{9.2}$$

In the reference arm of the interferometer, the frequency of the optical field is shifted by $\omega_S/(2\pi)$ (a frequency in the RF domain). The contributing electric field of this arm at the input of the photoreceiver is described by:

$$E_S(t) \propto E_{in}(t - \tau_{S1} - \tau_{S2}) \cdot e^{i\omega_S(t)} + c.c.$$

The other arm contains the DUT (the phase modulator). We restrict the discussion to the quasi-static limit. A description that includes the dynamic response of the modulator (and the driving network) is beyond the scope of this work. Also, it is not necessary for the investigation on the LEO, QEO effects addressed by this work. In the quasi-static limit, the response of the DUT to a modulation voltage $U_M(t)$ can be described by:

$$E_0(t) = E_I(t) \cdot [1 + \delta_M(U_M)] \cdot \exp\left(i\phi_M(U_M)\right)$$

where $E_I + c.c.$ is the optical field injected into the DUT, $E_O + c.c.$ the optical field retrieved from the DUT, δ_M the relative amplitude modulation (corresponding to the RAM), and ϕ_M the phase modulation imprinted onto the optical field by the DUT. At the output of the Mach-Zehnder interferometer, the fields of both arms are overlapped and interfere on a fast photoreceiver. The corresponding RF (voltage) signal at the photoreceiver output is proportional to $E_O(t) \cdot E_S^*(t) + c.c.$ and satisfies:

$$U_{PR}(t) \propto [1 + \delta U_{PR}(t)] \cdot e^{i\delta\phi_{PR}(t)} e^{i\omega_S t} + c.c. \tag{9.3}$$

where:

$$\begin{aligned} \delta U_{PR}(t) = &\, \delta_M \left(U_M(t - \tau_{D2})\right) + \delta_{LO}\left(t - \tau_{D1} - \tau_{D2}\right) \\ &+ \delta_{LO}\left(t - \tau_{D1} - \tau_{D2} + \Delta\tau\right) \\ &+ \mathcal{O}\left(\delta_M \cdot \delta_{LO}, \delta_{LO}^2\right) \end{aligned} \tag{9.4}$$

and:

$$\begin{aligned} \delta\phi_{PR}(t) = &\, \phi_M \left(U_M(t - \tau_{D2})\right) \\ &+ \delta\phi_{LO}\left(t - \tau_{D1} - \tau_{D2}\right) \\ &- \delta\phi_{LO}\left(t - \tau_{D1} - \tau_{D2} + \Delta\tau\right) \end{aligned} \tag{9.5}$$

Here τ_X with $X \subseteq \{D1, D2, S1, S2\}$ are the corresponding group delays for propagation of the optical signal through the interferometer (see figure 9.1), and $\Delta\tau = \tau_{D1} + \tau_{D2} - \tau_{S1} - \tau_{S2}$ denotes the group delay difference between the two arms of the interferometer. An electrical spectrum analyzer (ESA) carries out I&Q demodulation at IF frequency $\omega_S/2\pi$ of the signal provided by the photoreceiver. This makes it possible to reconstruct the modulation information, i.e. the phase modulation and noise $\delta\phi_{PR}(t)$, as well as relative amplitude modulation and noise, $\delta U_{PR}(t)$, of the RF beat note signal as a function of time.

The relative amplitude noise can be well approximated by $\delta_{LO}(t - \Delta\tau) \approx \delta_{LO}(t)$ for typical time scales of $\Delta\tau$ <0.17 ns (corresponding to arm length difference <5 cm), so that according to equations 9.2 and 9.4:

$$\delta U_{PR}(t) \approx \delta_M\left(U_M(t - \tau_{D2})\right) + \frac{\delta P_{LO}(t - \tau_{D1} - \tau_{D2})}{\langle P_{LO}(t - \tau_{D1} - \tau_{D2})\rangle_T} \tag{9.6}$$

Equation 9.6 shows that the relative amplitude modulation caused by the DUT is given by the relative amplitude modulation of the photoreceiver RF signal. Further, the relative *power* noise of the LO within the resolution bandwidth of the measurement limits the sensitivity of the measurement method to *amplitude* modulation imprinted by the DUT. Please note that for sufficiently small relative amplitude modulation, $|\delta_M| \ll 1$, the relative power modulation caused by the DUT equals twice the relative amplitude modulation.

Next, we consider the special case of a sinusoidal modulation. The modulation frequency is assumed to be small enough to regard the response of the DUT as quasi-static:

$$U_M(t) = \hat{U}_M + \Delta U_M \cdot \sin\left(\Omega_M t\right)$$

The phase modulation response of the DUT can then be written as (Taylor's expansion about $\hat{U}_M$):

$$\begin{aligned}\phi_M(t) =& \phi_M(\hat{U}_M) + \frac{1}{2}\partial^2_{U_M}\delta\phi_M(\hat{U}_M) \\ &+ \partial_{U_M}\delta\phi_M(\hat{U}_M)\cdot\Delta U_M \cdot\sin\left(\Omega_M t\right) \\ &- \frac{1}{2}\partial^2_{U_M}\delta\phi_M(\hat{U}_M)\cdot U_M{}^2\cdot\cos\left(2\Omega_M t\right) + \mathcal{O}\left(\Delta U_M{}^3\right)\end{aligned} \tag{9.7}$$

where the second and fourth terms in equation 9.7 are derived by using $(2\cos^2 x = \cos 2x + 1)$. It can be directly seen from equation 9.7 that fast Fourier transformation (FFT) of the time-domain phase modulation signal - or more precisely the Fourier component at the modulation frequency - delivers the linear phase modulation efficiency of the DUT at the working point $\hat{U}_M$:

$$\partial_{U_M}\delta\phi_M(\hat{U}_M) \tag{9.8}$$

The determination of the linear phase modulation efficiency at various working points $\hat{U}_M$ allows for the reconstruction of $\phi_M(U_M)$. Further, determining the FFT components at multiples of the modulation frequency delivers the non-linear response of the device at the working point $\hat{U}_M$.

The relative amplitude modulation can be determined in a analogous way. Linear relative amplitude modulation can be determined by FFT of the time-domain relative amplitude signal in equation 9.4 and subsequent identification of the level

$\partial_{U_M} \delta_M(\hat{U}_M) \cdot \Delta U_M$ as the spectral component at the modulation angular frequency Ω_M. Higher-order residual amplitude modulation is determined accordingly. Determination of higher order RAM is relevant for applications, where signal demodulation is carried out at harmonics of the modulation frequency in order to suppress the influence of RAM (present at the modulation frequency).

We emphasize that the I&Q demodulation is essential to this method. If the photoreceiver signal is analyzed with a scalar electrical spectrum analyzer (ESA), it would not in general allow for unambiguous separation of phase modulation from amplitude modulation. This is because the side bands for phase and amplitude modulation are coherent to each other, but amplitudes *and* relative phase of the side bands of phase and amplitude modulation cannot be reconstructed simultaneously from the RF power spectrum. Relative phases may be known *a priori* only in specific cases, e.g. in the quasi-static limit.

9.1.3 Sensitivity of novel method

From equation 9.5 we find that the phase modulation of the RF signal of the photoreceiver corresponds to the phase modulation caused by the DUT. Its sensitivity (within the resolution bandwidth of the measurement δf_{RBW}) is limited by the phase noise of the LO. However, the suppression of the LO phase noise at an arm length difference ΔL follows from the transfer function of the heterodyne interferometer that can be described by an effective first-order high pass filter for noise frequencies significantly smaller than $f_{HP} = 1/(2\pi\Delta\tau)$, where $\Delta\tau = \Delta L/c$, with c being the speed of light in vacuum. The expected phase noise for the measurement for modulation frequencies well below f_{HP}, i.e. $f_M \ll f_{HP}$ is then given by:

$$\delta\phi_{RMS} = \sqrt{S_f(f_M)/f_M^2 \cdot \delta f_{RBW}} \cdot (f_M/f_{HP}) \qquad (9.9)$$

Here, $S_f(f_M)$ denotes the frequency noise power spectral density of the laser. For example, if we assume that a sinusoidal modulation signal at $f_M = 500\,\text{kHz}$ is applied, the corresponding frequency noise power spectral density for a DFB laser (typically used for experimental implementation of the new method) $S_f(f_M) = 4 \times 10^5\,\text{Hz}^2/\text{Hz}$ [58]. As a result, the LO phase noise should be suppressed by 66 dB for the arm length difference of 5 cm, and by and by 46 dB for an arm length difference of 0.5 m. Hence, very small phase modulation amplitudes can be detected even without the need for narrow line-width lasers simply by matching the interferometer arm length sufficiently well.

9.2 Implementation of the novel method

The new method is experimentally implemented and applied to characterize a phase modulator chip from wafer C3059-3 from the process IV (operation wavelength is 1064 nm) and a phase modulator chip from wafer D2043-3 from process I (operation wavelength is 780 nm). Parts of the following results were published in [21].

9.2.1 Measurement setup

The setup is shown in figure 9.2. A DFB laser diode emitting at 780 nm or at 1064 nm is used as the local oscillator. An acousto-optic modulator (AOM, IntraAction

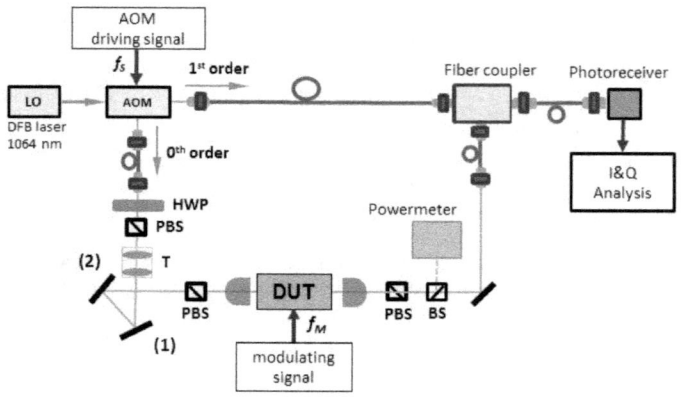

Figure 9.2: Experimental setup for in-depth characterization of GaAs-based phase modulators. (AOM: acousto-optic modulator, HWP: half wave plate, T: 2-1 telescope ($f_2 = 40$ mm,
$f_1 = 20$ mm), BS: 50/50 non-polarizing beam splitter, PBS: polarizing beam splitter).
Adapted/Reprinted with permission from Ref [21], [OSA].

ATM-200C1) implements a 200 MHz frequency shift as well as the input beam splitter
of the heterodyne interferometer. The driving signal for the AOM is provided by a
signal generator (HP 8657-B). It is then amplified by means of an RF amplifier (Mini-
Circuits ZHL-2-12). The 0th order output of the AOM is fed into the phase modulator
(DUT). The polarization optics (two polarizing beam splitters (PBS) and a half wave
plate, see figure 9.2) are used to set the required polarization at the input of the
DUT. A 2:1 telescope increases the mode overlap between the fundamental mode of
the waveguide and the incoming optical field by about 25%. Further, aspheric round
lenses ($f = 2.0$ mm) are used for the coupling into the phase modulator. Another
($f = 2.0$ mm) lens is used at the output of the phase modulator to collimate the
output beam. The beam is sent through a PBS to provide separate analysis for TM-
mode and TE-mode performance. A fraction of the beam is then picked of using a non
polarizing beam splitter (BS) in order to monitor the coupling efficiency by means of a
powermeter. A fiber coupler is used to combine the beam transmitted through the BS
with the 1st order output of the AOM (frequency shifted by $f_S = 200$ MHz). In order to
generate the RF beat note signal, the fiber coupler is connected to a fast photoreceiver
(New Focus 1544-A). Finally, the output of the photoreceiver is coupled into the
electrical signal analyzer (Rohde & Schwarz FSW26). The sinusoidal modulation
signal for the phase modulator is generated by means of a function generator (Agilent
33250A). Both, the internal clock of the modulation signal generator, and the internal
clock of the signal generator operating the AOM, are synchronized to the internal
clock of the signal analyzer. To run the measurement we employ the operation mode
analog demodulator of the FSW. In this operation mode the instantaneous phase and
amplitude modulation signals are derived and displayed by the signal analyzer in real

time. The signal analyzer then carries out an FFT of the time domain data to reveal the phase and amplitude modulation spectra, again in real time. The spectra are then saved an analyzed.

9.2.2 Measurement accuracy

Systematic errors can only arise in the measurement and data analysis through the dynamic response of the photoreceiver and systematic errors of the I&Q demodulator that is implemented by the RF signal analyzer.

Errors introduced by the photodetector can be minimized by using devices that feature a signal bandwidth significantly larger than the modulation frequency. For our measurements a New Focus 1544-A photoreceiver featuring a bandwidth of 12 GHz is used, and we measure at a beat note frequency of 200 MHz, with 0.5 MHz modulation sidebands. No estimate is available on how accurately the photoreceiver tracks the phase modulation of the beat note signal.

The I&Q demodulator tool of the signal analyzer Rohde & Schwarz FSW-26, Option B-126, has an I&Q demodulation bandwidth of 160 MHz. For the PM demodulation at modulation frequencies (PM rate) ≤ 1 MHz, the phase deviation uncertainty as per specification sheet is $\pm(0.002 \text{ rad} + 0.002 \times measured\ value)$. We have measured phase shifts of up to 100 deg (1.74 rad), so that the inaccuracy we expect to be introduced by the signal analyzer is on the order of 0.002 rad $\cdots$ 0.005 rad (0.1 deg $\cdots$ 0.3 deg). The amplitude demodulation uncertainty at an AM rate ≤ 1 MHz as per specification sheet is $\pm(0.2\% + 0.001 \times measured\ value)$.

Further, the spurious harmonics of the signal generator were measured with a spectrum analyzer and found to be 60 dB below the carrier. Therefore, their contribution to the phase shift signal (mainly at the quadratic component in the Fourier spectrum) can be safely ignored.

9.2.3 Preparation of modulator chips for characterization

The waveguide of the investigated chips was tilted with respect to the cleaved facets by 3°. This has been suggested by [59] in order to reduce the effective reflectivity by a factor of 10^3 to 10^4. Chips with 4 mm long modulators were cleaved and their facets were additionally AR-coated and then mounted on AlN-submounts. In order to electrically match the device to the modulation signal generator, a resistive load of 50 Ω was added in parallel to the phase modulator chip (see figure 9.3).

A sinusoidal modulation signal with a frequency of 500 kHz is used to drive the phase modulator. A sufficient reverse-bias voltage offset ($V_{DC} = -1.5$ V) is applied to operate the phase modulator.

The following two chips were investigated:

λ	process run	wafer	structure	chip	chip length
780 nm	I	D2043-3	table 4.2	080511	4 mm
1064 nm	IV	D3059-3	table 4.5	010118	4 mm

Table 9.1: List of characterized phase modulator chips using the spectral analysis.

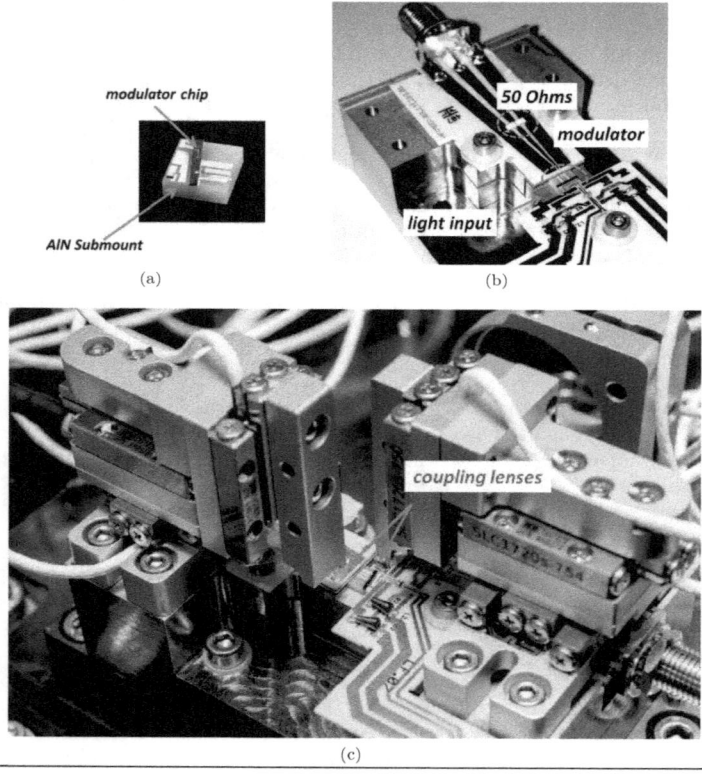

Figure 9.3: (a) Submount assimply: modulator chip on AlN submount, (b) fixture for sub-mount assembly, (c) part of measurement setup showing the submount assembly, the fixture for submount assembly and the motorized lens holders with lenses and electrical interfaces.

9.3 Measurement of the phase modulation efficiency

The spectrum of the phase modulation (PM) signals of a TE-mode for the two chips in table 9.1 are shown in figure 9.4.

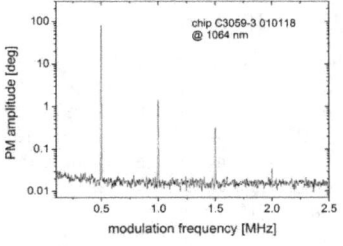 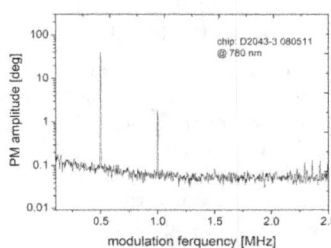

Figure 9.4: Spectrum of the phase modulation for TE-mode excitation of (left) phase modulator chip at 1064 nm, (right) phase modulator chip at 780 nm. The modulating signal amplitude corresponds to 1.4 V, offset voltage is $V_{DC} = -1.5$ V, and $\delta f_{RBW} = 3.8$ kHz.

Let us for example consider the spectrum of the phase modulation signal at 1064 nm in figure 9.4(left). The noise floor of about 0.02 degrees is due to the non-zero optical arm length difference between the arms of the interferometer and from the phase noise of the DFB laser. By taking into account the arm length difference of the interferometer in

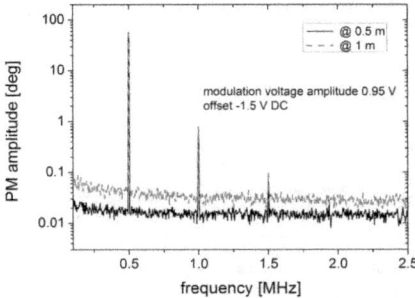

Figure 9.5: Spectrum of the phase modulation for TE-mode excitation at two different values of the arm length difference of the interferometer (at 50 cm and 100 cm). The amplitude of the modulating signal corresponds to 0.95 V, offset voltage is -1.5 V DC, and $\delta f_{RBW} = 3.8$ kHz.

the experiment setup which is about 50 cm, and the resolution bandwidth of $\delta f_{RBW} = 3.8$ kHz, which corresponds to $f_{HP} = 95.49$ MHz, using equation 9.9 we find that $\delta \phi_{RMS} = 0.023$ deg is consistent with our experimental findings, see figure 9.4.

The effect of the arm length difference on the noise floor can be clearly seen in figure 9.5. Initially, measurements were taken with an arm length difference of about 100 cm, then reduced it to about 50 cm which reduced the noise floor by a factor of 2 as expected. If the arm length difference were reduced to 5 cm, the noise floor would be reduced to 2×10^{-3} deg. However, at an arm length difference of 50 cm the noise floor is already small enough to provide a sensitivity significantly better than 0.1 deg which is sufficient for our application.

9.3.1 Phase modulator chip C3059-3 010118 at 1064 nm

In figure 9.4, the Fourier components at the modulation frequency f_M (linear component) describe the total phase shift due to linear effects. The Fourier component at the 2nd harmonic of the modulation signal can be solely attributed to the quadratic effects in the phase modulator chip which are the QEO effect and (possibly) quadratic contributions from carrier density-related effects. However, according to [23], carrier density-related effects contribute linearly to phase modulation in GaAs-based electro-optic phase modulators. Thus, the quadratic phase modulation can be attributed solely to the QEO effect and quadratic effects. The linear and quadratic components are attributed to the phase shift due to the linear effects and to the quadratic effects, respectively. The linear effects (not to confuse with LEO effect) include both, the LEO effect and linear contributions from the carrier density-related effects [23].

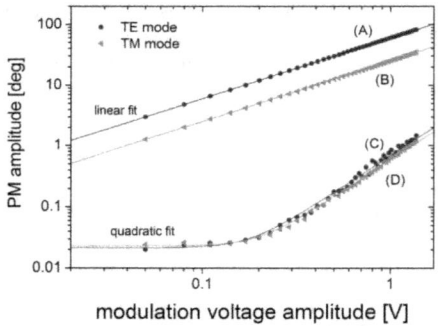

Figure 9.6: Fourier components of the phase modulation at the fundamental and at the 2nd harmonic of the modulation frequency as a function of the modulation voltage amplitude of the phase modulator chip C3059-3 010118 at 1064 nm. (A), (C): for TE-mode operation at fundamental and 2nd harmonic frequency, respectively. (B), (D): TM-mode operation at fundamental and 2nd harmonic frequency, respectively. The modulator offset is set to $V_{DC} = -1.5\,\text{V}$. Adapted/Reprinted with permission from Ref [21], [OSA].

The Fourier components of the phase modulation at the modulation frequency and its 2nd harmonic as a function of the amplitude of the modulating signal are shown for both, the TE and TM modes, in figures 9.6. The contribution of the quadratic effects to phase modulation is about two orders of magnitude less than that of the linear effects and the total phase shift can be well approximated by only the linear component of the Fourier spectrum of the PM signal. In order to determine the linear phase modulation efficiency, the amplitudes of the phase modulation at the modulation frequency f_M as a function of the amplitude of the driving signal (curves A and B in figure 9.6) are fitted using a linear function (enforcing $\phi_M(U_M = 0) = 0$). The resulting slope of the linear fit corresponds to $25.25\,°/V$ (fit standard error $0.01\,°/V$) for the TM-mode and $60.33\,°/V$ (fit standard error $0.03\,°/V$) for the TE-mode, which is the phase modulation efficiency of a $4\,mm$ long modulator. Therefore, the (linear) modulation efficiency (per mm) for TM and TE-modes correspond to $6.31\,°/(V \cdot mm)$ and $15.08\,°/(V \cdot mm)$, respectively.

To determine the quadratic phase modulation efficiency, the experimental data for the Fourier component at the 2nd harmonic of the modulation frequency (curves C and D in figure 9.6) are fitted using the function $y = \sqrt{A^2 + C^2 \cdot x^4}$ with A being the noise floor and C the corresponding (quadratic) phase modulation efficiency. The resulting fit values are ($A = 0.02°$, $C = 0.59\,°/V^2$) for the TM-mode and ($A = 0.02°$, $C = 0.69\,°/V^2$) for the TE-mode.

9.3.2 Phase modulator chip D2043-3 080511 at 780 nm

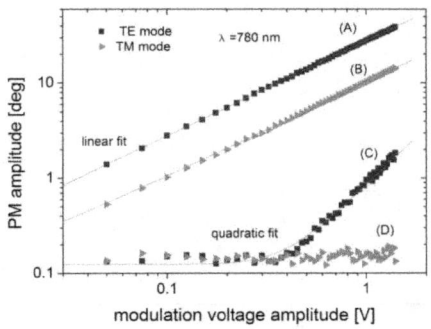

Figure 9.7: Fourier component of PM signal at the fundamental modulation frequency (A and B) and at its second harmonic (C and D) versus modulation voltage amplitude of TE and TM-modes. The phase modulator is biased at an offset $V_{DC} = -1.5\,V$. Operation at the wavelength $780\,nm$.

The Fourier components of the phase modulation at the modulation frequency and its 2nd harmonic as a function of the amplitude of the modulating signal are shown for both, the TE and TM modes, in figure 9.7.

The determination of the phase modulation efficiency follows in a similar way to the steps taken for the modulator chip at $1064\,nm$. The amplitudes of the phase modulation at the modulation frequency f_M as a function of the amplitude of the driving signal (curves A and B in figure 9.7) are fitted using a linear function $y = B \cdot x$ (enforcing $\phi_M(U_M = 0) = 0$). The resulting slope corresponds to $27.84\,°/V$ (fit standard error $0.03\,°/V$) for the TE-mode and $10.08\,°/V$ (fit standard error $0.02\,°/V$) for the TM-mode. Since the total length of the modulator is $4\,\text{mm}$, the (linear) modulation efficiencies for TE and TM-modes correspond to $6.96\,°/(V \cdot \text{mm})$ and $2.7\,°/(V \cdot \text{mm})$, respectively.

The analysis of the Fourier component at the 2nd harmonic of the modulation frequency follows in similar lines. The measured values in figure 9.7 (curve C) is fitted using the function $y = \sqrt{A^2 + C^2 \cdot x^4}$ with A is being the noise floor and C the corresponding (quadratic) phase modulation efficiency. The resulting fit values are ($A = 0.12\,°$,$C = 0.85\,°/V^2$) for the TE-mode. The PM Fourier components at the 2nd harmonic of the modulation frequency for the TM mode excitation lay beneath the the noise floor. Therefore, the corresponding quadratic phase shift could not be determined.

9.4   Residual amplitude modulation

For this measurement, we consider the chip C3059-3 010118 at $1064\,\text{nm}$. The relative amplitude of the RAM at the modulation frequency and its harmonics is directly read of the relative amplitude modulation spectrum, figure 9.8. According to [60], RAM

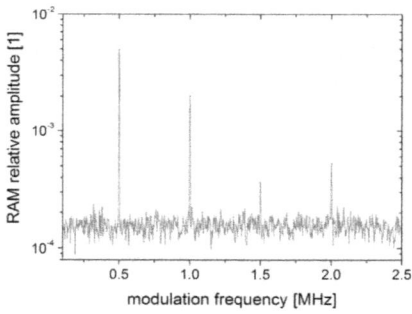

Figure 9.8: Spectrum of the RAM for TE-mode excitation of the phase modulator chip at $1064\,\text{nm}$. The modulating signal amplitude corresponds to $1.4\,\text{V}$, offset voltage is $V_{DC} = -1.5\,\text{V}$, and $\delta f_{RBW} = 3.8\,\text{kHz}$.

is proportional to the phase modulation efficiency. Hence, since the linear effects are dominant in phase modulation the same is expected for residual amplitude modulation, so that only the RAM signal at the modulation frequency has to be analyzed. Figure 9.9 shows the Fourier component at the fundamental frequency of the RAM as a function of the amplitude of the modulation voltage. The amplitude of RAM increases with increasing phase modulation, but it remains smaller than 5×10^{-3} for modulation amplitudes smaller than $1.4\,\text{V}$.

For the measurement of the RAM amplitudes in figure 9.9, the coupling efficiency of the incoming light beam (both TE and TM) into the modulator chip was optimized for minimum RAM at a modulation voltage amplitude of $0.1\,\text{V}$, then the RAM level as a function of the modulation voltage amplitude was recorded. The resulting data for

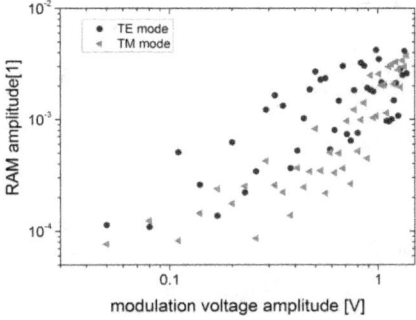

Figure 9.9: Fourier component of the residual amplitude modulation at the fundamental modulation frequency as a function of the modulation voltage amplitude for both, TE and TM-modes. Offset $V_{DC} = -1.5$ V. Adapted/Reprinted with permission from Ref [21], [OSA].

both TE and TM modes as shown by figure 9.9 are quite scattered with a general trend of increasing RAM level with increasing modulation voltage. The scattering behavior may be attributed to the alignment (coupling efficiency) of the optical mode into the phase modulator waveguide. To investigate the effect of coupling misalignment on RAM, we move the lens away from the optimum position, first in the lateral direction with respect to the modulator waveguide (parallel to the guiding layers), and then in the vertical direction (parallel to the pn-junction).

For a lateral misalignment of 500 nm, the RAM relative amplitude exceeds 10^{-2} and the output power of the phase modulator (detected by the powermeter, see figure 9.2) decreases by about 15%. This value apply to an operation at a bias voltage of -1.5 V with a modulation amplitude of 1.4 V. The strong dependence of RAM on the coupling could be attributed to the excitation of higher order lateral modes which interfere at the output with the fundamental mode. For coupling misalignment in the vertical direction we observed that the RAM level is significantly more sensitive to the position of the coupling lens. A vertical misalignment of the coupling lens of less than 100 nm increases the relative amplitude to 10^{-2}. The corresponding output power decreases by about 30%. We assume, that in addition to the possible excitation of higher order modes, the free carriers absorption of the optical field in the doped cladding layers may be responsible for this decrement in the output power by vertical misalignment. It is suggested that the effect of free carrier's absorption on the RAM is determined by further investigation of phase modulators with different doping profiles.

9.5 Modulation bandwidth

For this measurement, we consider the chip C3059-3 010118 at 1064 nm. Figure 9.10 shows the Fourier components of the PM spectrum at the fundamental modulation frequencies and at the 2nd harmonic of the modulation frequency for various modulation frequencies. It can be seen that the amplitude of the PM signals remains independent

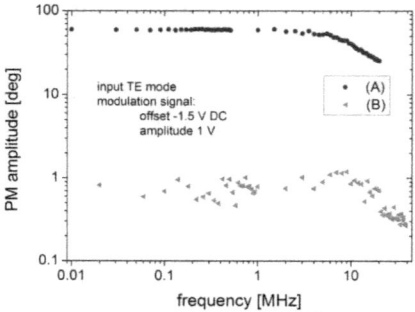

Figure 9.10: Amplitude of the phase modulation as a function of the modulation frequency. (A) and (B) are the Fourier components of the PM spectrum at the modulation frequencies and their corresponding 2nd harmonics, respectively. Input mode TE.

of the modulation frequency up to 10 MHz(within the resolution of the 50 Ω driving source). The dependence of the modulation amplitude on the modulation frequency can be described by a simple first order RC low pass filter, see figure 8.2. Hence, only the Fourier component at f_M can be considered.

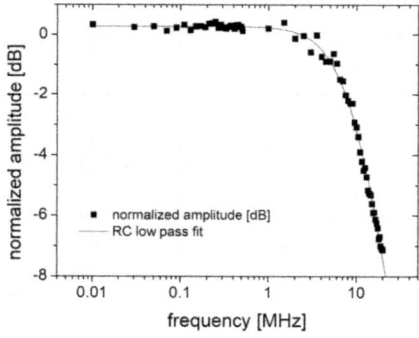

Figure 9.11: Normalized (to the PM amplitude at 1 V) amplitude of the Fourier components of the PM spectrum at the fundamental modulation frequencies and a fit to a simple RC low pass filter.

The transfer function of the low pass filter is given by $H(j\omega) = A/\left(1 + j\omega R_s C\right)$. The amplitude can hence be described by $f(\omega) = A/\sqrt{1 + \omega^2 \left(R_s C\right)^2}$. The amplitude of the Fourier components of the PM spectrum at the fundamental modulation frequencies f_M can then be fitted to the function $f(x) = A/\sqrt{1 + B^2 \cdot x^2}$ as shown by figure 9.11. The fit parameter B corresponds to $2\pi R_s C$, with R_s the series resistance, and C the modulator capacity. A is an amplitude scaling factor. Values of the series resistance at -1.5 V of 2 mm long phase modulators with ridge widths of 2 μm and 4 μm were found (see figure 8.3) to correspond to 125 Ω and to 65 Ω, respectively. Thus, for the 4 mm modulator chip with a ridge width of 3 μm, R_s is expected to be about 48 Ω. Hence, using the value of the fit parameter $B = 1.10 \times 10^{-7}$ sec, the modulator capacity is found to correspond to $C = 360$ pF. Please note that the junction capacity at $V_{DC} = -1.5$ V corresponds to 2.7 pF (the ridge width is 3 μm, the modulator length is 4 mm, and the depletion width is 0.5 μm). The capacitance of the modulator could be reduced by using PCB passivation between the upper cladding and the p-contact layer instead of the SiNx layer [19].

9.6 Determination of the electro optic coefficients

In this section, the heterodyne analysis of the phase modulation signal is used to determine the electro-optic coefficients of the investigated double heterostructures. The effects responsible for phase modulation in the GaAs/AlGaAs double heterostructures are the LEO effect, the QEO effect, and the carrier density-related effects. The layout of the tested modulators (see section 3.1.2 in chapter 3) is chosen so that the LEO effect contribute to phase modulation only in TE-mode operation. Hence, the contribution of the LEO effect to phase modulation can be extracted from the difference between the linear phase shifts of the TE and TM-modes [15]. For operation in TM mode, the linear phase shift is then solely attributed to linear contributions from the carrier density-related effects.

Results of the spectral analysis of the phase modulators are used to experimentally determine the electro-optic coefficients for GaAs at the wavelength of 1064 nm, and for $Al_{0.35}Ga_{0.65}As$ at the wavelength of 780 nm.

9.6.1 Electro-optic coefficients of GaAs at 1064 nm

Linear electro-optic coefficient

In figure 9.6, the linear effects are separated from the quadratic effects by means of spectral decomposition of the phase shift signal.

Using equations 3.15, 3.20, and 3.21, the LEO coefficient $\bar{r}_{41}$ is given by:

$$\bar{r}_{41} = -\left(\Delta\phi^{TE}(V) - \Delta\phi^{TM}(V)\right) \cdot \frac{\lambda}{\pi L \bar{n}^3} \qquad (9.10)$$
$$\cdot \frac{\int_{-\infty}^{+\infty} I(x)dx}{\int_{-\infty}^{+\infty} \left(E(V + V_{DC}, x) - E(V_{DC}, x)\right) I(x)dx}$$

where $\Delta\phi^{TE}(V)$, $\Delta\phi^{TM}(V)$ are the resulting phase modulation amplitudes of the TE mode and TM mode, respectively, , $\bar{n}$ here is the refractive index of the waveguide core, V is the amplitude of the modulating voltage signal, L is the modulator length, λ is the vacuum wavelength, $I(x)$ is the intensity distribution of the optical field which was found to be almost identical for the TE and TM modes, see figure 9.12). Further, $E(V + V_{DC}, x)$ and $E(V_{DC}, x)$ denote the electric fields for the respective modulation voltage signals. The values of $\Delta\phi^{TE}(V)$ and $\Delta\phi^{TM}(V)$ are taken from figure 9.6 (graphs A and B for TE and TM mode, respectively).

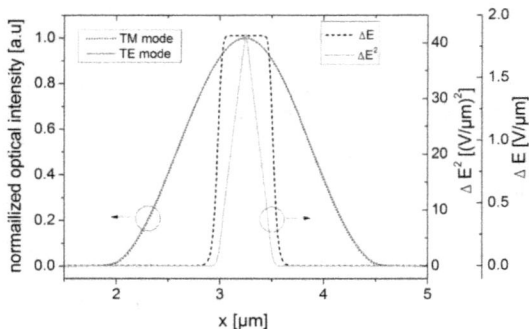

Figure 9.12: Calculated (vertical) field of the TE and TM modes of the modulator waveguide (at 1064 nm) and their overlap with the linear (ΔE) and quadratic (ΔE^2) electric field variations where $\Delta E = E(V + V_{DC}, x) - E(V_{DC}, x)$, and $\Delta E^2 = (E^2(V + V_{DC}, x) - E^2(V_{DC}, x))$. Adapted/Reprinted with permission from Ref [21], [OSA].

According to equation 9.10, and from the linear fit in figure 9.6, the resulting LEO coefficient $\bar{r}_{41}$ for the P-p-n-N GaAs/AlGaAs double heterostructure at $\lambda = 1.064\,\mu m$ is:

$$\bar{r}_{41} = -1.70 \times 10^{-10}\,\mathrm{cm/V}$$

In [61], the value of $\bar{r}_{41} = -1.80 \times 10^{-10}\,\mathrm{cm/V}$ was given for a phase modulator at $\lambda = 1.06\,\mu m$ with a p-i-n GaAs guiding layer. Besides, in [15] the values of $\bar{r}_{41}$ for GaAs-based phase modulators at $\lambda = 1.09\,\mu m$ and $\lambda = 1.15\,\mu m$ with P-i-N, and P-n-N doping profiles were found to correspond to $\bar{r}_{41} = -1.68 \times 10^{-10}\,\mathrm{cm/V}$ and $\bar{r}_{41} = -1.72 \times 10^{-10}\,\mathrm{cm/V}$, respectively. Hence, the value of $\bar{r}_{41} = -1.70 \times 10^{-10}\,\mathrm{cm/V}$ measured here is consistent with the literature (values reported in [61] and [15]).

Furthermore, in figure 9.13, the values of the LEO coefficient $\bar{r}_{41}$ are derived (using equation 9.10) from the individual data points in figure 9.6 at different modulation voltages. It can be clearly seen that the variation of the value of $\bar{r}_{41}$ is smaller than 0.5% within the modulation voltage amplitude range of 0.2 V to 1.4 V.

Quadratic electro optic coefficient

We follow the assumption made in [23], where quadratic phase modulation is assumed to be solely due to the QEO effect. Hence, the QEO coefficients for the TE and TM-modes can be calculated from the Fourier components of the phase modulation at the 2nd harmonic of the modulation frequency.

Following the lines of the discussion of the LEO coefficients, we use equation 3.15, equation 3.16, equation 3.20, and equation 3.21. The QEO coefficients are given by:

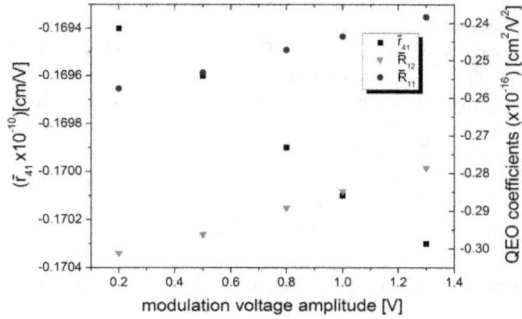

Figure 9.13: Values of the electro-optic coefficients $\bar{r}_{41}$, $\bar{R}_{11}$, and $\bar{R}_{12}$ for GaAs at 1064 nm determined using equation 9.10 from the individual data points in figure 9.6.

$$\bar{R}_{12,11} = -\phi^{TE,TM}(V) \cdot \frac{\lambda}{\pi L n^3}$$
$$\cdot \frac{\int_{-\infty}^{+\infty} I(x)dx}{\int_{-\infty}^{+\infty} \left(E^2\left(V + V_{DC}, x\right) - E^2\left(V_{DC}, x\right)\right) I(x)dx} \tag{9.11}$$

Where $\bar{R}_{11}$, $\bar{R}_{12}$ are the QEO coefficients and $\phi^{TM}(V), \phi^{TE}(V)$ are the quadratic phase modulation amplitudes for the TM and TE-modes, respectively. The values of $\phi^{TM}(V), \phi^{TE}(V)$ are calculated from the fit of the data points (C) and (D) in figure 9.6. The resulting values of the QEO coefficients for the GaAs/AlGaAs P-p-n-N double heterostructure are:

$$\bar{R}_{12} = -2.85 \times 10^{-17}\,\mathrm{cm^2/V^2},$$
$$\bar{R}_{11} = -2.44 \times 10^{-17}\,\mathrm{cm^2/V^2}.$$

As can be seen by figure 9.13, the variation of the values of $\bar{R}_{12}$, $\bar{R}_{11}$ is smaller than 8% within the modulation voltage amplitude range of $0.2\,V$ to $1.4\,V$.

Unlike to our findings regarding the LEO coefficient, the measured values here of the QEO coefficients are one order of magnitude smaller than the values that were reported in [61] and [15] for GaAs at the wavelengths of $1.06\,\mu m$ and $1.09\,\mu m$. Please note, that the value for LEO coefficient was derived from the phase modulation spectra at the fundamental modulation frequency and the measured value of the LEO coefficient agrees very well with the literature. If we further assume with [23] that the quadratic phase modulation is solely due to the QEO effect, then the QEO coefficients are expected to also be accurately determined from the phase modulation spectra, i.e. from the phase modulation amplitude at the 2nd harmonic of the modulation frequency.

In [15] and in [61] the authors used planar waveguide phase modulators. In their experiment in [15], the light signal was coupled onto both the [110] and $\left[1\bar{1}0\right]$ cleaved facets of the planar waveguide such that the phase shift due to LEO effect could be subtracted from the total phase shift using symmetry considerations. Then, the carrier density-related phase shift was calculated and subtracted from the remaining phase shift (see equations (3) and (4) in [15]). The authors emphasize that this approach relies on the carrier effect to be calculated accurately.

Hence, the discrepancy between our results and the results presented in [15] and [61] suggests, that in contrast to [23] other effects than the QEO effect may contribute to the quadratic phase modulation and/or the models used in [15] and [61] to calculate the carrier density-related effects may be inaccurate. We believe that further measurements on GaAs/AlGaAs double heterostructure phase modulators, e.g. for different waveguide orientations, are required to resolve this discrepancy.

9.6.2 Electro-optic coefficients of $Al_{0.35}Ga_{0.65}As$ at 780 nm

The determination of the LEO and QEO coefficients of $Al_{0.35}Ga_{0.65}As$ at the wavelength 780 nm follows from the measurements of the phase shift signal for both, the TE and TM-modes (figure 9.7). The procedure that was already applied to analyze the

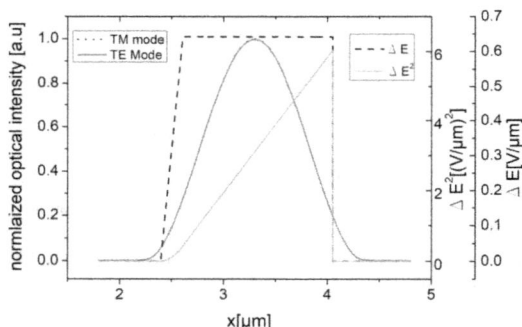

Figure 9.14: Calculated (vertical) field of the TE and TM modes of the modulator waveguide (at 780 nm) and their overlap with the linear (ΔE) and quadratic (ΔE^2) electric field variations where $\Delta E = E(V+V_{DC}, x) - E(V_{DC}, x)$, and $\Delta E^2 = (E^2(V+V_{DC}, x) - E^2(V_{DC}, x))$.

electro-optic coefficients of GaAs at 1064 nm can be applied here. Next, equation 9.10 is used to determine the values for the LEO coefficient for a P-p-i-n-N GaAs/AlGaAs double heterostructure at the wavelength of 780 nm. These values correspond to:

$$\bar{r}_{41} = -1.01 \times 10^{-10} \, \text{cm/V}.$$

This values agrees well with the value of $\bar{r}_{41} = -1.84 \times 10^{-10}$ cm/V that we estimated in section 4.2 for the LEO coefficient which is quite satisfying. Further comparison with values from the literature is not available. Please note that this is the first time a double heterostructure with $Al_{0.35}Ga_{0.65}As$ guiding core at the wavelength 780 nm is used to realize electro-optic phase modulators.

The value for the QEO coefficient $\bar{R}_{12}$ as determined from the evaluation of curve C in figure 9.7 using equation 9.11 is:

$$\bar{R}_{12} = -0.76 \times 10^{-16}\,\text{cm}^2/\text{V}^2.$$

In section 4.2 we estimated the value of $\bar{R}_{12} = -2.3 \times 10^{-16}\,\text{cm}^2/\text{V}^2$ which is about 3 times larger than the experimental value. However, the estimation of the QEO coefficient in section 4.2 was based on experimental values provided for the QEO coefficient for GaAs. We believe that the previous discussion regarding the experimental value of QEO for GaAs at the wavelength 1064 nm is also valid here. Namely, the discrepancy suggests that in the in contrast to [23], the quadratic phase shift may not solely be due to the QEO effects or/and the models used for the calculation of the free carriers effects may be inaccurate.

Furthermore, the Fourier components for the TM mode at the 2nd harmonic of the modulation frequency are below the noise floor (see curve D in figure 9.7). Hence, no experimental value of $\bar{R}_{11}$ could be determined for $Al_{0.35}Ga_{0.65}As$ at the wavelength 780 nm. One possible explanation would be that for the considered structure, $\bar{R}_{11}$ is significantly smaller than $\bar{R}_{12}$.

Please notice that in the literature, the values of the QEO coefficients $\bar{R}_{11}$ and $\bar{R}_{12}$ for GaAs at different values of the photon energy were reported to be very close to each other. This also agrees with our experimental findings for the QEO coefficients for GaAs at the wavelength 1064 nm. If our experimental finding for the QEO coefficients for $Al_{0.35}Ga_{0.65}As$ are corrects, then this may suggest that unlike to GaAs, for the $Al_xGa_{1-x}As$ material, the difference between the QEO coefficients $\bar{R}_{11}$ and $\bar{R}_{12}$ increases with increasing Al-mole fraction. As far as we know, no experimental values are available for the QEO coefficients for $Al_xGa_{1-x}As$, with $0 < x < 1$. Further investigations are required in the future to confirm or disagree with our suggestions.

9.7 Conclusions

The heterodyne analysis method described here is based on a heterodyne interferometer. The I&Q spectral analysis of the beat note signal delivers the amplitude and phase modulation in the time domain. The method can be applied to measure the RAM in real time and thus can be used to optimize the coupling efficiency for lowest RAM level.

The I&Q spectral analysis of the phase modulation signal delivers an accurate measurement of the phase modulation of less than 1 deg. It overcomes the limitation of the FP method that requires a phase modulation amplitude of at least 90 deg. The spectral analysis of phase modulation for both, TE mode and TM mode excitation has been further used to determine the individual contribution of the LEO effect, the QEO effect, and the carrier density-related effects to phase modulation in GaAs/AlGaAs double heterostructure phase modulators. The contribution of the free carriers effect to phase modulation can be calculated by subtracting the LEO contribution to the linear phase shifts of the TE and TM mode. Table 9.2 summarizes the measured (using the spectral analysis) phase modulation efficiencies of the two phase modulator chips at 780 nm and at 1064 nm and compares them to the theoretically expected values. A

Table 9.2: Experimental and theoretical modulation efficiencies of GaAs-based phase modulators.

λ [nm]	structure	LEO [deg/(V · mm)]		carrier [deg/(V · mm)]		QEO [deg/(V² · mm)]	
		theory	experiment	theory	experiment	theory	experiment
780	table 4.2	8.41	4.44	0.17	2.52	0.96	0.21
1064	table 4.5	8.46	8.77	1.41	6.31	0.88	0.17

good agreement between theory and experiment is found for the modulator at 1064 nm with respect to phase shift due to the LEO effect. For both, 780 nm and 1064 nm, the carrier density related effects turn out to be more pronounced than predicted by simulation. This suggests that the doping of the guiding layers are larger than the nominal values in table 4.2 and in table 4.5. Finally, the experiment shows that (as expected from the simulations) the contribution of the QEO effect to phase modulation is very small in comparison to the linear effects (LEO effect and free carrier effects). Furthermore, as a direct application, we were able to experimentally determine the electro-optic coefficients for GaAs at the wavelength of 1064 nm and $Al_{0.35}Ga_{0.65}As$ at the wavelength of 780 nm.

Chapter 10

Conclusions and Outlook

In order to be ready for leaving the labs, electro-optical systems for quantum precision experiments such as atom interferometers should be robust and compact to provide reliable mechanical and thermal stability. Laser radiation in the state-of-the-art electro-optical systems is achieved using compact and robust micro-integrated laser modules. However, passive components such as phase modulators, splitters, and fiber couplers that are required for the manipulation of the light signal (for example at 780 nm for rubidium spectroscopy and at 1064 nm for molecular iodine spectroscopy) are only commercially available on macro-scales. They are implemented in the electro-optical systems with a huge demand on space and from factor which correspond to a reduced robustness and mechanical stability. The miniaturization of the passive components to realize photonic integrated circuits or to micro-integrate them into laser and spectroscopy modules is a prerequisite for mature quantum sensors for applications in the field and in space.

In this work, GaAs-based electro-optic phase modulators for operation at the wavelengths of 780 nm and at 1064 nm and waveguide couplers at the wavelength of 780 nm have been developed, and experimentally investigated. Chip-based phase modulators provide the means to substitute crystal-based electro-optic modulators in the state-of-the-art optical systems. Waveguide couplers may replace the fiber couplers and are required in photonic integrated circuits (PICs). The monolithic integration of GaAs-based couplers with phase modulators is demonstrated by the implementation of a Mach-Zehnder intensity modulator at 780 nm.

10.1 GaAs-based phase modulators and waveguide couplers

The phase modulators that were designed and fabricated are based on a GaAs/AlGaAs double heterostructure, which allows for optical and electrical fields confinement for efficient modulation and to account for low free carrier absorption. The devices were realized based on the ridge waveguide optical design. The waveguide parameters were optimized to meet the micro-integration requirements of phase modulators with active devices such as edge-emitting GaAs-based lasers. Phase modulators with phase modulation efficiencies larger than 15 deg/(V.mm) have been designed.

We applied established techniques in order to determine the electro-optic performance of the phase modulators. The well-known Fabry-Perot (FP) method was used to determine the phase modulation efficiency and the propagation losses. The largest phase

modulation efficiency achieved using the FP method with a phase modulator designed
for operation at 780 nm (epitaxial design according to table 4.3) was found to correspond to 16 °/(V · mm) with propagation losses smaller than 1.2 dB/cm. This allows
for phase modulators that are 4 mm long, so that the half wave voltage can be as small
as 2.8 V. The capacity of the phase modulator (epitaxial design according to table 4.2)
at the wavelength of 780 nm was found to be 250 pF which allows for a modulation
bandwidth of 12.8 MHz when the phase modulator is driven directly with a 50 Ω signal
source, which is sufficient for example for generation of modulation sidebands for Rb
spectroscopy applications. In the future, the SiNx isolation layer could be replaced
by BCB passivation to reduce the capacity by one to two orders of magnitude so that
GaAs-based phase modulators can provide access to modulation frequencies beyond
1 GHz with direct driving from a 50 Ω signal source .

For phase modulators at the wavelength of 1064 nm, propagation losses of 2.7 dB/cm
and 4.3 dB/cm were determined experimentally (epitaxial design according to table 4.6 and table 4.5, respectively). The propagation losses measured for the devices
clearly demonstrate progress beyond state-of-the-art of GaAs/AlGaAs phase modulators (12 dB/cm for modulators at 1.06 μm [13]).

Waveguide couplers for operation at the wavelength of 780 nm have been demonstrated for the first time. The design of the couplers relies on the double heterostructure of the phase modulators at 780 nm (epitaxial design according to table 4.2 and
table 4.3). This is meant to ease the integration of phase modulators and couplers.
For the implementation of waveguide couplers two concepts have been analyzed, both
theoretically and experimentally. Multi-mode interference (MMI) couplers based on
the self-imaging principle in multi-mode waveguides were used to implement 1×2
and 2×2 couplers. Directional couplers based on evanescent mode coupling were
used to implement 2×2 couplers. The comparison between the MMI couplers and
the directional couplers showed the MMI couplers are less dependent on fabrication
tolerances related to the transverse geometry than the directional couplers. The MMI
couplers feature low excess losses (1.4 dB for 1×2 MMI splitter and 1.6 dB for a 2×2
MMI 3dB coupler) and low imbalance (0.2 dB for 1×2 MMI splitter and 0.2-0.6 dB
for a 2×2 MMI 3dB coupler) which allows for efficient integration of the couplers with
GaAs/AlGaAs double heterostructure phase modulators. The Mach-Zehnder intensity modulator realized using phase modulators and MMI couplers features a very low
excess loss (less than 3 dB), and the extinction ratio is larger than 10 dB.

10.2   In-depth characterization of phase modulators

The waveguide material of the GaAs-based phase modulator is transparent. Upon
propagation or upon coupling into the modulator chip, light scattered out of the mode
(into higher order modes) is expected to continue to travel through the transparent
waveguide material and thus to interfere at the output with the guided fundamental mode. This scattered light is a main source for residual amplitude modulation
(RAM). RAM is a main source of systematic errors, and hence, RAM is an important performance factor in the applications of phase modulators. The analysis of the
modulation efficiency, RAM, and the non-linearities in dependence of the operation
parameters (modulation voltage, coupling efficiency) is essential for the applications of
chip-based phase modulators. Even though the first GaAs-based electro-optic phase

modulators were presented many years ago, to the best of our knowledge, none of the previous works on GaAs-based phase modulators have included measurements on RAM or methods to quantify RAM.

In this work, a new method was developed to investigate linear and non-linear phase and amplitude modulation of electro-optic phase modulators. Unlike to the FP method that requires to determine the half-wave voltage, this method allows to determine phase shifts less than a degree so that, the modulation efficiency can be determined as a function of the bias voltage or of the modulation voltage. The method is based on a heterodyne interferometer (see figure 9.1). The optical field provided by a local oscillator is divided into two paths. The beam from the first path is coupled into the modulator chip where both, phase and amplitude modulation are imprinted. The second beam (reference beam) is frequency shifted, typically by several 10 MHz using an acousto-optic modulator (AOM). The reference beam interferes then with the output of the modulator on a fast photoreceiver. The in-phase and quadrature (I&Q) components of the resulting beat note signal are then analyzed following lines that were explained in section 9.1.2 in chapter 9. This novel method has been experimentally implemented (see section 9.2 in chapter 9) and applied to phase modulator chips designed for and operated at 780 nm and at 1064 nm.

The analysis of the I&Q components of beat note allows to separately analyze the information of amplitude modulation. The RAM is measured from the Fourier spectrum of the amplitude modulation (see for example figure 9.9). The measurement is carried out in real time. Thus, it can be applied for optimizing the coupling efficiency into the modulator waveguide for lowest RAM level. The measurement has shown that the RAM can be reduced to the 10^{-3} level by means of optimum coupling of the light signal into the guided fundamental mode of the phase modulator waveguide. It can be very advantageous to apply this method for RAM measurement, for example, during the micro-integration process of phase modulators into hybrid laser modules. In the future, the phase modulator waveguide may use a mode filter, e.g. a bent geometry, to reduce the overlap of undesired light with the modulated optical field which should account to further reduction of the RAM.

By applying the I&Q analysis to the phase modulation signal, the instantaneous phase shift could be determined. Using a Fourier transformation approach linear and quadratic response were determined. From the linear response for TE and TM mode operation, the linear electro-optic (LEO) coefficient as well as the phase modulation coefficient describing the effect of carrier density modulation could be determined. The quadratic response is solely due to the quadratic electro-optic effect and hence allows for determination of the quadratic electro-optic (QEO) coefficient. As a direct application of the separation of the linear and quadratic effects, we were able to experimentally determine for the first time the LEO and QEO coefficients of $Al_{0.35}Ga_{0.65}As$ at the wavelength of 780 nm and for GaAs at the wavelength of 1064 nm. This is also the first time the QEO coefficients were directly determined by an experiment. The values of the LEO coefficients derived from the experimental data agree very well with the values from the literature. However, the estimated QEO coefficients for GaAs at the wavelength of 1064 nm are one order of magnitude smaller than the values that were reported in the literature. Please note that the determination of the QEO coefficients was based on the assumption that the quadratic phase shift is solely due to the

QEO effects which is supported by literature. The discrepancy may be resolved by investigating modulator chips with different doping profiles in order to challenge this assumption and to investigate whether carrier density related effects also contribute to the quadratic response.

List of Abbreviations and Symbols

AlGaAs	Aluminum gallium arsenide
AlN	Aluminum nitride
AOM	acousto-optic modulator
AR	Anti-reflection
BCB	benzocyclobutene polymer
BPM	Beam Propagation Method
CCD	charge-coupled device
DFB	Distributed feedback
DH	Double Heterostructure
DLR	German Space Agency (Deutsche Zentrum füer Luft- und Raumfahrt)
DUT	Device under test
ECDL	External.cavity Diode Laser
EO	Electro-Optic
EZA	Electrical Spectrum Analyzer
FE	Finite Element
FEM	Finite Element Method
FD	Finite Difference
FOKUS	First Orbital Curing Experiment of University Students
FP	Fabry Perot
FWHM	Full width at half maximum
GaAs	Gallium arsenide
GPS	Global Positioning System
I&Q	In-phase and quadrature
KALEXUS	Kalium Laser-Experimente unter Schwerelosigkeit
LEO	Linear Electro-optic
LO	Local Oscillator
Milas	Mikro-Integrierte Diodenlasersysteme
MMI	Multi-Mode Interference
MOVPE	Metalorganic vapour phase epitaxy
MOPA	Master-Oscillator-Power-Amplifier
MZI	Mach-Zehnder-Interferometer
PBS	Polarizing beam splitter
PER	Polarization Extinction Ratio
PICs	Photonic Integrated Circuits
PM	phase modulation
QEO	Quadratic Electro-optic
RAM	Residual Amplitude Modulation
RBW	Resolution bandwidth

RF	Radio Frequency
RIE	Reactive ion etching
RW	Ridge Waveguide
RWA	Ridge Waveguide Amplifier
TE	Traverse Electric
TEC	Thermoelectric cooler
TM	Traverse Magnetic
VHBG	Volume Holographic Bragg Grating

A: GaAs ($Al_xGa_{1-x}As$) compound semiconductors

.1   Zinkblende structures

Examples of III-V compounds semiconductors that crystallize in the Zinkblende structure are InSb, InAs, InP, GaSb, GaAs, and GaP. The unit cell of GaAs is shown in figure 1. The crystallographic directions are defined by the components of a vector

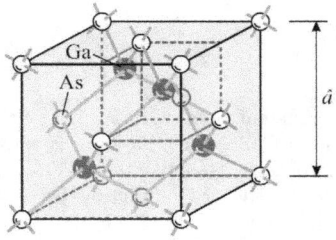

Figure 1: Unit cell of GaAs as example of the Zinkblende structure. $\hat{a}$ is the lattice parameter. Original picture in [30].

that is oriented in a given direction. For the cubic crystal (zinkblende), any direction can be fully described using the orthogonal basic vectors $\hat{a}$, $\hat{b}$, and $\hat{c}$ with the same length as can be shown in figure 2. A unit of three numbers from the group $\{0, 1, \bar{1}\}$ in square bracket describes then a given direction. Examples for these directions are

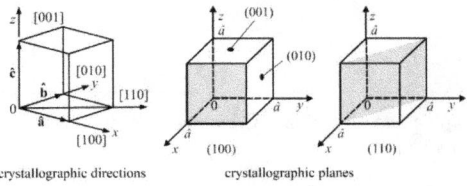

Figure 2: Crystallographic directions and planes in a cubic crystal. Picture taken from [30].

given in figure 2. Where 1 and $\bar{1}$ numerical codes refer to the opposite directions. The crystallographic planes are given by the Miller indices that determine the Intersection points of the plane with the axes $\hat{a}$, $\hat{b}$, and $\hat{c}$. The corrsponing planes are given in a units of three numbers within round brackets. For example, the crystallographic planes (110) and (100) are give in figure 2.

Figure 3: Photo of a model of GaAs crystal. The corresponding crystallographic directions are the vertical directions. Original picture taken from [30].

.2 GaAs wafers

In the zinkblende strcutures different atoms can occupy neighboring position in the crystal pattern. For example in GaAs, each Ga-atom is surrounded by 4 As atoms which are positioned at the edges of a regular tetrahedral. Figure 3 shows photos of a model of the GaAs pattern. The distribution of the Ga and As atoms in these models revels very important properties of the crystal. Suppose that the crystal is cleaved in the [111] direction. The resulting (111) layers would have Ga-atoms on the surface whereas the $(\bar{1}\bar{1}\bar{1})$ have As-atoms on the surface. The chemical properties of these two layers would then differ and are expected to respond in different manners to processing chemicals. The same argument is valid for layer planes in the [100]

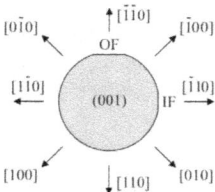

Figure 4: Crystallographic directions in a GaAs wafer. OF: orientation flat, IF: identification flat. Picture taken from [30].

direction where the Ga-atoms and As-atoms are positioned alternatively over each other in equidistant distance. The distance between atomic-layers are largest in the [111] direction. These layers are hold together with only one binding per atom. The same applies to atoms in the perpendicular direction to the [110] direction. However, the binding in the [110] direction is weaker as in the [111] direction. This is why the (110) crystallographic plane is considered as a natural cleaving plane [30]. As a direct advantage of this property, a GaAs wafer can be cleaved along this plane and the cleaved facets form perfect mirrors for edge-emitting semiconductor laser diodes. GaAs wafers are available in diameters of 2, 3, 4, and even 6-inches. A typical wafer surface is the (101) layer. The crystallographic direction in a GaAs wafer are typically (in Europe and Japan) given in the form in figure 4.

.3 Optical properties of GaAs

.3.1 Energy band gap and absorption in GaAs

The latice parameters of AlAs and GaAs are very close to each other as shown by figure 5. This makes $Al_xGa_{1-x}As$ at any value of x ($0 < x < 1$) lattice-matched to GaAs.

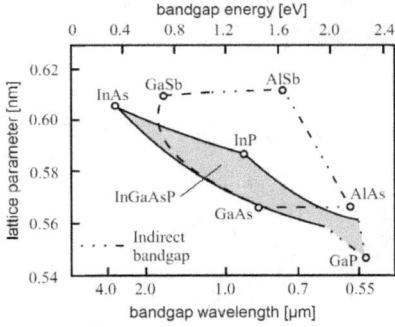

Figure 5: Energy bandgap and lattice constants of III-V semiconductors at 300 K.

.3.2 Refractive index of $Al_xGa_{1-x}As$

According to [62], below the direct band gap edge the real part of the refractive index $\bar{n}$ of a zinkblende material (such as $Al_xGa_{1-x}As$) can be expressed due to a simplified interband-transition model as:

$$\bar{n}(\lambda) = \sqrt{A_0 \left(f(\chi) + 1/2 \left[E_0 / (E_0 + \Delta_0) \right]^{3/2} f(\chi_{SO}) \right) + B_0}$$

with:
$f(\chi) = \chi^{-2} \left(2 - (1+\chi)^{1/2} - (1-\chi)^{1/2} \right)$
$\chi = \hbar\omega / E_0$
$\chi_{SO} = \hbar\omega / (E_0 + \Delta_0)$ A_0 and B_0 are constants. They are experimentally found to be written as $A_0 = 6.3 - 19.0x$, and $B_0 = 9.4 - 10.2x$.
E_0 and $E_0 + \Delta_0$ are critical point energies (see section VI in [62]).

The refractive indices of GaAs and $Al_xGa_{1-x}As$ are given in figure 7.

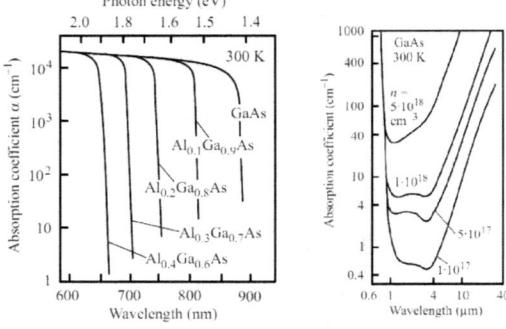

Figure 6: Fundamental absorption coefficient and absorption coefficients in AlGaAs (left), and in n-doped GaAs (right). Original picture taken from [30].

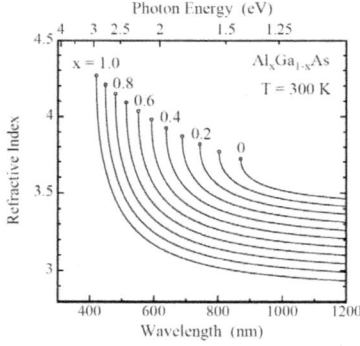

Figure 7: Refractive index of GaAs and AlGaAs a function of the wavelength. Picture taken from [30].

B: List of measured chips using the FP method

Table 1: List of chips measured to determine the phase modulation efficiency and propagation losses of phase modulators using the Fabry-Perot method. *chip number is determined by TFRRDD (TF: test field, RR: bar, DD: diode). Examples: (single chip 010212: TF=1, RR=2, DD=12), (012(a,b)02: two different chips at fractional lengths of one bar: RR=2, fractions a and b), (01(03,04)02): two different chips with diode number 2 at different bars 3 and 4), (012(a+b)02 chip on more than one section in one bar), (0102(01+02) chip extends at two diodes from the same bar).

Process ID	Wafer	*chip TTRRDD	λ µm	ridge width µm	length mm	Mount type	coating
	D2043-2	016a05	780	2	1	C-mount	no
	D2043-2	016d05	780	2	1	C-mount	no
	D2043-3	016d15	780	4	1	C-mount	no
	D2043-3	015(b+c)04	780	2	2	C-mount	no
Z1 6105	D2043-2	017(b+c)05	780	2	2	C-mount	no
	D2043-3	017(a+d)15	780	4	2	C-mount	no
	D2043-2	016(a+b+c+d)03	780	2	4	C-mount	no
	D2043-3	016(a+b+c+d)04	780	2	4	C-mount	no
	D2043-3	016(a+b+c+d)15	780	4	4	C-mount	no
Z1 6520	D2231-3	0001(01,02,03,04,05)	780	2.2	2	C-mount	no
	D2231-4	0001(01,02,03,04,05)	780	2.2	2	C-mount	no
	C3059-3	0201(17,18,19,20)	1064	3	2	C-mount	no
	C3059-3	0202(17,18)	1064	3	2	C-mount	no
	C3059-3	0203(17,18,19,20)	1064	3	4	C-mount	no
Z1 6894	C3059-3	0204(17,18)	1064	3	4	C-mount	no
	C3062-3	0201(17,18,19,20)	1064	3	4	C-mount	no
	C3062-3	0202(17,18)	1064	3	2	C-mount	no
	C3062-3	0205(17,18,19,20)	1064	3	4	C-mount	no
	C3062-3	0206(17,18)	1064	3	4	C-mount	no

List of Publications

The following scientific publications have been prepared in connection with this thesis:

Articles

Bassem Arar, Hans Wenzel, Reiner Güther, Olaf Brox, Harendra J. Fernando, Andre Maaßdorf, Andreas Wicht, Achim Peters, Markus Weyers, Götz Erbert, and Günther Tränkle,"*Double heterostructure ridge-waveguide GaAs/AlGaAs phase modulator for 780 nm lasers*", Appl. Phys. B, vol. 116, pp. 175-181 (2014).

Bassem Arar, Max Schiemangk, Hans Wenzel, Olaf Brox, Andreas Wicht, Achim Peters, and Günther Tränkle, "*Method for in-depth characterization of electro-optic phase modulators*", Appl. Opt. vol. 56, pp. 1246-1252 (2017).

Conference Contributions

Bassem Arar, Harendra Fernando, Olaf Brox, Andre Maaßdorf, Andreas Wicht, Achim Peters, Markus Weyers, Götz Erbert, and Günther Tränkle, "*Double Heterostructure AlGaAs/ GaAs W shaped Waveguide MZI Modulator for 780 nm Lasers*", Conference on Lasers and Electro-Optics (CLEO), OSA, ISBN: 978-1-55752-999-2, paper JW2A.51, San Jose (2014).

Bassem Arar , Hans Wenzel, Olaf Brox, Andre Maaßdorf, Andreas Wicht, Markus Weyers, Götz Erbert, and Günther Tränkle, "*GaAs-based Phase Modulator for Laser Radiation at 1070 nm*", Conference on Lasers and Electro-Optics/Europe (CLEO/Europe-EQEC 2015), ISBN: 978-1-4673-7475-0, paper CD-P-40, Munich (2015).

Bassem Arar , Hans Wenzel, Olaf Brox, Andre Maaßdorf, Andreas Wicht, Markus Weyers, Achim Peters, Götz Erbert, and Günther Tränkle, "*GaAs-based Phase Modulators for Frequency Stabilization of Diode Lasers at 780 nm and 1070 nm*", Semiconductor and Integrated Opto-Electronics (SIOE) conference, Cardiff (2015).

Bibliography

[1] C. Jekeli, "Cold Atom Interferometer as Inertial Measurement Unit for Precision Navigation," *Proceedings of the 60th Annual Meeting of The Institute of Navigation* pp. 604-613 (2004). [Online]. Available: https://www.ion.org/publications/abstract.cfm?articleID=5658

[2] E. Luvsandamdin, S. Spießberger, M. Schiemangk, A. Sahm, G. Mura, A. Wicht, A. Peters, G. Erbert, and G. Tränkle, "Development of narrow linewidth, micro-integrated extended cavity diode lasers for quantum optics experiments in space," *Applied Physics B*, vol. 111, no. 2, pp. 255–260, May 2013. [Online]. Available: https://doi.org/10.1007/s00340-012-5327-8

[3] E. Luvsandamdin, C. Kürbis, M. Schiemangk, A. Sahm, A. Wicht, A. Peters, G. Erbert, and G. Tränkle, "Micro-integrated extended cavity diode lasers for precision potassium spectroscopy in space," *Opt. Express*, vol. 22, no. 7, pp. 7790–7798, April 2014. [Online]. Available: http://www.opticsexpress.org/abstract.cfm?URI=oe-22-7-7790

[4] T. van Zoest, N. Gaaloul, Y. Singh, H. Ahlers, W. Herr, S. T. Seidel, W. Ertmer, E. Rasel, M. Eckart, E. Kajari, S. Arnold, G. Nandi, W. P. Schleich, R. Walser, A. Vogel, K. Sengstock, K. Bongs, W. Lewoczko-Adamczyk, M. Schiemangk, T. Schuldt, A. Peters, T. Könemann, H. Müntinga, C. Lämmerzahl, H. Dittus, T. Steinmetz, T. W. Hänsch, and J. Reichel, "Bose-Einstein Condensation in Microgravity," *Science*, vol. 328, no. 5985, pp. 1540–1543, 2010. [Online]. Available: http://science.sciencemag.org/content/328/5985/1540

[5] R. Nagarajan, M. Kato, J. Pleumeekers, P. Evans, S. Corzine, S. Hurtt, A. Dentai, S. Murthy, M. Missey, R. Muthiah, R. A. Salvatore, C. Joyner, R. Schneider, M. Ziari, F. Kish, and D. Welch, "InP Photonic Integrated Circuits," *IEEE Journal of Selected Topics in Quantum Electronics*, vol. 16, no. 5, pp. 1113–1125, Sept 2010. [Online]. Available: http://ieeexplore.ieee.org/document/5398834/

[6] M. Lezius, T. Wilken, C. Deutsch, M. Giunta, O. Mandel, A. Thaller, V. Schkolnik, M. Schiemangk, A. Dinkelaker, A. Kohfeldt, A. Wicht, M. Krutzik, A. Peters, O. Hellmig, H. Duncker, K. Sengstock, P. Windpassinger, K. Lampmann, T. Hülsing, T. W. Hänsch, and R. Holzwarth, "Space-borne frequency comb metrology," *Optica*, vol. 3, no. 12, pp. 1381–1387, December 2016. [Online]. Available: http://www.osapublishing.org/optica/abstract.cfm?URI=optica-3-12-1381

[7] A. N. Dinkelaker, M. Schiemangk, V. Schkolnik, A. Kenyon, K. Lampmann, A. Wenzlawski, P. Windpassinger, O. Hellmig, T. Wendrich, E. M. Rasel,

M. Giunta, C. Deutsch, C. Kürbis, R. Smol, A. Wicht, M. Krutzik, and A. Peters, "Autonomous frequency stabilization of two extended-cavity diode lasers at the potassium wavelength on a sounding rocket," *Appl. Opt.*, vol. 56, no. 5, pp. 1388–1396, February 2017. [Online]. Available: http://ao.osa.org/abstract.cfm?URI=ao-56-5-1388

[8] D. F. Nelson and F. K. Reinhart, "Light modulation by the electro-optic effect in reverse biased gallium phosphide P-N junctions," *Appl. Phys. Lett.*, vol. 5, no. 7, pp. 148–150, 1964. [Online]. Available: http://dx.doi.org/10.1063/1.1754092

[9] H. G. Bach, J. Krauser, H. P. Notling, R. Lagon, and F. K. Reinhart, "Electro-optic light modulation in InGaAsP/InP double heterostructure diodes," *Appl. Phys. Lett.*, vol. 42, no. 8, p. 692, 4 1983. [Online]. Available: http://dx.doi.org/10.1063/1.94075

[10] A. Alping, X. S. Wu, T. R. Hausken, and L. A. Coldren, "Highly efficient waveguide phase modulator for integrated optoelectronics," *Appl. Phys. Lett.*, vol. 48, no. 19, pp. 1243–1245, 5 1986. [Online]. Available: http://dx.doi.org/10.1063/1.96992

[11] J. Faist, F.-K. Reinhart, and et al., "Orientation dependence of the phase modulation in a p-n junction GaAs/AlxGa1xAs waveguide," *Applied Physic letters*, vol. 50, no. 2, pp. 68–70, 1 1987. [Online]. Available: http://dx.doi.org/10.1063/1.97875

[12] U. Koren, T. L. Koch, H. Presting, and B. I. Miller, "InGaAs/InP multiple quantum well waveguide phase modulator," *Applied Physics Letters*, vol. 50, no. 7, pp. 368–370, 1987. [Online]. Available: http://dx.doi.org/10.1063/1.98201

[13] J. Mendoza-Alvarez, L. Coldren, and A. Alping, "Analysis of depletion edge translation lightwave modulators," *Journal of Lightwave Technology*, vol. 6, no. 6, pp. 793–808 (1988). [online]. Available: http://ieeexplore.ieee.org/document/4068/

[14] R. J. Deri, E. Kapon, J. P. Harbison, M. Seto, C. P. Yun, and L. T. Florez, "Low-loss GaAs/AlGaAs waveguide phase modulator using a W-shaped index profile," *Applied Physics Letters*, vol. 53, no. 19, pp. 1803–1805, 1988. [Online]. Available: http://dx.doi.org/10.1063/1.99786

[15] J. Faist and F. Reinhart, "Phase modulation in GaAs/AlGaAs double heterostructures. II. Experiment," *Journal of Applied Physics*, vol. 67, no. 11, pp. 7006–7012, 1990. [Online]. Available: http://dx.doi.org/10.1063/1.345046

[16] J. F. Vinchant, J. A. Cavailles, M. Erman, P. Jarry, and M. Renaud, "InP/GaInAsP guided-wave phase modulators based on carrier-induced effects: theory and experiment," *Journal of Lightwave Technology*, vol. 10, no. 1, pp. 63–70, January 1992. [Online]. Available: http://ieeexplore.ieee.org/document/108738/

[17] Y. T. Byun, K. H. Park, S. H. Kim, S. S. Choi, J. C. Yi, and T. K. Lim, "Efficient single-mode GaAs/AlGaAs W waveguide phase modulator with low propagation loss," *Applied Optics*, vol. 37, no. 3, pp. 497–501, January (1998). [Online]. Available: https://www.osapublishing.org/ao/abstract.cfm?uri=ao-37-3-496

[18] H. S. Park, J. C. Yi, Y. T. Byun, S. Lee, S. H. Kim, M. Takenaka, and Y. Nakano, "Investigation of the Modulation Efficiency of InGaAsP/InP Ridge Waveguide Phase Modulators at 1.55 micrometer," *Japanese Journal of Applied Physics*, vol. 42, no. 7A, p. 4378, 2003. [Online]. Available: http://stacks.iop.org/1347-4065/42/i=7R/a=4378

[19] B. Arar, H. Wenzel, R. Güther, O. Brox, A. Maaßdorf, A. Wicht, G. Erbert, M. Weyers, G. Tränkle, H. N. J. Fernando, and A. Peters, "Double-heterostructure ridge-waveguide GaAs/AlGaAs phase modulator for 780 nm lasers," *Applied Physics B*, vol. 116, no. 1, pp. 175–181, July 2014. [Online]. Available: https://doi.org/10.1007/s00340-013-5671-3

[20] B. Arar, H. N. J. Fernando, O. Brox, A. Maassdorf, A. Wicht, A. Peters, M. Weyers, G. Erbert, and G. Tränkle, "Double Heterostructure AlGaAs/GaAs W-shaped Waveguide Mach-Zehnder Intensity Modulator for 780 nm Lasers," in *CLEO: 2014*. Optical Society of America, 2014, p. JW2A.51. [Online]. Available: http://www.osapublishing.org/abstract.cfm?URI=CLEO_AT-2014-JW2A.51, ©IEEE.

[21] B. Arar, M. Schiemangk, H. Wenzel, O. Brox, A. Wicht, A. Peters, and G. Tränkle, "Method for in-depth characterization of electro-optic phase modulators," *Appl. Opt.*, vol. 56, no. 4, pp. 1246–1252, 2 2017.[online]. Available: http://ao.osa.org/abstract.cfm?URI=ao-56-4-1246

[22] S. S. Lee, Y. S. Kim, R. V. Ramaswamy, and V. S. Sundaram, "Highly efficient separate confinement PpinN GaAs/AlGaAs waveguide phase modulator," *Applied Physics Letters*, vol. 55, no. 18, pp. 1865–1867, 1989. [Online]. Available: http://dx.doi.org/10.1063/1.102155

[23] J. Faist and F. Reinhart, "Phase modulation in GaAs/AlGaAs double heterostructures. i. theory," *Journal of Applied Physics*, vol. 67, no. 11, pp. 6998–7005, 1990. [Online]. Available: http://dx.doi.org/10.1063/1.345045

[24] S. Spießberger, "Compact semiconductor-based laser source with narrow linewidth and high output power," Ph.D. dissertation, TU Berlin, 2011, http://dx.doi.org/10.14279/depositonce-3353.

[25] J. Shin, Y.-C. Chang, and N. Daglia, "0.3V drive voltage GaAs/AlGaAs substrate removed Mach-Zehnder intensity modulators," *Appl. Phys. Lett.*, vol. 92, no. 201103, 5 2008. [Online]. Available: http://dx.doi.org/10.1063/1.2931057

[26] L. B. Soldano and E. C. M. Pennings, "Optical Multi-Mode Interference Devices Based on Self-Imaging: Principles and Applications," *Journal of Lightwave Technology*, vol. 13, no. 4, pp. 615–627, 1995. [Online]. Available: http://ieeexplore.ieee.org/xpls/abs_all.jsp?arnumber=372474

[27] J. S. Cites, and P. R. Ashley, "High-performance Mach-Zehnder modulators in multiple quantum well GaAs/AlGaAs," *Journal of Lightwave Technology*, vol. 12, no. 7, pp. 1167-1173, 1994. [Online]. Available: http://ieeexplore.ieee.org/stamp/stamp.jsp?tp=&arnumber=301809&isnumber=7452

[28] H. Klein, "Integrated InP Mach-Zehnder Modulators for 100 Gbit/s Ethernet Applications using QPSK Modulation ," Ph.D. dissertation, TU Berlin, 2010. [Online]. Available: http://dx.doi.org/10.14279/depositonce-2598

[29] K. J. Ebling, *Integrierte Optoelektronik.* Berlin Heidelberg: Springer Verlag, 1989, doi. 10.1007/978-3-662-07945-4.

[30] K. J. Ebling, R. Michalzik, and J. Mähnß, "Optische Informationstechnik," Winter-Halbjahr 2009/2010, Universität Ulm http://www-opto.e-technik. uni-ulm.de/lehre/opto1/script/oit-vorlesung.pdf.

[31] W. Haung and H. A. Haus, "A simple variational approach to optical rib waveguides," *Journal of Lightwave Technology*, vol. 9, no. 1, pp. 56–61, 2013. [Online]. Available: http://ieeexplore.ieee.org/document/64923/

[32] Q. Wang, G. Farrell, and T. Freier, "Effective index method for planar lightwave circuits containing directional couplers," *Optics Communications*, vol. 259, no. 1, pp. 133–136, 4 2006. [Online]. Available: http://www.sciencedirect.com/science/ article/pii/S0030401805009077

[33] R. A. Soref, J. Schmidtchen, and K. Petermann, "Large single mode rib waveguides in GeSi-Si and Si-on-SiO2," *IEEE J. Quantum Electron.*, vol. 27, no. 8, pp. 1971–1974, 1991. [Online]. Available: http://ieeexplore.ieee.org/ stamp/stamp.jsp?tp=&arnumber=83406&isnumber=2719

[34] S. P. Pogossian, L. Vescan, and A. Vonsovic, "The Single-Mode Condition for Semiconductor Rib Waveguides with Large Cross Section," *Journal of Lightwave Technology*, vol. 16, no. 10, pp. 1851–1853, 1998. [Online]. Available: http://ieeexplore.ieee.org/stamp/stamp.jsp?arnumber=721072

[35] F. Kish et al., "System-on-chip photonic integrated circuits," *IEEE Journal of Selected Topics in Quantum Electronics*, vol. 24, no. 1, pp. 1–20, Jan 2018. [Online]. Available: http://ieeexplore.ieee.org/stamp/stamp.jsp?tp=&arnumber= 7954965&isnumber=7985001

[36] A. Melloni, F. Carniel, R. Costa, and M. Martinelli, "Determination of bend mode characteristics in dielectric waveguides," *Journal of Lightwave Technology*, vol. 19, no. 4, pp. 571–577, 2001. [online]. Available: http://ieeexplore.ieee.org/ stamp/stamp.jsp?tp=&arnumber=920856&isnumber=19910

[37] B. E. A. Saleh and M. C. Teich, *Fundamentals of Photonics.* John Wiley and Sons, Inc., 2004, Print ISBN: 9780471839651.

[38] S. L. Chuang, *Physics of Optoelectronic Devices*, Wiley Series in Pure and Applied Optics. Wiley, 1995, [Online]. Available: https://books.google.de/ books?id=ect6QgAACAAJ

[39] L. A. Coldren, S. W. Corzine, and M. L. Masanovic, *Diode Lasers and Photonic Integrated Circuits, Second Edition.* John Wiley and Sons, Inc., 2012, ISBN: 978-0-470-48412-8.

[40] M. T. Hill, X. J. M. Leijtens, G. D. Khoe, and M. K. Smith, "Optimizing Imbalance and Loss in 2x2 3-dB Multimode Interference Couplers via Access Waveguide Width," *Journal of Lightwave Technology*, vol. 21, no. 10, pp. 2305–2313, October 2003. [Online]. Available: http://ieeexplore.ieee.org/stamp/stamp.jsp?tp=&arnumber=1236502&isnumber=27720

[41] S. Adachi and K. Oe, "Linear electro-optic effects in zinkblende-type semiconductors: Key properties of InGaAsP relevant to device design," *Journal of Applied Physics*, vol. 56, no. 1, pp. 74–80, 1984. [Online]. Available: http://dx.doi.org/10.1063/1.333731

[42] S. Adachi and K. Oe, "Quadratic electro-optic (Kerr) effects in zincblende-type semiconductors: Key properties of InGaAsP relevant to device design," *Journal of Applied Physics*, vol. 56, no. 5, pp. 1499–1504, 1984. [Online]. Available: http://dx.doi.org/10.1063/1.334105

[43] R. Hiroyama, Y. Nomura, K. Furusawa, S. Okamoto, N. Hayashi, M. Shono, and M. Sawada, "High-power and highly reliable 780 nm band AlGaAs laser diodes with rectangular ridge structure," *Electronics Letters*, vol. 37, no. 1, pp. 30–31, 2001. [Online]. Available: http://ieeexplore.ieee.org/document/894346/

[44] S. Yamashita, S. Nakatsuka, K. Uchida, T. Kawano, and T. Kajimura, "High-power 780 nm AlGaAs quantum-well lasers and their reliable operation," *IEEE Journal of Quantum Electronics*, vol. 27, no. 6, pp. 1544–1549, June 1991. [Online]. Available: http://ieeexplore.ieee.org/document/89975/

[45] J. T. Byun, S. J. Kim, and S. H. Kim, "Linear electro-optic coefficient of GaAs/Al(0.4)Ga(0.6)As phase modulator," *Journal of Korean Physical Society*, vol. 45, no. 5, pp. 1162–1164, 11 2004. [online]. Available: http://www.jkps.or.kr/journal/view.html?uid=6419&vmd=Full

[46] S. B. John, M. Heaton, Michelle M. Bourke et al., "Optimization of deep-etched, single-mode GaAs/AlGaAs optical waveguides using controlled leakage into the substrate," *Journal of lightwave technology*, vol. 17, no. 2, pp. 267–281, Febraury 1999. [Online]. Available: http://ieeexplore.ieee.org/xpls/abs_all.jsp?arnumber=744237&tag=1

[47] B. M. A. Rahman and J. B. Davies, "Finite-Element Analysis of Optical and Microwave Waveguide Problems," *IEEE Transactions on Microwave Theory and Techniques*, vol. 32, no. 1, pp. 20–28, 1 1984. [Online]. Available: http://ieeexplore.ieee.org/stamp/stamp.jsp?tp=&arnumber=1132606&isnumber=25130

[48] H. C. Casey and M. B. Panish, "Stimulated emmission in semiconductors," in *Heterostructure lasers: Part A: Fundamental Principles*. San Diego, California 92101: Academic Press Inc., 1978, ch. 03, p. 175.

[49] J. Faist, F.-K. Reinhart, et al., "Comparison of the Phase Modulation of GaAs/AlGaAs Double Heterostructures," *Electronic Letters*, vol. 23, no. 25, pp. 1391–1392, 1987. [Online]. Available: http://ieeexplore.ieee.org/document/4259202/?reload=true&arnumber=4259202

[50] D. Gallagher, "Industry Research Highlights, Photonic CAD Matures," *IEEE LEOS Newsletter*, pp. 8–14, 2008. [Online]. Available: https://www. photonicssociety.org/images/files/publications/Newsletter/leosNL_feb08.pdf

[51] R. Ulrich and T. Kamiya, "Resolution of self-images in planar optical waveguides," *J. Opt. Soc. Am.*, vol. 68, no. 5, pp. 583–592, May 1978. [Online]. Available: http://www.osapublishing.org/abstract.cfm?URI=josa-68-5-583

[52] R. Anderson et al., *Progress in Optics*, E. Wolf, Ed. Amesterdam: Elsevier Sience B. V., 2000, vol. 41. ISBN: 978-0-444-50568-2

[53] R. G. Walker, N. I. Ameron, Y. Zhou, and S. J. Clements, "Optimized Gallium Arsenide Modulators for Advanced Modulation Formats," *IEEE Journal of Selected Topics in Quantum Electronics*, vol. 19, no. 6, pp. 138–149, 2013. [Online]. Available: http://ieeexplore.ieee.org/document/6523958/

[54] S. Sze, *Semiconductor devices, physics and technology*. Wiley, ISBN: 978-0-470-53794-7 (2012).

[55] R. Regener and W. Sohler, "Loss in Low-Finesse Ti: LiNbO3 Optical Waveguide Resonators," *Applied Physics B*, vol. 36, no. 3, pp. 143–147, 3 1985. [Online]. Available: http://link.springer.com/article/10.1007/BF00691779

[56] Y. T. Byun, K. H. Park, S. H. Kim, and et al., "Single-mode GaAs/AlGaAs W waveguides with a low propagation loss," *Applied Optics*, vol. 35, no. 6, pp. 928–933, 1996. [Online]. Available: https://www.osapublishing.org/ao/abstract. cfm?uri=ao-35-6-928

[57] L. Li, F. Liu, C. Wang, and L. Chen, "Measurement and control of residual amplitude modulation in optical phase modulation," *Review of Scienctific Instruments*, vol. 83, pp. 43111, 2012. [Online]. Available: http://dx.doi.org/10.1063/1.4704084

[58] M. Schiemangk, S. Spiessberger, A. Wicht, G. Erbert, G. Tränkle, and A. Peters, "Accurate frequency noise measurement of free-running lasers," *Appl. Opt.*, vol. 53, no. 30, pp. 7138–7143, October 2014. [Online]. Available: http://dx.doi.org/10.1364/AO.53.007138

[59] A. Klehr, H. Wenzel, J. Fricke, F. Bugge, and G. Erbert, "Generation of spectrally stable continuous-wave emission and ns pulses with a peak power of 4 W using a distributed Bragg reflector laser and a ridge-waveguide power amplifier," *Opt. Exp.*, vol. 22, no. 20, pp. 23 980–23 989, 2014. [Online]. Available: https://www.osapublishing.org/oe/abstract.cfm?uri=oe-22-20-23980

[60] J. Sathian and E. Jaatinen, "Intensity dependent residual amplitude modulation in electro-optic phase modulators," *Appl. Opt.*, vol. 51, no. 16, pp. 3684–3691, June 2012. [Online]. Available: https://doi.org/10.1364/AO.51.003684

[61] S. S. Lee, R. V. Ramaswamy, and V. S. Sundaram, "Analysis and design of high-speed high-efficiency GaAs-AlGaAs double heterostructure waveguide phase modulator," *IEEE Journal of Quantum Electronics*, vol. 27, no. 3, pp. 726–736, 1991.

[online]. Available: http://ieeexplore.ieee.org/stamp/stamp.jsp?tp=&arnumber=81383&isnumber=2667

[62] S. Adachi, "GaAs, AlAs, and $Al_xGa_{1-x}As$ Material parameters for use in research and device applications," *Journal of Applied Physics*, vol. 58, no. 3, pp. R1–R29, 1985. [Online]. Available: http://dx.doi.org/10.1063/1.336070

Innovationen mit Mikrowellen und Licht
Forschungsberichte aus dem Ferdinand-Braun-Institut, Leibniz-Institut für Höchstfrequenztechnik

Herausgeber: Prof. Dr. G. Tränkle, Prof. Dr.-Ing. W. Heinrich

Cuvillier Verlag
Internationaler wissenschaftlicher Fachverlag

Innovationen mit Mikrowellen und Licht
Forschungsberichte aus dem Ferdinand-Braun-Institut, Leibniz-Institut für Höchstfrequenztechnik

Herausgeber: Prof. Dr. G. Tränkle, Prof. Dr.-Ing. W. Heinrich

Cuvillier Verlag
Internationaler wissenschaftlicher Fachverlag

Innovationen mit Mikrowellen und Licht
Forschungsberichte aus dem Ferdinand-Braun-Institut, Leibniz-Institut für Höchstfrequenztechnik

Herausgeber: Prof. Dr. G. Tränkle, Prof. Dr.-Ing. W. Heinrich

Cuvillier Verlag
Internationaler wissenschaftlicher Fachverlag

Innovationen mit Mikrowellen und Licht
Forschungsberichte aus dem Ferdinand-Braun-Institut, Leibniz-Institut für Höchstfrequenztechnik

Herausgeber: Prof. Dr. G. Tränkle, Prof. Dr.-Ing. W. Heinrich

Band 30: **Christian Fiebig**
Diodenlaser mit Trapezstruktur und hoher Brillanz für die Realisierung
einer Frequenzkonversion auf einer mikro-optischen Bank
ISBN: 978-3-95404-690-4, 26,30 EUR, 140 Seiten

Band 31: **Viola Küller**
Versetzungsreduzierte AlN- und AlGaN-Schichten
als Basis für UV LEDs
ISBN: 978-3-95404-741-3, 34,40 EUR, 164 Seiten

Band 32: **Daniel Jedrzejczyk**
Efficient frequency doubling of near-infrared diode lasers
using quasi phase-matched waveguides
ISBN: 978-3-95404-958-5, 27,90 EUR, 134 Seiten

Band 33: **Sylvia Hagedorn**
Hybrid-Gasphasenepitaxie zur Herstellung von Aluminiumgalliumnitrid
ISBN: 978-3-95404-985-1, 38,00 EUR, 176 Seiten

Band 34: **Alexander Kravets**
Advanced Silicon MMICs for mm-Wave Automotive Radar Front-Ends
ISBN: 978-3-95404-986-8, 31,90 EUR, 156 Seiten

Band 35: **David Feise**
Longitudinale Modenfilter für Kantenemitter im roten Spektralbereich
ISBN: 978-3-7369-9116-3, 39,20 EUR, 168 Seiten

Band 36: **Ksenia Nosaeva**
Indium phosphide HBT in thermally optimized periphery for
applications up to 300GHZ
ISBN: 978-3-7369-287-0, 42,00 EUR, 154 Seiten

Band 37: **Muhammad Maruf Hossain**
Signal Generation for Millimeter Wave and THZ Applications
in InP-DHBT and InP-on-BiCMOS Technologies
ISBN: 978-3-7369-9335-8, 35,60 EUR, 136 Seiten

Band 38: **Sirinpa Monayakul**
Development of Sub-mm Wave Flip-Chip Interconnect
ISBN: 978-3-7369-9410-2, 44,00 EUR, 146 Seiten

Band 39: **Moritz Brendel**
Charakterisierung und Optimierung von (Al, Ga) N-basierten
UV-Photodetektoren
ISBN: 978-3-7369-9465-2, 49,90 EUR, 196 Seiten

Band 40: **Erdenetsetseg Luvsandamdin**
Development of micro-integrated diode lasers for precision quantum optics
experiments in space
ISBN: 978-3-7369-9479-9, 39,00 EUR, 126 Seiten

Cuvillier Verlag
Internationaler wissenschaftlicher Fachverlag

Innovationen mit Mikrowellen und Licht
Forschungsberichte aus dem Ferdinand-Braun-Institut, Leibniz-Institut für Höchstfrequenztechnik

Herausgeber: Prof. Dr. G. Tränkle, Prof. Dr.-Ing. W. Heinrich

Cuvillier Verlag
Internationaler wissenschaftlicher Fachverlag